The Princess and The Laird

A Highland Secrets Prequel

The Princess and the Laird

a highland secrets prequel

by

C.A. Szarek

other books by c.a. szarek

<u>Highland Secrets Trilogy & Companions</u> — Historical Fantasy Romance

The Princess and The Laird (Highland Secrets Prequel)

The Tartan MP3 Player (Book One)

The Fae Ring (Book Two)

The Parchment Scroll (Book Three)

Highland Valentine (A Highland Secrets HEA Story)

Highlander's Portrait (A Highland Secrets Story)

<u>Highland Treasures</u> — Historical Fantasy Romance

Highland Oath (Book One)

Highland Essence (Book Two)

Highland Skies (Book Three)

<u>The King's Riders</u> — Fantasy Romance

Sword's Call (Book One) — *Also in Audio*

Love's Call (Book Two) — *Also in Audio*

Rogue's Call (Book Three) — *Also in Audio*

Fate's Call (A Novella from the World of the King's Riders) — *Also in Audio*

<u>Crossing Forces</u> — Romantic Suspense

Collision Force (Book One) — *Also in Audio*

Cole in Her Stocking (A Crossing Forces Christmas) — *FREE read!*

Chance Collision (Book Two) — *Also in Audio*

Calculated Collision (Book Three) — *Also in Audio*

Collision Control (Book Four) — *Also in Audio*

Weekend Collision (A Crossing Forces HEA Story) — *FREE read!*

Superior Collision (Book Five) — *Also in Audio*

Incendiary Collision (Book Six) — *Coming Soon!*

<u>The Giovanni</u>

King of Hearts (Book One) — *Also in Audio*

Queen of Diamonds (Book Two) — *Coming Soon!*

Dedication

To one of my besties, and fab author and editor in her own right, Susie! Thanks for dropping everything and making time to meet Alana and Alex when I was freaking out. (I tend to work in at least 1000 freak-outs with every book I write...)

chapter one

"Nay, Alana. 'Tis foolish. And dangerous."

"Then stay here." She flashed a grin at her cousin's frown. Of course, as her royal bodyguard, he had to be the voice of reason, but could he not smile? "Where's your sense of adventure?"

Xander's frown slid into a scowl. He patted the sword sheathed at his waist and flexed his iridescent wings. "I'd rather not be forced to kill a hapless human because *you* need to see their realm."

She giggled and flitted around the Fae Warrior. "Nothing bad will happen, cousin."

"Famous last words, Your Highness."

Alana paused, drawing her brows tight. He only called her by an honorific when she'd tapped into his ire. "Relax."

"Nay. I will not. Until you get this idea out of your head."

She flopped down on her bed with a sigh. "I have to get out of here."

Concern flashed in his eyes, and she tried to swallow her sense of triumph.

I have him now.

Xander was familiar with the desire to run away. "Did something happen?" He took a step toward her.

Alana smiled softly and shook her head. "Nay."

He narrowed his eyes and tilted his head, his white-blond warrior braid shifting with the movement. His hair was tightly plaited, like all Fae Warriors, and her cousin's fell past his waist, denoting his strength and prestige.

Like most Fae soldiers, he stood well over six feet, just as broad and muscular. She was short in comparison at about five and a half feet tall—and small for a Fae woman.

His wings were iridescent, with colors dancing over them as he moved. They were long and elegant, extending a foot or two higher than his already impressive height. Although, looks could be deceiving; Fae Warrior wings appeared delicate, but they were as strong as the men themselves.

They shuddered and shifted, even though he stood unmoving before her, the slight vibration showing his irritation as sure as his tight shoulders. Xander was still wearing his sword and hunter green armored chest-plate, as if he'd come to her from sparring with his brothers-in-arms.

"I…need to go."

His violet stare—just like her own—narrowed to slits. "Why?"

Alana sighed. "I need away. From the castle. From Court. From…Father."

"Has he been hassling you about picking a suitor again?"

She shook her head. "Nay. Not really."

Her cousin adjusted his giant weapon and took a seat next to her on the oversized bed. "Then why now?

Beltane's feast is days away."

The jewel-encrusted chandelier above them alit, its magic sensing the fading day outside. Rubies, diamonds, and sapphires twinkled in the newly magic-born light, adding to the soft glow awakening in her suite. The fireplace, which also had precious gems embedded in the brick, would give birth to a fire soon, warming the room just enough for her to sleep comfortably.

The opulence of her rooms held little appeal, even though the suite was the only area of the vast Fae palace she'd ever been able to call her own. Her *safe* place, but as she'd told Xander, she didn't feel anything but *trapped* as of late.

"Exactly. *Now* is the perfect time to away, when there are so many visitors. When I can manage to not be noticed."

He arched an eyebrow. "You are the Crown Princess. No matter the circumstances, your absence will be noticed."

"Please do this for me, Xander. *With* me."

"Nay." Her cousin crossed his arms over his broad chest and leaned away from her.

"I'll go without you." Alana shot to her feet and whirled around, her royal purple gown billowing, but she ignored the moving air that caressed her legs.

"You will not." He stood as well, intentionally towering over her, his eyes flashing.

She glared. "*You* will not order *me* around."

"My vow is to protect your life."

"As you will. As you always do."

"Aye. But I cannot allow you to be so reckless."

She sighed and paced in front of him. "The last thing I want is to be cross with you, Xander."

His hard expression softened a bit, and he sighed as he sat back on the edge of her bed. "Alana…"

They were more than cousins. More than guard to princess. They were friends. *Best* friends. She loved him like the brother she'd never had. They'd been inseparable since they were wee.

"I love you, too," she whispered, moving closer so she could hug him.

He didn't wrap his arms around her right away—a sure sign she was far from forgiven. However, when he embraced her, it was tight.

Alana pulled away several seconds later, then tugged his face down to press a kiss to his cheek. "I need to do this."

"Why?" he asked for the hundredth time.

She couldn't put it to words, but she didn't want to admit that. Nor could she explain the restlessness worming its way from her belly to her limbs. If she didn't hold herself together, she'd be shaking in front of him. "I just *have* to."

"I do not like it."

"I know." Alana rested her hands on his shoulders and met his gaze. "I *will* go without you. Not a threat. It's a promise."

"You won't." Xander sighed and broke their eye contact. His tone was resigned.

Her stomach jumped but she kept her face impassive. If she showed her victory, her cousin would remain irritated with her — or worse, regain his anger. "You'll go with me, then?"

"As if I have a choice." The acquiescence was a mutter, but it was still what she wanted to hear.

"Thank you, cousin."

He grunted.

She grinned.

"You still look like a princess." Xander's gaze burned as it assessed.

"I do not. I have on trews and a leine." Alana spun around, grinning.

"Of the finest material."

She sighed. "You're not going to lighten up at all, are you?"

They'd decided to wait until the next morning, but even after a night to sleep on things, her cousin appeared as grumpy as ever.

She was lucky he'd shown up as agreed upon.

"Nay." His voice was hard, and the frown was likely to mar his handsome face permanently at this rate.

"Cousin, please — "

"I will do my duty to keep you safe, Your Highness. But I shall not pretend to like this. Or be accepting of your recklessness."

"Goddess, you sound like my father."

Xander scowled. "Keeping you safe is the *only* thing he and I agree upon."

Alana ignored him and snapped her fingers. A

short mantel appeared from nowhere. It was brown—instead of her normal color—royal purple being her favorite shade for its darkness, but she often wore purple of all hues. She donned it, pulling the hood up to cover her head.

She'd bound her long hair, but her tresses were too fine to stay so; they never did. The cloak fell mid-thigh and would keep her concealed enough, she hoped. "Let's go to the Faery Stones."

"How do you propose to fool the guards? The Stones are spelled against stealth magic."

"I know."

"Well?" Xander arched a fair eyebrow.

"I shall figure it out when we get there." Alana stepped closer as her cousin snorted. That wasn't exactly the truth, but she didn't want to confess everything just yet. He could read minds, so she quickly built mental walls, lest he be cross with her.

Again.

"Do you even know where the Stones *are* in the Human Realm?" her cousin asked.

"Nay. But we shall find out."

"If you want an adventure, why the Human Realm? Why don't we just go to the falls? We can swim in the hot springs and stay as long as you like."

"We're not children anymore. It won't satisfy." She shook her head. "That's a poor adventure."

The caves riddled with natural springs they'd discovered at the Grànnda Falls years ago were private, hidden behind the giant waterfall, but not what she needed. Alana could have a warm bath at home.

Fae avoided the area because unlike most of the bright colored foliage in their realm, it resembled the muted browns and greens of the Human Realm. *Grànnda* was the Fae word for *ugly*. Rumor had it, the whole area was cursed. There were some villages of exiled Fae living in the area, but they didn't interact with society.

"Just fly us to the Field of Light. Please." She wrapped her arms around his waist.

Xander flexed his wings. "I will not harm a Fae Warrior for your whims, Alana."

"Harm? Who's going to come to harm?"

"The guards will not let you just walk to the Faery Stones and do as you please, princess or not. They will not obey any orders to step aside and allow you access. You know that, right?"

"The area will be unguarded."

"How so?" His question was sharp.

"I...adjusted the schedule." Her neck warmed, but she made herself maintain his gaze.

Xander's eyes widened. "My father will not be pleased."

Her uncle was captain of the entirety of the king's soldiers, as well as leader of her father's personal guard. He was in charge of all Fae watch schedules, for the Faery Stones and the palace alike.

"Uncle Daegus will not find out. If we hurry. 'Tis an overlap of an hour. No more. We must go now."

"How about when we return?"

Alana gnawed her bottom lip. "I had not—"

"Thought ahead," Xander finished for her, frown

firmly back in place.

She squared her shoulders. "I am the princess. I shall do what I please. Take me now." Her order was clear.

Her cousin grunted in answer, narrowing his eyes, but wrapped his arms around her and pulled her into his chest. He pumped his wings once, then twice, and lifted them into the air.

She held on and hid her smile against him.

Xander's grip in return was almost too-tight, as if he meant her to feel his ire.

She could anyway—part of her magic was empathic—but she didn't comment. She really did regret his upset with her. She was closer to no one.

Alana lifted her head as the Field of Light came into view. She'd moved the times and the names around on the guard schedule, so they'd all think another patrol group was present. When the Warriors returned shortly, they'd report that the Faery Stones had been left unguarded, but hopefully no one would trace the lapse back to her. Her uncle might get chastised by her father, but there hadn't been another way.

She winced. Uncle Daegus was stern at best. If he discovered it was, *she* who caused problems for him with King Fillan—well, her status wouldn't save her from punishment.

Damn.

Xander's deep voice pulled her focus from the unladylike curse. "Ah, your choices are finally dawning on you, are they?" His words were dry, and she cursed the fact he could read minds.

The same had been a talent of her mother's, and as a child it'd never boded well for her. The queen's dark eyes and smiling face danced into her mind and Alana frowned.

She'd been dead for years now, but it didn't make her miss her mother any less. They'd always been close. The queen had been as soft and loving as her father was cruel and hard.

"Don't think of Aunt Elysia now and make me feel guilty for being mad at you," her cousin said.

"Guilt? I didn't know you could suffer such," Alana quipped. "Maybe I should cause it more often."

Xander said nothing, and when she looked at him, he flexed his jaw and looked straight ahead, as if he was avoiding her gaze.

She'd at least expected a smirk. "Xander—"

"'Tis fine." His voice was curt.

Alana should've known better than to tease where her mother was concerned. Queen Elysia had been a mother to him as well, in many ways. *He* missed her, too. She could feel it coming off him.

His own mother—a former princess, and her father's sister, had given up her status to marry down—his father, the winged Fae Warrior Captain. They'd snuck off when the king had forbidden them from marrying and bound themselves with magic so they couldn't be forced apart without both of them perishing.

King Fillan had never forgiven his sister, but he had Uncle Daegus. Xander's mother, her Aunt Aileana, hadn't been able to cope. She'd turned to smoking Acana root after Xander's birth.

The root came from the maroon-barked trees that Fae healers used for their medicinal properties, but because the tree flourished all over the realm, the powder harvested was widely abused. Her aunt had powerful healing magic and unlimited access to the drug.

Her mother had pretty much taken Xander in; Aunt Aileana was always in a drugged haze, and couldn't care for her son—or select a nursemaid to do so. Even now, Alana's aunt was an addict and rarely fully lucid.

They'd been raised and educated together, until her cousin had started Warrior training at her uncle's insistence, around age twelve. He'd said his son wasn't a prince and shouldn't be considered as one.

Uncle Daegus treated him harshly, although Xander rarely talked about it. He wasn't the captain's son; he was just another Fae Warrior under his command.

"At any rate, I'm sorry," she whispered, but he didn't comment. She'd let it go for now—he never stayed mad for long, and Xander would feel her sincerity.

Her eyes swept the home of the Faery Stones. Their people called the grassy knoll *the Field of Light* because when the Stones were alight, the magic-born crystals glowed with a white-gold radiance, especially the center Stone.

Xander landed at the foot of the dais that elevated the Faery Stones from the long swaying blue and orange grass that covered the area.

A huge Acana tree stood not ten feet from the

raised platform, its pink and purple leaves swaying in the gentle breeze on thick maroon branches.

The weather was nice — mild, as it always was. Her father employed the best weather mages to keep it not too hot, not too cold. They kept the sun shining and the rain away until it was needed.

So irritating.

Could not even the weather be as it was *supposed* to?

Her father had to control *everything*.

The vast area was usually patrolled by a half Wing of Fae Warriors — six men made up a guard unit and rotated out with the other half of each Wing.

"Let us be quick about this trickery," Xander said, crossing his arms over his hunter green chest-plate.

Alana sighed and shook her head. "Thank you for coming with me," she pushed out, instead of the retort on her tongue. It would do no good, and she wanted her cousin by her side. More than that, she wanted him to enjoy himself.

He snorted. "Not likely."

"Don't read my mind then," she snapped. She needed to reinforce the spell to block her thoughts. Because she trusted him, it wasn't something Alana normally did, but most Fae used magic to block such an invasion. Mind reading was a common trait.

Instead of waiting for his answer, she jogged up the dais and inhaled fresh air.

The Faery Stones hummed in her head, magic moving over her form like a caress. She'd always had a strong draw to the Stones and had been able to open them without issue.

Not all Fae could hear the melody they omitted. Each Stone had a different tone; Alana could already feel the thrumming, although she'd barely caressed the crystals.

They were made up of five clustered natural formations, originating in a cave before being relocated to the Field of Light. There were contradicting legends about why and how the Faery Stones had been moved, but they'd been here so long—probably six or seven long Fae generations—most accepted the grassy knoll as their rightful home and birthplace.

They were perfectly spaced from each other in a loose circle. One was centered, and the other four surrounded it. The crystals atop the five rough pillars were forged in magic. The one in the middle was larger than the rest. It was the key to making the others work. They had to be in tune as a whole to open a magical doorway.

She touched the Stones in order, continuing the pattern required. All five crystals lit up from the inside, and power coursed through her, making her limbs tingle.

A lyrical, rhythmic hum reverberated, becoming louder every second, and she repeated the song in her head as well as aloud, humming the order.

Alana pushed more magical energy into the movement of her hands, begging the Stones to be quick about their task.

The first *pop* sounded, indicating the portal *would* open. Then she heard the sound of tearing parchment.

The following *pop-pop-pop* was each louder than the last, and a magic-born gale swirled around her; her hair had already worked itself loose, flying in her eyes. Her mantle, too, was disturbed, dancing around her thighs. The hood flapped against her shoulders.

Xander stood in her periphery; his long plait was also soaring, but she didn't spare her cousin a glance.

Their time was even shorter now; she needed to work fast so they could go.

White light shot straight up toward the sky, cresting the tall Acana tree from the center crystal of the Faery Stones, the last step before the gateway's birth.

Anticipation hit Alana in waves, making her breath hitch, and she released her hold on the final crystal.

A shimmering orb appeared beside the dais, hazy and wobbly as it grew and hovered over the orange grass. The larger it got, the more the fuzziness started to clear, but she couldn't make out what was on the other side.

The view held a glistening darkness, as if it was night. That didn't make sense; time in the Fae Realm followed that of the Human Realm. Day was day and night was night in the same stretch of hours.

A sliver of fright sliced down her spine, and she chided herself. Perhaps it was just dark where the Faery Stones' twin set was located?

The portal stopped growing, and light was visible shining through from the other side. Probably from the Human Realm's Stones.

Alana jumped off the side of the dais in front of the magic bubble instead of going down the stairs. She shot her cousin a glance and peered through the way to the other realm. "Sand? Do you see sand?"

Xander offered a curt nod and drew his sword. "Aye. Let's get this over with."

She sucked back a sigh as his sense of danger, his wariness, washed over her magic and chased her fascination away. "Don't ruin this for me, cousin."

"Stay close."

Alana shook her head but obeyed, falling in behind him. She bid her exasperation to go away; peril *could* be near; they were entering a realm other than their own, so her cousin was right to be cautious, but she still wanted to go.

They stepped through the portal, and it closed behind them with a *pop*.

chapter two

"Yer all done, brother."

"Thank ye, lass."

Janet grinned as she brushed hair from his shoulders with a piece of linen. Then she slid around to the front of him and scrutinized her work. "Looks good, though I ne'er imagined ye'd want yer hair short."

Alex flashed a grin and ran his hand through his newly shorn locks. His hair had been down to the middle of his back. Looking at all the loose dark patches on the floor, perhaps he didn't have much left at all. "Now people dinnae get Duncan an' me mixed up."

His younger sister arched a dark eyebrow "Is that what 'tis abou'?"

He shook his head. "Nay. I wanted a change."

"'Tis a change all right." His twin pushed off the wall, studying him as their sister had. "Ye look…odd."

"Thank ye." Alex kept his voice dry, eliciting a grin from Duncan.

"Dinnae listen ta him, I'm sure you'll still catch tha eye of all tha lasses." Janet winked.

He groaned. That was the *last* thing he wanted.

In the months since he'd become laird, the lasses were already all over him. They always had been, but now all hoped to be the one he'd catch and call wife, Lady of the Castle.

Alex was two and twenty, *dammit*.

Not ready to wed.

Their father, Iain, hadn't broached the subject yet, but the time was no doubt coming. Alex couldn't be a proper laird without a wife…and an heir. Duncan was lucky he'd been born second.

"Aye." His brother chuckled. "Now ye can see his bonnie face better."

Janet giggled.

"Bonnie?" Alex growled.

His twin beamed.

"I s'pose ye suffer from tha same fate then, little brother. As ye have tha *same* face."

Duncan crossed his arms over his broad chest and tilted his head to one side, shifting his long dark hair. "Aye. Yet I'm no' complainin' abou' attention from tha lassies."

Janet rolled her eyes. "If Da catches you tupping one more maid, you may no' be 'round much longer. No' ta mention, I shall ne'er see tha wine cellar in tha same light." She scrunched up her nose, looking very much her age of five and ten. Adorable, too.

Alex laughed, but he was torn. He should admonish his sister. She shouldn't have knowledge of such things. "Again?"

At least their brother had the decency to blush. "Aye." Duncan looked down. Shifted in his deer-hide boots.

"Who this time?"

"Helen."

"Ah." The lass hadn't been working at Dunvegan

long, but she was a pretty petite blonde—what his brother liked.

"Peg is why Da is angry," Janet said. "He threatened ta dismiss her."

Duncan pulled an uncomfortable expression, fidgeting again. His boots made a shuffling noise as if he'd rubbed the stone wall behind him. His brow was tight, and his blue eyes darted all around. He avoided looking at either sibling.

"Peg?"

"Aye." Their sister nodded. "Peg knows he was caught wit' Helen, and is—"

"Makin' things difficult." Duncan's voice was as reluctant as his expression. Embarrassed.

Alex shook his head. "Jesu, brother. Why dinnae ye jus' go ta tha tavern like everaone else?"

"T'would be wise." His twin swallowed, making the apple of his throat bob.

"Nay." Janet glared. "T'would be *wise* ta stop your impure ways. Or take a wife."

Duncan scowled and shuddered, his wide shoulders shaking.

Alex chuckled. "Ye have tha right of it, sister." He gestured to the lass, who was wise beyond her years. "Ye should listen ta her, brother."

"Dinnae tell Mother. She's got enough ta deal with," Duncan whispered. His cheeks were still tinged pink, and he rubbed the back of his neck.

Silence fell, and now all three of them avoided each other's gazes.

Their mother had been sick for over two years, and

no matter what healer their father had brought to Dunvegan, she'd failed to improve.

As of a few months past, they currently had a man from Clan Beaton living with them permanently. The Beatons were famous all over Scotland for their healing skills, yet Malcolm Beaton had yet to help their mother. He'd succeeded in keeping her comfortable, but he'd been realistic from the start.

It was only a matter of time.

Their father spent his time devoted to her, so the duties of laird had partially fallen to Alex. Since Malcolm had pronounced things had worsened, however, his father had officially stepped aside. He rarely left their mother's suites.

Iain MacLeod was open in his declaration that the woman he'd married was the love of his life. He said it was his duty to show it.

Alex shook his head.

Love. Marriage.

Not for him. Not *yet* anyway.

He loved the lasses — though his brother's activities and appetite put his own to shame, but he wasn't tempted to find one for keeps.

Not even for the sake of his clan.

He'd always known he'd be laird. It'd just come too soon. Now he wrestled with selfishness that did nothing but keep guilt churning in his gut. As much as he loved his parents, it was unfair.

His sister suffered just as much. Since their mother had taken ill, Janet had acted as Lady of the Castle. A slip of a lass, running Clan MacLeod's massive

Dunvegan Castle. Yet she did her duty without complaint, and she did it well.

Alex stood and brushed the remaining hair from his leine, watching it dust the stone floor. He tugged Janet in his arms and kissed her forehead. "Thank ye, lass."

She stared; her expression quizzical. Concern danced in her sapphire eyes. "You already thanked me. And 'tis no' necessary, brother."

"I appreciate ye, nonetheless."

"Are you well, Alex?" She squeezed her arms around him.

"Aye, lass."

Even Duncan looked worried when their eyes met. "Alex?"

"Both of ye stop lookin' a' me like tha'. I'm braw."

Their brother nodded, but the concern didn't fade from his eyes.

"I need some air." Alex sighed.

Janet stepped away, her countenance mirroring his twin's.

"I shall go ridin'," Alex said. "Bán could use exercise, no doubt."

"I've ta go collect rents. Ye wan' ta accompany me? I'm bringin' Cormac, amongs' tha men," his brother said.

He shook his head. In years past, he and Duncan had gone to collect the tithing from all the MacLeod holdings, but his heart wasn't in duty at the moment. Alex wanted to run away. "Nay. Our cousin should do ye well. I'll see ye in a fortnight or so? Surely a good plan, ta disappear fer a while."

"Aye, I think bein' away will help tha Helen and Peg situation. Cool Da's ire, too."

He smirked. "Ye are a coward, brother."

Duncan grinned but didn't disagree. "I have duties ta see ta, is all."

"Aye, 'tis that, a'course."

Janet rolled her eyes again but flashed a grin.

"Mayhap, ye can console Peg, brother?" His twin winked.

"Nay, I dinnae tup MacLeod maids." Alex mock glared. "An' neither should ye."

"I'd say he learned his lesson," their sister said. "Da threatened ta throw him ou' on his ear."

"He ordered me ta muck stalls fer a month."

Alex crossed his arms over his chest. "Then how 'tis yer leavin' ta collect tha rents?"

"He volunteered." Janet grinned. "Ta get back inta Da's good graces."

"Och, lass, ye talk too much," Duncan accused, but he rammed his hand through his dark hair.

Alex chuckled. "Then off wit' ye."

His twin bowed at the waist. "Aye, my laird." He winked again, when he straightened, and Janet fell into a fit of giggles as Duncan whirled from the laird's chambers with a flourish.

"Our brother is too charmin' fer his own good."

Alex harrumphed. "I dinnae ken abou' tha'."

His sister grinned again and shook her head, making her ebony locks dance over her shoulders.

The wind danced around his face, but no longer did it rustle his hair along with his leine and the MacLeod plaid he wore. It was odd, having cropped locks, but it was good.

Different is good.

Alex sat high on the ridge on Bán's wide back, surveying the castle gates he had no desire to go back through.

His stallion nickered as he adjusted his hooves, and the sound vibrated under his thighs.

"Nay, laddie. We dinnae be goin' home."

For now.

He couldn't avoid Dunvegan forever.

The horse's gray mane shifted over his snowy coat as another gust caressed them both, and Alex shivered. It wasn't cold exactly, Beltane was around the corner, but spring was teasing Skye more than presenting itself.

He sighed and turned his mount away from the castle he should be riding toward. They'd go back to the beach until he was ready to face…reality.

Alex hadn't visited his mother since the previous day, and he should. Speak to his father, and maybe affirm that his brother and the men had ridden out to collect the rents.

The laird should know that, right?

Later.

He'd handle it all later. When he had to.

The water was rough today, the surf frothy as it slammed into the loamy beach, each wave bigger than the one before, splashing higher; demanding to be noticed. He watched from the safety of his mount before he kneed him forward.

Observing the mild violence on the shore made Alex fidget. He wanted to dive in, have a swim, as much as he wanted to run from it. As if the sea would make him feel worse, since it was a visual example of his churning stomach.

He let the big stallion guide him, his hold on the reins looser than it should be.

Bán whinnied and tossed his head, but he paid him no mind as the horse wandered down the beach at a walk.

The stretch before them was deserted, but Alex needed to at least pay attention to where they headed. He had no desire to tangle with Clan MacDonald — the laird was a tough man, and the tenuous peace between their clans had only been in existence since he and Duncan were lads.

He couldn't jeopardize that by mere distraction. Their lands bordered each other, and they shared the beach.

Hugh, the son of the laird and heir, was a few years their junior, and had been in a few tussles with Duncan. The lad was an arseling, at best. He was braw, almost as tall, and broad as they were, so he'd given his brother a run for his coin the last time. Hugh

MacDonald didn't need a reason to fight, other than their differing surnames.

Alex sighed. If only all his…issues…could be solved with something as simple as a fist fight. He'd take on any challenger.

Ye dinnae be able ta run from life, lad.

He could hear his da's words in his mind. Of course, the man had been referring to caring for his sick mother, but the sentence resonated.

Is that what I'm doing?

Running? From duties, responsibilities…*life*, as it was?

Bán nickered and slowed, swishing his tail.

Alex smiled and gripped the horse's reins, encouraging him to continue on, but the stallion had his head down, nibbling on the long grasses at the edge of the sandy area to his left.

"Ah, yer bein' stubborn taday, are ye?" He chuckled and threw his leg over to dismount. His boots hit the sand with a soft *thud.*

He left his loyal steed to his desires and patted Bán's neck, running his hands over his coarse mane while he grazed. Or tried to. There wasn't much vegetation, but the horse seemed determined to get it all. The grinding sound of him chewing brought another smile to Alex's lips.

Voices caught his attention, and he whipped his head up, scanning the beach in front of him. No one was visible.

There were rocks—large and small alike to

obscure his view—and of course the water was loud, but he'd definitely heard voices.

The expanse ahead was made up of a series of small caves, leading up to cliffs. On the other side of them ended MacLeod lands and began what belonged to Clan MacDonald.

Were members from his rival clan coming at him?

"Who goes there?" Alex called, one hand on the hilt of his claymore, but he didn't draw it. He narrowed his eyes and took a few steps away from his still-grazing stallion.

It'd be more prudent to mount and turn—go home—but something kept his boots glued to the ground.

They were coming closer, and he was able to discern a little, even though he couldn't make out the words, but so far, he still saw no one. The deeper voice had to be a man, and was speaking in harsh tones that betrayed irritation, but the softer one—female—answered in quick snaps that sounded like commands.

He moved forward to where the terrain started to incline. Alex could climb up the rocky hill to have more visibility, but their volume told him they would join him soon enough. He only heard two people, so he relaxed his hold on his weapon.

Indeed, it was only two, for the figures appeared in a few moments, moving into view around a large boulder. Both were fair-haired, and the man was tall, around Alex's own height of six feet, five inches. He looked broad, too.

A warrior.

The lass was petite; the man towered probably a foot over her. They were speaking in hushed tones now, apparently oblivious that he was only a few feet from them.

Bán nickered behind Alex, and the man's head shot up. He shoved the lass behind him, but she didn't stay put.

She hurried around him, slipping from his grasp and looked in Alex's direction.

Their eyes locked.

The lass froze, and her hip-length flaxen locks were the only thing that remained in motion, swaying around her like an aura. She wore a short brown mantle that stopped mid-thigh, but instead of skirts or a gown, she wore trews — *purple* trews.

However, it was her ethereal face and unusual eyes that held his attention — and wonder. He'd never seen a more beautiful creature.

She recovered first and inclined her head. "Good day." Her voice — no longer the angry snap it had been — was sultry, just like it should sound, and washed over him.

Alex shivered, and it had naught to do with the wind. He blinked. Cleared his throat so he'd be able to speak. He echoed her nod, and gripped Bán's reins with white knuckles. Somehow, he needed his stallion beside him. "Good day." He winced. The greeting had been barely a croak.

Out of the corner of his eye, there was movement, and he tensed.

The large man rushed in front of her again, his hand on the hilt of a sword, but it was still in its scabbard. His breastplate was odd—dark green in color, and Alex had never seen colored armor before. His hair was the same white-blond as the lass', but it was in a thick plait, dancing as he adjusted his stance. He leveled Alex with a narrowed glare.

"I mean ye no harm." Alex dropped the reins and threw his palms out—keeping his hand away from his claymore.

The lass peered around her protector—as best she could, since she was so diminutive behind him. "'Tis all right, Xander," she whispered.

The warrior didn't move, nor look at his charge. "Nay. 'Tis *not*." His voice was the same hard tone Alex had overheard before he could see them.

Their accents were Scottish but had a refined edge that was different from his own brogue. They weren't from the Highlands.

"Are ye lost?" He forced a breath. "These are my lands. I'm tha Laird MacLeod."

The gorgeous lass perched delicate hands on her guard's thick arm but couldn't seem to budge him this time. She flashed a smile from around him instead. "Nay. What're you called?"

The tall man glared harder. "Your Hi—" He pushed words out through gritted teeth, his jaw was hard, and his eyes deadly slits.

She threw him a frown, and he stopped talking.

"Alex." He inclined his head again, and wanted to take a step forward, but wasn't fond of the idea of that big sword being pulled—or being run through.

The lass managed to slide around her protector, despite his growl and obvious disapproval. "I'm Alana." She put her hand out and Alex hid his amusement, lest he offend her.

'Twas a man's greeting.

"Alana." Her name was clearly all warning, but she ignored the tall blond man.

Alex's eyes darted to him, then back to the lass. He put his hand against her much smaller one, and a bolt of energy shot up his arm, into his bicep. He fought shudders and swallowed and fell into her alluring gaze.

Her eyes were—violet?

They were definitely more purple than blue. He sucked back a gulp.

Surprise lit her pretty face, and she looked at their joined hands before meeting his eyes again. Her mouth fell open—just a touch, and a little pink tongue darted out to moisten her bottom lip.

Alex swallowed a groan as the need to taste her rolled over him.

What?

The uncomfortable shifting of her protector broke whatever spell held him captive, and when Alana tugged, he released her hand, but Alex could feel her reluctance.

Her fair brow was drawn tight, as if she thought her guard's presence was an intrusion—like *he* did. She swallowed and he wanted to kiss her throat.

Alex looked from one to the other, spotting a resemblance. Not only the hair, but the two people before him had the same color eyes. "I mean ye no harm," he repeated, but her guard's shoulders didn't loosen.

Are they siblings?

They could be. Looked enough alike to be so.

Relief flooded him. If she was…*with* the man…or married…it would bother him.

Where's that coming from?

He had no right to be jealous of a man concerning a lass, when he knew neither party.

"Alana, let us go," the man barked.

"Nay, Xander." She glared up at him, then looked back at Alex. "Forgive my cousin, my laird. He's rude."

Ah, her cousin. Good.

He didn't like just how pleased he was with the information.

Xander harrumphed, but finally released the hold on his sword, only to cross his arms over his broad chest.

Alex squared his shoulders and exhaled but didn't want to reveal his nerves. Nor did he want either of them to notice his…intrigue…with the lass. Although, no doubt by the way she'd looked at him; she'd felt something, too.

Why does that please you?

"Nay, 'tis no bother." He forced polite words out. He looked the cousins up and down. Other than the unusual armor, their clothing wasn't odd — except perhaps the hue of the lass' trews. The fabrics looked like they were made of the finest materials.

Who were these people?

It'd be rude to demand that knowledge, even if they were on MacLeod lands unannounced.

Alana was studying him as much as he studied them, and Alex heard her guard make a noise in his throat.

"Are ye lost?" he repeated his earlier question.

She looked at Xander before answering. "Nay. We're…visiting."

"Visitin'? From where?" He scanned the waters. "I dinnae see a ship. An' ye've no mounts. Is all well?"

Silence descended as the cousins again exchanged a look.

Alex narrowed his eyes. "Where're ye from?"

Alana fidgeted in the sand.

Xander stepped forward and muttered a word that sounded Gaelic, but it was off somehow.

Alex didn't understand it. He opened his mouth

to speak, but no words came out. His limbs suddenly weighed four stone a piece and he wavered on his feet. His vision narrowed and he couldn't keep his eyes open.

Then the world went black.

chapter three

"Xander!" Alana rushed forward to the handsome dark-haired laird and knelt at his side without a backward glance at her cousin. She'd not even waited for a response to her shout.

Alex was in a heap in the pebble-ridden sand, but his chest rose and fell in an even rhythm.

He was just asleep.

Relief washed over her, and she had to suppress the odd urge to caress his beardless cheek. He had high cheekbones, and sculpted features that added to his appeal. His eyes were closed, but they were sapphire, and 'twas a shame she couldn't get a better look, since she was closer now. She'd remember their deep hue for all her days. His gaze had captivated her, as if the MacLeod laird had cast a spell. He couldn't have. He was only human, after all.

She glared over her shoulder at her overprotective hovering bodyguard. "*Why* did you do that?"

Xander growled. "You have to ask?"

"He was just making conversation! Showing concern for our wellbeing."

"Nay." The word was hard, and her cousin's eyes narrowed. "He was asking questions we *cannot* answer."

"He meant us no harm." Alana repeated the

handsome laird's words and frowned. "If he had, he would've drawn his sword."

Xander harrumphed and stayed a few feet away. "Let us go, Your Highness."

"Do not call me that here," she snapped. "And I won't leave him like this. Something bad could happen to him."

He cast his eyes skyward and said a very rude word in Fae that should never be uttered in the presence of a lady, let alone his princess.

She arched an eyebrow but didn't respond; the unconscious laird demanded all her attention.

Alex wore an ivory long-sleeved leine with ties at the neckline, tucked into the plaid belted around him. The rich pattern consisted of greens and blues, along with a yellow and red stripe, and currently flapped in the wind, revealing part of a powerful thigh, and Alana couldn't tear her eyes away.

Dark hair lightly smattered the flesh of his knees and down his calf, as well as that tempting expanse of tanned skin above, and intrigued her even more. Fae had no body hair, and the difference in front of her made her want to see what it would feel like beneath her fingertips.

The ties of his shirt had come loose, and the vee hung open, hinting at the supple skin of his neck and collarbone. He looked peaceful in his repose; despite the fact sleep had been forced by magic.

"What spellword did you use? You didn't wish him harm, did you?" Alana whipped her head around and pushed accusation into her tone.

Intent was everything in magic. If her cousin had wished him to never wake when he'd done the spell, Alex would not.

Then again, Xander's magic was diminished in the Human Realm. When they'd arrived, her cousin's wings had not, and he'd been disoriented for moments that had felt like hours.

She'd panicked and tried hard not to *show* it, half-surprised he didn't demand for her to reopen the Faery Stones and go right back home. She hadn't expected him to be wingless. Then again, they wouldn't have been able to explain wings to any human. Maybe it was a kind of protection for Fae Warriors.

Alana didn't feel any different, magically speaking, and her powers were much greater than his. She'd thrown a few spells around in the cave that housed the Faery Stones in this realm—everything had worked, as did her empathic powers, because she'd still felt Xander's unease, which had only worsened without the ability to fly.

His wings weren't his source of power, but her cousin was like most Fae Warriors, and relied on the iridescent flesh for strength and prestige. Fae tended to be proud, and in that her cousin was the same—as far as his Warrior accomplishments were concerned. Otherwise, her protector didn't have a haughty bone in his body. He was a good—no, a *great*—man.

"Nay. He should wake shortly. An aching head at most. I meant him no harm." Amusement wrapped the last of his words, but then his expression fell, and he frowned. "Evidently, I don't have true power…here."

"Xander—"

"I didn't kill him, and I could have. I'm sworn to protect you." This was harder, with a touch of bitterness.

"He wasn't *trying* to harm me," she repeated.

"Alana, I shall not argue with you." He averted his violet gaze and sighed. "Get away from him. Let us go from here."

Alana ignored him and stared at Alex MacLeod again. He looked young, yet he'd said he was *the* laird. It was hard to judge human age—Fae lived two to three times longer and aged slower—so if she was home, she'd say he appeared to be of an age with her five and fifty, but it was likely he was much younger.

Unlike the Fae, humans lived in clans, so he was the leader of his? Perhaps he wasn't that young after all?

Alana shuddered, and it wasn't from the blustery day. Why was she so fascinated with this sleeping man? Was he more lad than man?

She wanted to touch him. Explore his body. His legs and thighs were full of muscle, and even though his leine was loose—also rustling in moving air—she could sense his chest and arms were the same. It was a shame the fabric didn't cling like her cousin's armor.

Alex's shoulders were broad, and his waist trim. She was more attracted to him than she'd ever been to any Fae man she'd dabbled with.

Attracted? To a human?

Aye.

She wanted to *kiss* him. Cuddle close and feel his body hair against her skin. A startled awareness tingled down her spine — like when he'd touched her. Alana had experienced a jolt of energy from a being with no magic? She *had*.

Sometimes, in her realm, a reaction like that was an indication of fated mates. She jumped, her heart hammering.

Nonsense.

A human — handsome or not — couldn't be meant for *the* Fae Princess of Scotland. Her father would kill him on sight.

The big white horse nickered as he grazed but didn't come closer.

Alana let her eyes sweep the hilly area behind the stallion, then looked back at the sleeping laird. "Alex…MacLeod he said. So, I guess we're on Skye."

"Of *course*, you know what this place is called, and who lives here." Xander's words were dry, his fair eyebrow arched.

She shrugged. "I studied the human lands and their clans, as well as Fae geography. There's nothing wrong with being educated."

He snorted. "Nay, but your fascination with the Human Realm leads to things like this." Her cousin gestured to Alex's unmoving form.

She chose not to answer his accusation, even if it was the truth. "Are you going to help me with him or not?"

"Not."

"Xander! *You* did this to him."

He scoffed. "I put him to sleep for his own good. If he's of a strong constitution, he'll be fine. Mayhap his head won't ache when he wakes. We need to leave."

Alana climbed to her feet and whirled on her guard. "Nay."

"I do *not* like your thoughts about him."

Heat slapped the back of her neck and inched into her cheeks. The wind made it worse, and even her ears burned. "Then stay out of my head," she snapped.

Xander sighed.

She muttered a spellword. "There. Now you can't hear my thoughts."

"You were thinking *loudly,* and—"

"I do not need you to regale me with my own...thoughts." She swallowed and shifted in her boots. She'd been about to say "*desires.*" Alana couldn't admit that to her cousin. She threw Alex MacLeod a glance over her shoulder.

There was no doubt about it.

She *desired* things about this man—doing things *with* the human laird—a lady of worth would never want from someone she didn't know. Someone she'd just met.

Alana turned to look back over his sleeping form.

I want him.

She shouldn't. *Couldn't.*

"We can't just...leave him like this." Alana cleared her throat when her statement wavered, and heartbeat kicked up. Thank the Goddess she'd said her thought-suppression spell. Her cousin didn't need to know her recent ideas—*at all.*

"We can, and we *will.*"

Before she could answer, Xander swung her up

over his shoulder and said a spellword to bind her there.

"Xander!" She punched at his back, but his chest-plate protected him from so much as an *"oomph."*

He shifted her higher, wrapping his arms around her legs—presumably so she couldn't kick him. Her sworn bodyguard ignored all her protests and carried Alana back toward the cave that held the Faery Stones.

Something was…nibbling at him?

What was the chomping sound in his ear?

Alex grimaced and tried to shift away, but the grinding of heavy teeth just got louder, then a soft muzzle bumped his cheek, as if insistent. "Bán?"

Had he fallen asleep in the stables?

His stallion nickered and nudged him again, this time his neck and shoulder. There was a wet sweep of a huge tongue against Alex's skin.

Fresh sea air rolled over his senses and his eyes flew open. He scrambled to sit up, ignoring the poke of sharp pebbles biting into his palms. He looked around as the encounter on the beach hit his memory full force. He gasped. "Alana?"

Where were the lass and her guard?

All Alex could see were waves crashing against the rocks, more violently than before.

"What the hell happened?" He groaned as he gained his feet, and his temples throbbed. He slid his arms around Bán and leaned into his beloved mount. He rested his forehead against the stallion's warm white coat and inhaled, concentrating to take breath deep into his lungs.

He was dizzy. His temples throbbed, like a preview of a bad headache.

Why?

The happenstance with the big blond man and the gorgeous lass ran on a loop in his mind, leaving him with more confusion.

Who are they?

"Where are they now?"

When he'd gathered his wits, Alex mounted his horse and ran his hand through his hair. He startled when his fingertips ran out of locks, then remembered his sister had cut it before he'd left Dunvegan.

He rode up and down the beach in search of Alana and her guard but failed to locate them. He repeated his path over and over until the chill in the air indicated the evening wasn't far and promised to be cold.

Alex had always been a fair tracker — although his cousin Cormac was better — but there were no clues left as to where his new acquaintances could've gone.

No footprints, and the water wasn't so high that they wouldn't have left any. He could see the imprints of Bán's hooves everywhere *they'd* traveled.

"Dinnae make sense," he whispered. "They dinnae…just disappeared…" He rubbed his chin and felt rough stubble.

How long had he been out?

How long had it been since he'd left his clan's stronghold?

He'd half a mind to retrieve his cousin and bring him back to the beach, but he couldn't. Cormac had gone with his twin to collect the rents.

Alex sighed again and shook his head. He turned his stallion and let Bán lead the way back to Dunvegan. It was time he returned home anyway.

Supper was being served when he sauntered through the great hall. He'd been gone all day, so there was no wonder his stomach was a knot, belching angry growls with its demand for sustenance.

He didn't care. Wasn't hungry.

Instead, violet eyes and flaxen locks haunted his mind's eye.

Alana.

A short brown mantle stopping mid-thigh, purple trews, and her touch, which had shot lightning through his body.

Alex hadn't imagined their encounter, had he?

Nay.

If it'd been a fantasy, he would've done more than shake her hand. Not to mention, he would've omitted the large, angry protector.

"Alex?"

"Lad, where've ye been?"

Two voices called at the same time.

He met the concerned gazes of his father and Janet. Surprise washed over him to see his da. Iain rarely came down to the hall to sup. He usually ate with his wife in her suites.

Alex jogged up the three steps attached to the dais and told himself to relax. "Is *Mamaidh*, well, Da?"

The older man's expression softened, and his shoulders loosened. His father had begun to gray at the temples a few years past, but everyone said he and Duncan looked just like him.

Since their mother had fallen ill, silver now streaked Iain's long locks all over, but he was still a tall broad MacLeod, like his sons.

"She's restin'. But 'tis *ye* I'm worried abou'."

"Me?" Alex grunted as he took his seat at the head of the table.

The housekeeper, Mairi, hurried over and put a trencher of a steaming venison steak and small loaf of bread in front of him, and he muttered thanks.

"Aye, ye, brother!" His sister's voice was urgent, and when he spared the lass a glance, she was leaning into the table, her dark brows furrowed. Her plate was empty, and she wrung her hands on her lap.

"Why?"

"The lass says ye've been gone all day, lad."

Ah, so *that* was why their father had ventured to the great hall.

Alex swallowed a sigh and bit back the urge to

correct the man. Their father hadn't said *'my laird'*. "I'm hale. Hungry, though."

Iain harrumphed and Alex felt his searching gaze even though he couldn't meet his eyes.

He tore the bread open and slathered it with honey butter. It was still warm, his favorite.

His family was silent, and he did his best to ignore them as he shoveled food into his mouth. In the very least, he could appease his stomach.

"Duncan an' tha men got underway?" Alex cleared his throat and went for a distraction.

"Aye," his father said, and nothing more.

One word.

Iain MacLeod at his most dangerous.

Alex finished his meal under the scrutinizing eye of his da, but he didn't speak, and neither did the retired laird. He tried not to shudder in his seat. Couldn't meet the blue eyes that matched his own. There'd be questions there he didn't want to answer, and besides, he didn't want to give his father another worry.

He'd nothing more to say for the evening. Alex put his fork down and pushed his chair back from the table but was keenly aware his father and sister both still watched him. "If ye'll excuse me, I'll go see Mother, then seek my bed."

His father inclined his head, but he still didn't stop staring Alex down.

"Good night, Da. Janey." He left the dais and

tried to convince himself not to run from the great hall.

His sister cornered him before he was halfway down the corridor. She must've dashed to catch his hurried pace. "Alex…"

He cocked his head to one side and studied her open face. She was too young to have so much worry in her pretty countenance. Someone her age should be concerned with a new brooch or what style to order her new gown in. Even wonder what the lasses were doing with their hair these days, chittering, and laughing with other lasses like her.

Guilt jumped up and bit at Alex, but what did *he* have to feel that way about?

It wasn't anyone's fault their mother was ill and would most likely die. It wasn't anyone's fault their father felt his place was at her side, leaving a lass of five and ten to run the castle and a lad of two and twenty as laird.

Wait…he was a man, was he not?

Aye, I am.

So, no one was at fault. Other than…God?

Alex shook himself. Thoughts like that could lead to no good. Anger with no outlet. "What, lass?"

Janet hesitated, then grabbed his arm and squeezed. "First ye ask me ta cut yer hair…then ye disappear fer tha day. Dinnae be like you. What's goin' on, brother?"

"Nothin'."

"Nothin'? Her blue eyes held more maturity than they should've been capable of. "If ye were Duncan, I might expect—"

"All is well, Janey." He gripped her hands, but her expression said she wasn't convinced. "I went fer a ride an' lost track a' time s'all." Alex had no intention of revealing his odd encounter on the beach. He needed to figure Alana and Xander out before he could recount it to anyone—if he even wanted to share.

What really happened?

His sister swallowed and opened her mouth, but he beat her to speaking.

"Do ye want ta go wit' me ta see *Mamaidh*?"

She rolled her plump bottom lip between her teeth. "Alex—"

"Janet MacLeod, I'm yer laird an' I've no need fer a second mother. Especially no' *ye*." He clenched his jaw when her sapphire eyes widened and went misty. His chest burned when the first tear made its way down her cheek.

"I dinnae know abou' a *second* mother, but I surely wish fer *ours!*" Janet snapped. Her dark locks flew about her shoulders as his sister whirled away and stalked down the hall.

When she disappeared into their mother's suite, he felt about two inches tall.

Alex sucked back a wince. He shouldn't have said that. Any motherly statements had a bite, no matter the context. A glaring reminder that theirs wasn't her effervescent self, running Dunvegan as she always had.

His sister held their family together in many ways, keeping their father's temper in check regarding their brother's antics, and keeping their mother calm, free of worries about family.

Janet was probably the strongest of them all, and he'd made her *cry*. Even as young as she was, it wasn't something she did often.

He was the biggest wretch of them all.

Alex sighed for the hundredth time of the day. He needed to gird his loins before he had the bollocks to join his sister in his mother's rooms. He wouldn't be able to withstand more tears.

CHAPTER FOUR

Alana woke in her own bed. Her temples throbbed and she cradled her head as she sat up and oriented. She groaned and used her magic to chase the pain away.

It only took a moment for the veil to clear and normalcy to descend. She breathed a sigh of relief when the discomfort fled. That little spellword was handy for headaches, even ones from over-imbibing.

She hadn't gotten drunk at any feast. Didn't remember drinking wine or mead, or anything else for that matter.

What happened?

Alana had no memory of…getting back here. She looked around her room, familiar with its sense of suffocation, but that was equal to her sense of security, despite the contradiction. This was the only place that was *hers*.

Her eyes rested on her things—her desk, her chest of drawers, the fireplace, as well as the wardrobe that held her many gowns.

She stared at the arched doorway that led into her sitting room, and to the exit of her suite. Like the rest, it was encrusted with jewels.

Alana exhaled and closed her eyes.

Home.

Right?

Funny, she could've done just as well without the extravagance. Xander's room in the Warrior Barracks was much more pleasant in many ways, his furniture simpler, his decorations sparse, even if masculine.

Females were forbidden there, but she made regular visits to see her cousin anyway—nearly as much as he was present in her rooms, but at least *he* was permitted in his role as her personal guard.

Of course, as the princess, she wasn't questioned openly for being in the Barracks, only chided by her father when he found out.

Word *always* got back to the king.

King Fillan had already lost one princess to a Fae Warrior, so he was especially keen that she stay away from winged soldiers. However, unlike her aunt, Alana had no romantic interest in any of them, especially not her blooded cousin.

Not that her father cared. He just expected to be obeyed without question, as a good daughter should. So of course, she'd upped her discretion after his last lecture, but didn't heed him.

At least Uncle Daegus never shooed her away when they'd encountered each other at the Barracks or near the fighting grounds, but who knew, the captain probably tattled on her to the king as well.

She always had to *blink* into Xander's quarters when she wanted to see him. Alana had the magical ability to picture where she wanted to go, concentrate, and she could appear there, but she couldn't do it sight-unseen. She had to visit a place once before she could *blink* to it subsequently. She couldn't teleport between realms.

Realms —

She gasped.

The Human Realm.

Alex.

The handsome laird…

Her cousin had ripped her from his side when he'd still been unconscious on the beach. Xander had thrown her over his shoulder and taken off running.

After that, things got fuzzy.

Alana didn't remember returning to the cave that held the Human Realm's Faery Stones. She didn't remember them being opened or coming home.

Obviously, her cousin had been able to open the portal without her. However, if she couldn't remember anything…that meant Xander had used magic on her. To keep her asleep.

Probably the same spell he'd knocked the laird out with. That didn't answer the question of how he'd gotten through the wing of Fae Warriors in the Field of Light, but she could figure that out later. When she spoke with him.

Damn him.

He'd taken her away from Alex MacLeod and brought her home against her will.

"How *dare* he?" she growled aloud. Alana swung her legs over the side of her bed and cursed Xander to all five levels of Fae Hell.

She hadn't gotten to say goodbye to Alex. Or make sure her cousin's magic hadn't really harmed him. She could've at least placed him on his mount's back and told the stallion to go home. She could've done so with magic.

Alana stood and said a quick spellword to don a gown. Warm air swirled around her, making her hair dance as the rich lavender day-dress settled over her body and she caressed the front as it formed to her breasts and stomach. It was one of her simpler designs, with white and dark purple stitching up and down the front, forming stripes, and made of the softest Fae silk. It had a higher bodice than most of her attire, and the sleeves were off shoulder.

She glanced over her reflection in the full-length mirror, then left her sleeping room, heading to the exit. She turned the decorative knob, but it was locked.

From the outside.

Alana tried again, then yelped as white-hot pain shot up her wrist, into her elbow, and blue sparks flew at her from the lock-spell, floating down to the floor as if innocent before dissipating.

What the…

"I'm sorry, Princess, you've been sealed inside." The deep voice from the other side of the door was *not* her cousin.

"*What?*" Her head reeled and she took a step back, ignoring the fluffy furniture surrounding her in the lavish sitting room. "Who's there?"

"Rannick, Your Highness."

Alana expelled a breath. The guard wasn't a winged warrior, but one of the many castle men-at-arms. He was oversized, but he'd always been kind to her. "Rannick, can you please open the door so we can speak?"

"Nay, I cannot, but I know a spell."

In a few heartbeats, a window opened through the thick panel, and she could see into the corridor, but experience told her it was for viewing only, not a true opening. She'd be unable to leave her suite, even if her guard allowed a large enough space.

"What happened?" Alana looked up and met the yellow-gold eyes of the big Fae man.

He was even larger than Xander, probably seven feet tall, and just as broad. He had long sable locks, and a neatly trimmed beard. His coloring made his eyes all the more stunning, like a lion with a dark mane. He was handsome, wickedly so, like most Fae.

Rannick carried two swords, so large he had to strap them crisscrossed on his wide back. His palace uniform was blue with silver trim, and an ivory under-tunic spanning his wide chest. The neckline and sleeves were only partially visible.

"I know not, Princess. I was ordered to guard you, and not permit your exit. The mages sealed your locks."

"For how long?"

"Until His Majesty calls for you."

What did Xander do?

"Where's my cousin?"

"I was not told, Your Highness."

Alana frowned.

"Worry not, food will be brought shortly."

She pursed her lips and swallowed some unladylike curses. It wasn't Rannick's fault he was following orders, or that he'd been the one saddled with her. She'd always liked him. "Thank you, Rannick. I appreciate your explanation. If you see my cousin, can you tell him to come to me?"

As her personal bodyguard, Xander would be permitted entry to her suites even if she was banned egress, as frustrating as *that* was.

The man-at-arms gave a curt nod and waved his hand.

Alana stared as the door clouded and returned to its normal carved dark wood panel. If the mages had spelled her locks, they also *blink*-proofed her suite, because her father knew her too well. She always escaped at first chance she got.

She went back to her sleeping quarters and plopped onto her bed, sighing for the twentieth time since she'd woken. *'Until His Majesty calls for you,'* Rannick had said. Well, if she'd tapped into her father's ire, it could be days, maybe even weeks. Once he'd left her confined to her suite for a month.

However, he couldn't do that this time, if only to save face. The Feast of Beltane was around the corner, and King Fillan was hosting a lavish ball.

Most of the Scottish Court would be there, but also the kings and queens from the English, Welsh, and Irish Fae Courts would be in attendance as well.

So her father would dress her up and put her on display; he couldn't hide Alana away or let it be known she was a constant *'problem'* for him. Appearances were everything to him.

Besides, if she was locked up, he couldn't parade her in front of the Irish Crown Prince, Seamus. He'd been trying to get her to entertain a betrothal with Seamus for years, but the Irishman was a buffoon. Not to mention a womanizing rake, and she couldn't stand him to look at him.

Promiscuity didn't bother her; it was commonly accepted for young Fae to have several lovers before marrying, but monogamy was expected after vows were exchanged, and Prince Seamus was under the impression royal blood made him an exception.

He was quite open with such information, which spoke loudly to the fact he was yet unwed; and he was older than she.

She'd had her fair share of dalliances, but she'd never given her maidenhead away. Kisses and intimate touches were pleasant—both giving and receiving—but she'd never met a man she'd fancied enough to consider having inside her.

Alex MacLeod's sapphire eyes and handsome features popped into her mind. His short dark hair was an oddity to most males she knew. It made him more tempting. Then…there was the jolt that'd felt like magic when they'd touched.

What is that?

She wanted to go back to the Human Realm and see him. See if they had any more…sparks.

No, she *needed* to.

Alana paced her sleeping room, and a flash of ivory caught her eye. A small scroll rested on her bedside table; it was a wonder she hadn't spotted it before.

She broke the plain red wax seal and unrolled it. The familiar hand of her cousin was scrawled inside.

I won't apologize.
-X

She harrumphed and threw the offending parchment down. "Of course, you won't." Alana rolled her eyes and couldn't help her desire that Xander was somewhere being punished too.

Xander brought her a well-laden tray of food a few hours—that felt like days—later. She'd expected a servant, but perhaps her father had also ordered her handmaidens away. It wouldn't be the first time.

"Where've you been?" Alana demanded as she whirled toward him in her sitting room as soon as the door to her suite shut with a soft *thud*. She ignored the sizzling sound of the lock-spell reengaging and the blue glow that pulsed around the oversized handle.

Her cousin sighed and set his burden on the table next to her favorite purple chaise lounge. His posture was stiff, even with his movements, and his wings vibrated, revealing his ire, and reflecting the light in the room. The moving iridescence was pretty, belying his obvious mood. "Dealing with consequences of *your* choices."

"What?" She stilled but couldn't pry her hands off their perch on her hips.

"First, I was chided by my father for allowing you to rein me into your antics. Captain Daegus is not pleased with you, and he's embarrassed by me, as usual. Then I appeased my *dear* uncle," his voice dripped disdain, "by vowing I'd never listen to your orders again."

Alana gasped. "What?" She blinked.

"You're lucky I'm still charged with your protection, *Your Highness*. Only my Oath saved me. My father," he cleared his throat, "convinced yours not to bind me to my word with any kind of magic, but I've no idea why. I've not seen the king quite *that* angry in some time. The mages were standing at his side like eager pups, the bastards."

Apprehension settled low in her gut and her stomach quivered. She swallowed. Inhaled slowly. "Are you being punished?" Her voice cracked, more of a whisper than she'd intended.

"Aye, I was given ten lashes." He delivered it matter-of-factly, but that didn't stave off her wince.

She squeezed her eyes shut and told herself to breathe. "Xander, I'm—"

He held a palm high. "Alana, don't bother. I told you your little adventure would lead to no good, and *shockingly*, I was right."

Remorse hovered, then settled in her chest. "I didn't think—"

"I *know*. You never do, and the rest of us must deal with what happens after."

Alana reared back as if he'd slapped her. Her cousin was her rock. He'd rarely snapped at her. Tears pricked her eyes, and she couldn't hold them back. "Xander—"

He looked her up and down and exhaled audibly. Closed his eyes before taking a seat on the overstuffed lavender sofa. "Don't cry." The words weren't for comfort. "Just *don't*. You've got to lie in the bed you made. And I wouldn't count on getting out of here before Beltane."

Tears were born and scalded her cheeks, but Alana didn't care about Beltane or being confined. She cared about Xander being cross with her. No, not cross. *Seriously angry.* "What happened?"

His brow furrowed. "What d'you mean?"

"You…knocked me out? I've no memory."

Her cousin sighed again and reclined into the sofa, his long plait over one shoulder, down his chest and pooling on his lap. He flexed his wings. Despite being seated on purple upholstery, he couldn't have looked more masculine. "I'd no choice."

"I'm not angry."

Xander snorted, as if asserting she shouldn't *dare* have the right to be upset.

"I'm sorry, Xander," Alana whispered. She wanted to reach for his hand, but he wouldn't have it right now. Magic and instinct alike confirmed it. She took a seat across from him on her chaise and looked at the food he'd brought.

A stew of some sort, and some bread. Nothing close to the normal feast she was presented with. Her father obviously wanted her to be treated like a servant as a part of her punishment.

She didn't care. Had always preferred simpler meals. A good rabbit stew was actually her favorite. As empty as her stomach was, as much as she needed sustenance, Alana couldn't eat.

Not until her cousin forgave her.

"How did we get caught?" She kept her voice low and tried to project calm on him with her magic.

"Stop it."

"Stop what?"

"I feel the ripples of your powers. Just...stop. I won't be coerced, Your Highness."

Alana grimaced and muttered another apology, but he shook his head.

"Remember how you didn't *account* for the Stones being guarded upon our return? Well, that's *how*." Xander finished with a curt nod.

"I'm so sorry." Repetition wasn't helping, if his expression was any indication.

"I had to tell them you fled from me, and I went after you. I told them we encountered no one; I caught you right on the other side of the Faery Stones and brought you home."

Alana sucked in a breath. He'd *lied*. A great risk, considering her father had mages that could detect dishonesty. If Xander had been discovered—

"Right. It wouldn't have been as simple as ten lashes." A scowl marred his handsome face.

She didn't dare chide him for reading her mind.

"Don't apologize again, I told you I don't want to hear it, cousin." This was softer, with less of an angry edge, but she was far from forgiven.

She deserved that.

"Are you...does your back hurt?"

He shook his head, making his braid dance. "Nay, I was permitted to see a healer, though I suspect my father didn't make that known to the king."

Alana looked at the bowl of stew again, not sure what to say, so she didn't try.

"This isn't as simple as when you flit around our realm, and it's discovered. If they knew you'd seen a human—"

"I know. My father would order his death even though we didn't tell him we're Fae." Her heart thumped.

Alex.

Alana couldn't be the reason he was harmed—or worse.

"Aye." Xander nodded when their gazes brushed. He appraised her, and his eyes softened again, but only a touch. They remained like hard violet jewels, and his expression matched. "Eat." He stood and took a breath.

"Where're you going?" Her heart sank to her gut and stayed there. Her muscles twisted and churned for good measure.

If she did eat, there was no way food would stay down.

Alana made no magical effort to hide her thoughts…her regret and sorrow. If anything, she projected them, so he had no choice but to feel how she did.

"The problem with that, my dear cousin, is that you don't *regret* going. You're just sorry we got caught, and that *I* was punished. And while I love you as I always have, I'm not quite ready to forgive you."

She startled.

He was gone before she could tell him she respected his honesty or assert she loved him too.

Xander had been right.

If they hadn't gone, she wouldn't have met Alex. Despite the consequences, she *couldn't* regret the trip.

Where was the laird now? In the Human Realm when she was literally trapped in the realm of the Fae. Not to mention, the closest person to her was angry with her.

She had *neither* of them.

Alana stared at the door. She'd never felt more alone.

She threw herself down in her chaise and sobbed so hard her body shook.

chapter five

alex rode—well, it was more like stalked—the length of the beach for hours, letting the task consume his morning just like he had yesterday, and the day before.

It'd been three days.

"Nothin'." He shook his head, and the semi-warm breeze caressed his face, washing the fresh scent of the sea over his form. As calming as it normally was, now it just tore him up inside.

Gulls called to each other above, but he ignored the pesky birds and their screeches.

He'd failed to find even the smallest clue of the gorgeous petite blonde and her oversized guard. Still, he couldn't employ his cousin Cormac's help, because Duncan and the men were still gone, and would likely be so a fortnight.

"Dammit."

Bán nickered and tossed his head, either chiding him for his language or asserting that their feat was useless.

Which would you prefer?

It wasn't like he didn't have duties. At present, there was a pile of scrolls on his desk in the laird's ledger room the steward had bid him to go over and declare yay or nay. They were to have a meeting that afternoon, and his side of things was supposed to be completed by then; decisions made.

Instead, Alex was wasting time on the beaches of Skye, and if Hamish went to his father to report his important request had gone unheeded, he'd only worry Iain more. He risked a chiding as well, but his father couldn't do more than that, really. *He* was laird now, after all.

However, Alex had no use for another conversation with his father where he did little more than grunt and nod. He'd barely survived the one from last night, when the retired laird had cornered him much like his sister had the evening he'd met Alana.

Alex was fine, but if he shouted as much, they'd peer at him in shock for speaking as such. Something like that was much more Duncan-like than something *he'd* do.

Was he really fine?

Doubt crowded his thoughts and pushed them around. He hadn't been *fine* for days.

Since the moment he'd met *her*.

The tempting lass had haunted Alex's dreams, leaving him restless and fatigued come daylight. He'd seen her naked. Touching him. Teasing him. Kissing him while she rode him.

"Perhaps I've gone mad," he muttered.

He'd seen her once — and very much clothed. How could his mind conjure up such vivid images of someone he'd seen *one* time?

Without a single stitch of a garment.

Alex had woken hard and aching. Unfulfilled,

since his hand's skill paled in comparison to the nightly visions of a flaxen-haired sprite.

He rubbed his wrist and forearm, remembering the shock of energy when they'd touched. That small moment of their skin coming together preoccupied him as much as his dreams. He kept replaying the moment—the feeling—over and over.

"What am I doin'?"

Bán whinnied as if in answer and hoofed the loamy ground. Was his stallion asserting that he hadn't a clue?

Aye, I don't either.

Since *when* did Alex talk to himself so much?

"C'mon, laddie, let us hie ta Dunvegan." He put his knees to his mount's sides, feeling the powerful animal's muscles ripple as he turned them around.

His horse had taken only a few steps when tingles of awareness coursed down his spine, and Alex swallowed. He tugged Bán to a halt with a quick apology.

"Wait," he whispered.

Don't go home. Look again.

Alex didn't stop to question his gut. He slid off the stallion's back and whirled. Riding down the beach would be faster, but something was driving him forward on his own two feet. He left Bán where he was, with only one glance over his shoulder.

The horse had already made his way up the incline of the smaller cliff, and he was again grazing on the long sparse grass, as if telling him there was no hurry.

He chuckled and shook his head, increasing his speed to round the large rocks he'd first seen her by. His heart jumped and he skidded to a halt, kicking up sand and pebbles as soon as the ridge was visible unencumbered.

Alana sat up there with her knees to her chest, arms wrapped around them. Her chin rested atop, as she leaned into herself, and her long pale mane played in the wind. She stared into the water. Didn't notice him down on the beach.

She was a vision of platinum and purple because, this time her mantle matched her trews. The hood was down and flapped in the dancing gales.

As if Alex had called her name, the gorgeous lass' eyes found his, and he had to swallow. Twice.

She straightened and smiled, but it had a touch of sadness he didn't like.

He wanted to demand what had upset her so he could slay it.

"Alex…"

His name was breathy on her lips and made his cock twitch. She'd said his name in his dreams in much the same manner, especially when she was rocking her naked body over his.

Alex fought a shudder and forced a smile. "Alana, are ye well, lass?" He framed his mouth so his voice would carry.

"Come sit with me?"

He obeyed without pause, scampering up the ridge like he and Duncan had done so many times as wee lads. Alex planted his behind next to her and gave her a onceover.

Alana sat on the ground, not on a blanket or plaid

as expected. Sorrow seemed to leak from her pores, despite the small curve of her luscious lips.

"Alana?"

Saying her name pulled her gaze from his bare legs, and he was again startled at the hue of her eyes. Gorgeous, and definitely more purple than blue.

"Are ye real?" The query tumbled out unbidden.

Her laughter washed over Alex like a caress, and he blew out a breath. His heart cantered, and it shouldn't. It hadn't taken that much energy to ascend the ridge.

"Aye, I'm real."

"I've been lookin' fer ye fer days…"

Alana swallowed, and he wanted to kiss her throat. "I'm sorry. Honestly, I shouldn't have come then, and I most certainly shouldn't be here now."

"Why?"

Her gaze raked his face, and she lifted her hand, but when their eyes met, she dropped her arm.

Had she been about to touch him?

His insides wobbled. He wanted to assure her she could touch him wherever and whenever she wanted.

"I…"

When she faltered, Alex reached for her hand.

Just like the first time they'd touched, energy shot upward, all the way into his biceps and shoulder. It didn't hurt.

It made him yearn all over.

For more.

As if the small skin-to-skin contact hadn't been innocent.

His manhood shifted and jumped as it became interested, too. He'd be granite in moments if Alex didn't shut his desire down.

He didn't want to. He wanted to explore it.

Push her down and touch her.

Taste her. Take her.

"What…happened?" Alex cleared his throat. The intensity didn't make sense. He didn't know this lass.

Her shoulders straightened. "So…you felt that?"

"Aye. What 'tis tha meanin'?"

"I don't know. But it doesn't scare me." With every word, Alana leaned closer, until their mouths were millimeters apart and their breaths mingled. She licked her bottom lip, a little pink arrow darting out to tempt him.

"Scare…ye?" Alex forced out, but his eyes were glued to her mouth. His own watered, and his need was a living thing about to consume him.

"Nay. Alex—"

He dipped down, covering her lips with his; swallowing whatever she'd been about to say. He groaned at first touch, but it melted away as she let him inside the warm recesses and rubbed her tongue against his.

Alex was lost, even more so when she gripped his leine with two small fists to haul him closer. He pulled her into his arms without breaking the seal of their kiss, and allowed Alana to slant deeper, taste him fuller.

How she'd taken such complete control should've registered, but her flavor burst, like wine and summer berries. So good he didn't care who led.

She moaned against his lips and the vibration went straight to his cock. Tremors chased each other down his spine and heat settled low in his bollocks. Alex was so hard he throbbed. His body begged him to take her.

Alana pressed ever closer, until she snaked her arms around his neck and pushed his back to the ground. The gorgeous lass followed him down, lying on his chest and gripping his head while their kiss went on. She tunneled her fingers in his hair, and he shivered; it was so perfect.

Alex held her just as tightly, barely aware of the smooth material of her mantle. His thoughts scattered when he felt the soft press of her breasts into his chest.

The lip-lock made its way into nips, licks and nibbles. He couldn't get enough of her. He mapped her back and cupped her bottom as she started to rock against him.

Shame she hadn't straddled him. She pushed her pelvis into his hip, and he wanted—no, *needed*—so much *more*. Moans and whimpers made his blood sing, and he squeezed her delectable rear end, encouraging her.

Alana slid her hand downward, teasing his abdominal muscles over the fabric of his leine, and it wasn't enough.

He wanted her hands on his bare skin. They needed to get naked—

When she gripped his erection on the outside of his plaid, Alex reared back and cursed.

Their eyes locked, and he groaned at the flushed hue of her alabaster skin. She was pink to the tips of her ears, and he wanted to see if he could make every inch of her flesh that particular shade.

They panted in time with each other.

"Alex? Did I hurt you?" Alana breathed.

He blinked to clear his head. "Nay. Jus'…surprised me."

"Oh." Her blush deepened and she withdrew her hand.

Alex grabbed it and brought it to his mouth, kissing her knuckles. How could he tell her—and save her embarrassment—he'd never been with a lass so forward?

He'd never had a woman reach for him like that—been the one to initiate the intimate touch. Not that he minded. He wanted Alana to touch him where she would.

All over.

"Most Fae men prefer a lover that…that…knows where a man likes to be touched."

He stilled. "Fae?"

Her gorgeous eyes widened until the whites showed. Alana slapped a hand over her mouth and sat up, breaking their physical contact.

She was bright red now, but it wasn't from their shared passion. "Oh, Goddess!" The words were muffled behind her slender fingers.

Alex tilted his head. "Did ye say, *'goddess'*?"

Alana nodded slowly, dropping her arm, but her expression was filled with dread. She'd paled out, and her slender shoulders were shaking.

Protective instincts flared all over his body. He sat

up, pulling her to him. He wrapped her in his arms and inhaled her sweet scent. It was like her taste, a mixture of heady wine and berries.

She didn't fight him; only burrowed into his chest and hid her face against his neck. Still trembled, so he rubbed her back in long soothing strokes.

"Alana-lass, talk ta me. What yer sayin' makes little sense."

"I'm Fae. I…am…a princess."

Alex blinked. Swallowed. Perhaps he was dreaming, after all.

Or the lass in his arms *was* mad.

"Say something," she whispered, her warm breath tickling the skin under his chin.

"Fae?" was the only thing he could manage.

Alana met his eyes and grimaced. "Aye. I snuck to the Human Realm using the Faery Stones, and—"

"Tha…Human…Realm? Faery…Stones?" Alex had heard of the Standing Stones before, were they the same thing?

She nodded, speaking normally, as if they were discussing the weather. "The first time, I just wanted to see, well, *here*. Your world. But this time, I-I-I had to…see *you*."

"Lass—"

Alana frowned. "Don't look at me like that, Alex MacLeod. I've not lost my wits, nor am I mad. I speak true. I'm the Scottish Fae Princess, daughter of King Fillan and Queen Elysia, though my mother is dead now." Grief passed over her expression briefly, but it was replaced with the haughtiness of her declaration.

She has the commanding tone well enough.

"Fae…"

Alana nodded. "Surely you've heard stories of the Faery Folk."

"Oh, aye. Since I was a wee laddie."

Her frown deepened, and she narrowed her eyes. "I'm not mad. Or daft."

"I believe ye." Alex's gut shouted that she spoke the truth—he didn't stop to question *why*. He should examine that, but he couldn't look away from *her*.

Astonishment darted across her gorgeous face and those vivid eyes. "You do?"

He nodded. "In my family—my clan—there's a legend."

"Go on…" Alana swallowed, and it lured him, so he wanted to kiss her throat again. Her visage shouted caution, as if she wasn't sure she could believe *him*.

"Some time ago, actually, a *long* time ago, hundreds a' years, a Fae Princess married tha Laird MacLeod. There are some MacLeods tha' believe…we are…part Fae."

His da believed the clan legend with all his heart. Something Alex and his siblings had always scoffed at. Could it actually be true?

How could the Fae be real?

There was one item his father claimed to be proof. A tattered scrap of formerly fine material Iain kept under lock and key. It was called the Faery Flag and came with a story about the Fae and wishes made upon it to save his clan. Legend had it, two wishes had been made and one remained, and that a Fae Princess would save them all.

Alex had believed *that one* even less than the Fae blood that supposedly ran through his veins.

'Tis all nonsense. Right?

Alana gasped and blinked. "That might explain what happens when we touch." She reached for his hand, and he jumped. "Alex…are you afraid of me now?" She entwined their fingers as he shook his head.

"Nay, lass. I could ne'er be afraid of ye." He drew their joined hands to her chin and tilted it up. "I've no idea why, but I feel as if I've known ye fer years. I'm drawn ta ye, Alana."

Her lovely face streaked the most adorable shade of pink.

Alex pressed his lips to each cheek, savoring the heat of her skin and craving more.

"I feel the same way." This was another whisper, but her expression said she wanted to say more. However, she did not.

Her discomfort washed over him; he wanted to make her feel better. "Where's yer guard?"

Alana averted her eyes, telling him he'd missed the mark. "I…left him. I didn't exactly have permission to leave my rooms."

"Ye snuck away?"

"Aye."

His belly quivered when her enchanting orbs found his again.

"I just *had* to see you," she whispered.

Alex cupped her cheeks. "I'm glad. *I* had ta see *ye*, as well." He needed to taste her again, more than he needed his next breath.

He dipped down and took her mouth, but she was right there, kissing him with the same fervency as the first time, slipping her arms around his neck and squeezing him almost too tight.

Alana climbed onto Alex's lap, and they trembled against each other as he deepened the kiss and settled his hands at her hips. Their tongues danced and dueled as they swapped control back and forth.

His cock was so hard, there was no doubt she could feel it.

She shifted against him, the soft pressure of her bottom only a tease of friction that wasn't nearly enough.

He broke the seal of their mouths on a groan. "Alana, we need ta stop, before I dinnae be able ta. I've ne'er wanted a lass tha way I want ye."

Alana panted against his chest, her perfect breasts rising and following in a rhythm he couldn't tear his eyes from. "I feel the same way. Never before have I wanted someone like I *need* you."

Alex growled; he couldn't help it. "Ye've had lovers?" Chiding himself didn't stop the rage and jealousy swirling in his gut. Neither did the reminders that he didn't know this lass, this supposed Fae Princess. His need for her was swift, demanding, and shocking in its concentration. He wanted her in his bed in the laird's rooms, and he'd never let her leave.

The thought should've alarmed him, but it only burned yearning low in his gut.

"Yay...and nay."

He'd expected her gaze to waver, but she met his eyes dead on.

"Meanin'?"

Alana slid her hand through his short hair, and then rested her palm against his cheek. "I've..." She cleared her throat and took a breath. Licked her kiss-swollen lips. "I've touched and kissed a man. I've been touched and kissed. I've never...had a man inside me."

His heart tripped and his mouth went dry. "Yer innocent?"

The smile that lit her face made his gut quiver. "My maidenhead is intact, but I'm not naïve." She laughed. "I've not been called innocent for many years."

"Years? Yer barely grown." Alex's cock pulsed a disagreement. This was no child in his arms. She kissed with experience enough to tie him in knots and send him to oblivion.

He sucked back a growl, trying not to imagine her small hands on another man—especially an intimate touch she wasn't afraid to make.

It bothered him *much* more than it should.

Alex shouldn't care if she'd given herself to a dozen men, but even if it was just one, he more than merely *cared*.

It was wrong, if it wasn't *him*.

He wanted to mark her; claim her.

Alana's smile dimmed. "How old are you, Alex?"

"Two and twenty summers."

She swallowed, and a shadow danced over her features. "Fae live much longer than humans. I...I was five and fifty on my last nameday."

Air rushed from his lungs. "Ye dinnae look more than eight and ten."

Her laughter surrounded them, tickling like the wind. "I wouldn't go that far. I'd like to think I look no older than you. I'm not a child, nor an old woman."

God's blood she wasn't a child. Of course, she wasn't *old*. Age could explain her experience with men, as much as he didn't like it. "Five and fifty?" Older than his father by a few years. He wouldn't point it out in case she'd take offense.

Alana nodded and cupped his cheeks. "I'm considered young by Fae standards. A *'lass'*, as you say. My father is over one hundred years old."

He gulped. "One hundred?"

"Aye, and he has many more years left."

Alex's head spun with the unbelievable information. There was nothing but truth in her pretty eyes, even if logic told him she couldn't be correct. "Then…"

"I will live much longer than you." She looked so sad he tugged her back to him and kissed her forehead.

"'Tis nothin' tha' matters."

"It does matter. I—"

"What, lass?" Alex prompted when she trailed off.

Alana trembled in his arms again, then shook her head. "You're right. It doesn't matter. *Shouldn't* matter because I shouldn't be here." She gently broke the circle of his embrace and climbed to her feet. She faced the sea without another word and silence descended.

His heart ached.

What could have her so sad?

Alex wanted to yank her to him and run back to Dunvegan with her in his arms.

Keep her forever.

He made it to his feet and brushed off the back of his plaid but studied her beautiful profile. Her mantle rustled in the wind, and the waves crashed into the beach, but nothing took his focus off her.

She was dressed in purple from head to foot, although several different shades. Even her boots were a dark shade of the color.

"Why do ye keep sayin' that, Alana?" he whispered. He liked the way her name rolled off his tongue.

Alana whirled on him, and jumped, as if he'd startled her, like she'd forgotten he was there. "I have to go."

"Nay. Why?"

"I have to, Alex. Now." Her words shook and her expression was grief-stricken.

His stomach dipped to his toes. "When will I see ye again?"

Her eyes went misty, making their hue shine like amethyst, and he wanted to snatch her back into his arms and force that sorrow away.

"I...I don't know. I'm not sure you will." A tear rolled down her creamy cheek.

Alex couldn't help himself, he darted forward and cupped her face, thumbing it away. "Dinnae cry, lass."

"I...Alex...I..." Alana gripped his wrists and squeezed. "This trip...it was supposed to be goodbye. I didn't even know if I'd see you, but I convinced myself

I would."

"And ye did."

She nodded in his grip, and he wiped new tears away. "But… I cannot come back. I just…can't. This *has* to be goodbye."

His gut—or maybe it was his *heart*—rejected her words.

He didn't shout, '*nay!*' again, as he'd wanted. Alex dipped down and claimed her mouth like she'd claimed *him*.

Alana had branded him from their first kiss, or maybe it was their first touch, days ago.

She kissed him until he was hard and aching all over again, and she held his waist tightly, as if her grip could erase her words. Her tears mingled with the movement of their lips, and he could taste the salt, but it was sweet somehow, just like his princess.

"Then dinnae go," Alex breathed against her lips.

She whimpered and looked down. "I cannot stay. Goddess, I want to, but I cannot."

His heart slid to his toes and his chest constricted like he'd run the length of the beach. Alex *hurt* all over his body. "I dinnae let ye go." His voice was a croak.

"We don't even know each other," Alana whispered.

Somehow, even though it was the truth, it didn't relieve the pressure in his lungs. "I ken it." He inhaled, trying to force the air down. "But it dinnae feel as if tha' were so."

She covered her mouth with her hand and nodded.

Each tear destroyed him a bit more than the one

before.

"Goodbye, Alex," Alana sobbed.

He didn't get a chance to respond.

Alex blinked and she was gone.

chapter six

ow could she tell him who she was?
What she was?
She'd broken every rule she'd ever been taught. Fae and humans were *enemies*, dating back from their first encounter a millennia ago.

Of course, there'd always been rebels like her, or the humans of Scotland would've never have known of the Faery Folk—as Alex had attested.

Alana shook her head and her vision blurred, making the crystals in the cave of the Faery Stones waver until they were just a bright blob in her line of sight. Her teeth chattered and she sucked in one breath, then another as the shudder passed over her whole body.

She needed to open the Stones and go home, but she couldn't make her feet move. Stood like a statue—except that she was shaking all over, so maybe she was a crumbling statue.

Her mantle *swooshed* as the fabric shifted against itself.

Alana needed to gather her wits, too. She was lucky to have gotten out of her rooms undetected—she'd used the secret passageway behind her hearth to get down to the numerous escape tunnels that spilled out into the forest.

She hadn't wanted to risk *blinking* inside the palace,

so she'd waited until she was well away from it before going to the Field of Light.

From there, she'd used an invisibility spell and had caused a small explosion in the woods at the edge of the Field. The Fae Warriors—all six of them—had left the Stones unguarded to investigate.

Uncle Daegus would not be pleased with their carelessness, but it'd been to *her* advantage, and she'd made it to the Human Realm without incident.

Her plan had been to seek Alex out, but she hadn't been confident she'd find him. Alana had sat on the ridge, enjoying a genuine breeze and the scent of the waters, instead of Fae magic-induced always pleasant weather.

That he'd happened upon her had been an accident.

Or is it really fate?

What she was feeling made no sense. She didn't know Alex MacLeod.

Well, *know* was a relative term, was it not?

Alana knew his mouth.

His taste.

She knew his body—at least on the outside of his clothing. He was adept at kissing and had aroused her without touching her intimately when no other had been able to do so. He'd run her desire so high her blood had boiled. She'd throbbed between her legs and would've let him strip her trews down and take her innocence had he not stopped.

Although she mourned his choice, it confirmed he was a good man. Magic and Alex's words alike solidified that the draw she felt was mutual.

He was even part Fae — if the Clan MacLeod legend was true.

So why are you leaving?

Alana crushed her eyes on the answer she didn't want to even think, let alone say out loud.

I could get him killed.

Would get him killed if anyone discovered she'd seen him, let alone told him she was Fae. Or that she was the princess.

His 'crime' would only be considered greater if anyone discovered they'd been intimate, no matter it hadn't gone beyond kissing.

Goddess, she could hear her father dooming Alex in her mind. His deep voice would be harsh, his violet eyes sharp slits. His broad shoulders held tight, and a glare on his handsome bearded face.

Just like this morning.

Her father had finally called Alana from her rooms three full days after being imprisoned, and his hours' long lecture had involved threats — and promises — that should have her shaking in her boots for reasons other than a human laird's kisses and caresses.

She'd made a practice of sneaking away from the palace and disobeying the king. This time, she'd left the protection of the Fae Realm, '*carelessly*', her father had ranted. He'd commanded she mind him this time, or he'd seal her in the tower.

It wasn't that Alana didn't believe her father's vow; she just wasn't afraid.

The only thing that *had* impacted her was when the

king had reminded her she was no longer a child—
funny, considering how he treated her—and that her
mother would be so disappointed. She feared her father
was right.

King Fillan had imparted that he would be
respected. *Obeyed.*

What had she done instead?

She'd snuck back to the Human Realm the very
morning of her admonition, partly because he'd not
answered her demand of how long he planned to keep
her locked up, and partly because she *had* been driven
to see her human laird.

I'm sorry, Mother.

Even then, Alana didn't regret her second trip to
where she'd been forbidden. Hopefully, her mother
could've understood—she and the laird were fated.

Alex…he'd begged her to stay.

Her head spun and her chest ached. "Breathe, just
breathe." The whisper bounced around the low ceiling
of the humid cave.

The space wasn't large, and opposite of the Faery
Stones on the dais in the Field of Light, the ones on this
side looked as if they belonged here. Like their twin set,
the Stones were made up of five clustered natural
formations, rising from the cavern's floor, perfectly
spaced from each other, in a loose semi-circle.

The shape they sat in was perfect, as if it'd been
placed there, not grown. That was probably the case, but
likely they'd been created in a cave in her realm.

The main Stone called to her, brightening and
humming, as if in welcome.

Alana wanted to reject the call; stay in the Human Realm with Alex, but she couldn't.

She sighed as she approached. Her fingers hesitated before the first touch of the largest crystal, and the start of the pattern.

Typical of her behavior—as Xander would tout—she hadn't contemplated how she'd get home. The half-Wing of guards would still be in the Field of Light, and would no doubt be ready to defend the Stones and the realm from the moment the portal opened.

What would she do?

"What *can* I do?"

Light glinted off the largest crystal, as if it was trying to answer.

Alana could knock them out with magic, but there was no way she wouldn't end up with more *consequences* for this jaunt to see Alex.

She groaned. Magic was on her side, but nothing her powers were capable of couldn't be sensed or discovered by her father's mages. As her cousin had mentioned—they were a vindictive lot. Always eager to inflict pain at the king's will.

Apprehension skidded down her spine when she made her fingers move over the Stones. Her magic wasn't in tempo with their internal chords, so she had to breathe deeply and try again.

They hummed as if to admonish her, but soon Alana played the pattern out and the small cavern filled with artificial gales, rustling her hair and clothing.

All the history scrolls said the Human Realm had no magic and Fae powers were diminished here, but this was the first time she'd felt the like.

She stepped back when the portal opened, and her tears were already falling again. No matter how many times she swiped at her face, her eyes went blurry over and over.

I'm leaving. For good.

"I'll never see him again."

Alana sucked back a large sob and focused on the orange and blue grass visible beneath the dais through the shimmering bubble. She chided herself to calm and stepped through to her realm.

She met the shocked dark gaze of an ebony-haired Fae Warrior standing next to the raised platform. She didn't know his name.

"Princess?" He flexed his wings and the grip on his sword at the same time. His posture screamed hesitation, but her empathic powers told her he was determined, too.

Determined to what? Should I run?

She had no answer for him and turned away. The dais only had three stairs…

A sound, like the breath rushing from someone's lungs hit her ears, then a *thud*, and Alana gasped. She whirled and her eyes collided with her cousin's.

The thick black plait of the Fae Warrior was the only movement as he now lay in the orange grass.

Lying in heaps around the dais on the ground—also unconscious—were two more soldiers. That meant three were missing, but *where* they were wasn't obvious.

Xander sheathed his large weapon and stalked over to her. He grabbed her arm, and practically dragged her away from the Faery Stones.

"D-d-d-id you kill them?"

"Nay," he growled. "But *you* are going to get *me* killed. What in Five Hells do you think you're doing?"

Heat swirled at the back of her neck and scorched her cheeks. He wouldn't like the answer, so Alana didn't want to tell him. "Will they remember what happened?" she asked instead.

"I hit Braelyn with the hilt of my sword, from behind, so no. I knocked Garreth and Meninx out with magic. I also said a thought-scatter spell."

"Xander—"

"Not a word." This was a hard command he shouldn't dare give *her*.

Before Alana could take the fortifying breath she very much needed, her cousin swung her up into his arms and pinned her to his chest. His green armor bit into her shoulder, despite its curvature. That was partially due to the breastplate and partially due to Xander's muscled body.

"I need to get you back to your rooms, so when this mess is discovered, *you* can look innocent. By the Goddess, *Your Highness*, what were you *thinking*?"

"You said not to say anything."

He narrowed his violet eyes and pumped his wings hard. Looked away from her as if he couldn't endure otherwise.

Alana said the invisibility spell she'd used in order to gain access to open the Faery Stones. It would hide them both in flight. Her heart rebounded against her ribs.

What can I say?

Xander hadn't forgiven her for their joint trip to the Human Realm; there was no way he'd understand her drive—her desperate *need*—to see Alex again.

She magically clouded her mind so he wouldn't hear her thoughts. They might help him understand, but when he was so angry, it wouldn't be of any assistance.

"How did you get out?" he demanded, right above her ear.

"The winding stairwell behind the hearth in my sleeping room. Whichever mage Father used to seal my suite didn't spell it. It was a longshot, but it worked. How did you know I was gone?"

"I brought your morning meal, and you weren't in your rooms. I assumed the rest." The words were a low urgent growl, and he gritted his teeth.

"I wasn't gone long."

"Through the kitchen tunnels, then?" Xander asked, ignoring her statement.

"Aye."

Her cousin's voice lost its angry edge, but it was only temporary. Her gut shouted as much.

The secret passageways that ran beneath the palace were dank and smelled of old dirt, but Xander pulled her through at such a speed they didn't have time to offend her lungs.

The dark walls of packed earth were a blur, and soon he was pushing the ancient door behind her fireplace shut with touch and a strength spellword.

He only needed the magic because he hadn't put her down yet, but that quickly came to an end when her cousin dumped her unceremoniously on her bed. Xander growled, glared and started to pace. "Explain. Now."

Alana sighed and righted herself. Pulled her mantle off and tossed it on the trunk at the end of her bed. "Good thing I'm wearing trews. You would've made me indecent."

He narrowed his eyes again.

Obviously, her cousin didn't appreciate her small jest or the attempt to diffuse his ire. Nor did it appear to work.

"I'm not hearing what I want to hear."

She harrumphed. "In case you forgot, *I* am the princess. You're supposed to take orders from *me*, not the other way around."

Amusement darted in his eyes, but it was gone almost as soon as it was born. "Do you not remember your father's mandate? I'm not *allowed* to take orders from you anymore. At least for the time being."

Alana rolled her eyes.

"Well," Xander prompted. His wings shifted, as if he would pump them to rise any second now. His whole form bled irritation and dark emotions rolled over her empathic powers.

She shuddered, but irritation was better than anger. Perhaps they were getting somewhere? "You know the answer, so why do you stand there and interrogate me?" she snapped.

He frowned. "The human?"

Alana lifted her chin. "His name is Alex."

Her cousin cursed under his breath, but it was too

low to make out.

"I think we're fated, Xander."

That shut him up, but now his mouth was a hard line. He didn't say anything. Stopped his movements and crossed his arms over his chest, glaring.

She took a big breath and reached for the right words. "When Alex and I touch," her cousin scowled harder, but she ignored him, "I *feel* something. Almost…magic. But more than that, *he* feels it too."

"He's *human*, Alana."

"Not wholly so," she retorted.

Disbelief darted across his handsome face.

"I speak the truth. His grandmother, albeit many times removed, was a princess."

"Fae?"

Alana nodded.

Xander narrowed his eyes. "How many times removed?"

"I don't know. But I was planning on visiting the archives."

The vast library was in the basement of the palace, but above the dungeons. The head scribe, a lovely older woman name Eirini, adored her. Alana wouldn't need to bribe or wheedle, or even sneak. She'd be allowed free reign to find whatever information she could about Alex's princess great grandmother—as long as she hadn't been erased from the histories.

Most Fae believed there was no lower lifeform than humans. To *breed* with one was an embarrassment—not to mention a death sentence, for mother *and* child. For a princess to do such a thing, banishment would be a gift.

Also, unlikely. Whoever she was, if she left the Fae Realm, she surely never returned. She'd probably fled in secret.

"You will not leave this suite again." Another hard command from her bodyguard.

"Xander—"

"I mean it. You caused me to harm *three* of my brothers today. Not to mention forced me to *lie* to make the guard light. It's only a matter of time before I'm discovered. Captain Daegus will lash me more than ten times, Your Highness."

She winced. "What did you do?"

"Memory scatter spells."

"That's not so bad."

Xander gave her a long look.

"What? It's not."

"Easily discovered," her cousin muttered.

Alana swallowed. "I can't explain it to you. I can only tell you how I feel here." She placed her palm over her heart.

He scoffed. "You do not know him. He's *human*." Her cousin spat the last word as insult.

"I know." Heat suffused her cheeks when she remembered Alex's mouth moving over hers. It didn't matter that they'd just met.

It should—even setting all the forbiddeness aside.

She'd been truthful with him—Alana *wanted* him. After all these years, she'd finally found the only man she'd wanted to give herself to—completely.

She couldn't.

If Alex had been willing, she would've given him

her innocence right there on the ridge, in view of anyone who cared to see.

That desire shouldn't be floating in her head. It was wrong. Not just because he was human. Alana had never been loose with her favors. The dalliances she'd had, had only been after getting to know each man.

How could she be so drawn to a human?

A voice whispered that it would do no good—she couldn't have him, but she ignored it and told her best friend what was in her heart. "He's for me, cousin. I can't tell you how or why I know. It's...fate." She shrugged.

Alarm was stamped all over Xander's expression. "Goddess, you really believe this."

"Aye."

He restarted his pacing. "Oh, *Goddess*." Her cousin shook his head, making his thick plait bounce around him like a moving aura. "Fated mates are rare enough amongst *our* people. This must be nonsense, Alana."

She ignored him and pushed on. Wanted to convince him, as impossible as it seemed. "It's not nonsense. Maybe this is why I could never entertain a betrothal..."

Xander wrenched his head around, and his braid followed like a whip. "Don't you *dare* start trying to...justify this foolishness."

Alana sighed. "I'm just saying. No Fae man drew me. Ever."

"You're not so old that you've met all your choices. Don't judge by that useless Irish Prince, Seamus."

She quirked a small smile. "I wouldn't dare; I

agree. I'm not judging *all* Fae men by him, of course. But you should take care not to speak as such about royalty, even if everyone agrees, and he's not from our Court."

Xander paused. "Why? Are not your rooms magically soundproofed?"

"Oh, aye. I reinforced the spells before I left so Rannick wouldn't catch me. I'm just saying."

He tugged his plait, something he only did when he was agitated.

"What can I say to make you know I speak true, cousin? I speak of what I feel inside," she whispered.

"How do you know about his supposed Fae blood?" he shot back, stopping at her bedside.

Alana flushed to her toes and wanted to avert her eyes but didn't look away from the gaze that matched her own. Xander wasn't going to like her answer. *At. All.* However, she wouldn't lie to him. "I told him who I am."

After an audible intake of the obviously shocked breath, her cousin smashed his eyes shut and stood very still. His wings vibrated. When he finally spoke, it was a string of curses in Fae. Low. Deadly.

"There's nothing you can say to me that I do not *know*, cousin," she said.

"Then do not be a fool." He started pacing again. His wide shoulders shook as hard as his wings and he wore a path on her shiny marbled floor. Xander started ranting, repeating everything she'd assured him she was aware of.

Every caution, every black promise that wasn't far from the truth. Things he didn't have the power to keep her from. Things that made them both shake in fear.

The more he talked, the more doom settled over Alana. She couldn't have Alex. Hearing her cousin confirm it just made her feel worse.

"You don't have to worry, anyway." She pushed the words out, low but clear. Misery settled over her and she wanted to sink into her bed.

The look on Alex's face when she'd said goodbye had just about obliterated her. Made her want to take the words back immediately, vowing she'd come back to him. Be with him.

Stay with him.

Alana's head and gut agreed with everything her cousin was raving about.

Too bad her heart refused.

Concern crossed Xander's expression, but it was much preferred to anger. "What happened? Did he hurt you?"

She shook her head. "Nay." Tears burned, were born and spilled. She couldn't help it, and she didn't bother trying to wipe them away, there would only be more.

"Alana?"

"I hurt *him*, Xander. I hurt myself, too."

"What d'you mean?"

"I said goodbye." Alana *hated* that there was relief in her cousin's eyes. Her chest was so tight every breath was a dagger to her soul.

chapter seven

The Beltane celebration was going on around her, yet all she could see…all she could *feel,* was a misery so great it threatened to consume her.

The opulence of her surroundings was suffocating—so many jewels on display, the sheen and shine from bouncing light was bound to give Alana a headache. Spinning gemmed chandeliers, encrusted serving wear—even the eating utensils.

Glimmery tablecloths, magically infused with extra shimmer—it was all bound to make her hurl what little food she'd shoved down.

She preferred her punishment rations of soup and bread to the glamorous stuffed swine, duck and swan on display as the residents and the guests of the palace ate.

If Alana had ever wanted to run away, the urge had never been greater than it was at the moment. She'd always enjoyed feasts.

After her last jaunt to see Alex, and Xander's rescue in the Field of Light, her cousin had made her vow she wouldn't try again. They'd not gotten caught, despite the spells they'd both used.

The explosion had been explained as a trick by unknown lads in official reports—Goddess knew where that idea had come from.

The memory charms and scatter spells had

worked—nothing else was said officially; or unofficially that her cousin had been able to discover from Warrior chatter. If any of the three winged soldiers had remembered anything, they must've been too embarrassed to report waking up on the ground while on duty. More likely, they feared punishment from Captain Daegus and had formed a pact of silence.

Xander stood very much in her periphery, hovering and shooting her disapproving looks from time to time.

She tried to ignore him, and his not-so-subtle visual admonitions.

Act normal. Her cousin's voice was in her head, not in her ears. He'd spoken telepathically and shoved through her mind-barriers.

Alana didn't acknowledge him. Just swirled sweet red wine around in her golden-jeweled goblet. She'd already had three full glasses. Shouldn't imbibe any more, even if it might numb the hurt. Then again, it hadn't worked so far, other than wiping out the mental strength to rebuild her walls, although she should try.

Mind reading wasn't an unusual Fae trait, especially with the strong magic of so many nobles present for Beltane, most in the great hall right now. Entourages from Wales, England, and Ireland were in attendance, in addition to all the members of the Scottish Court. The best of the bloodlines, her father had boasted in his welcome speech not thirty minutes before.

She didn't need anyone else to know why she was so melancholy, especially by plucking it from her thoughts.

A fortnight.

It'd been two whole weeks since she'd seen Alex MacLeod on her second stolen visit to the Human Realm.

"Who's Alex MacLeod?" The Irish Crown Prince, Seamus, sidled up to her, winking as he bit into a plump shiny pink fruit from the blue-barked Sùbh tree.

He didn't bow, which was rather rude, considering who she was. However, not surprising, considering the source.

Alarm shimmied down her spine and Alana straightened. She hastily rebuilt her mental blocks and internally shouted the spellword that would keep Prince Seamus — and anyone else — out of her head.

Xander, who'd always had excellent hearing, shot a murderous look in their direction; although she couldn't be certain if it was for her or the prince.

Or both.

She swallowed a gulp and cleared her throat, forcing a smile. "Excuse me, Your Highness?"

About a decade her senior, Seamus was sinfully handsome, which made her skin crawl with extra vigor since good looks were so wasted on him. His eyes were a crystal-clear light green hue, and alluring. There was no doubt why he commanded most of the female population.

His hair was loose today and fell around his shoulders in ebony waves. Alana wasn't tempted to touch them, unless yanking counted. She'd always been of the opinion that his hair was as crooked as he was, since the almost-curl was natural.

The prince was tall and broad and had as much muscle as the average Scottish winged Fae Warrior. She'd never seen him fight, but it was rumored he could hold his own with a sword.

He was dressed as finely as she'd always seen him—the heir to the Irish throne was as arrogant as royalty came. Prince Seamus wore the greens of his lands from head to foot—his leine matched his eyes, and his over-doublet was embroidered and shiny, with twinkling emeralds lining the whole thing. His trews were a richer shade of green and tight—no doubt with a purpose to display his *personal* jewels.

Alana refused to glance down because he'd love the perusal and get the wrong idea.

Very very wrong.

"Who is Alex MacLeod?" the prince repeated, flashing an irritating dimpled smile that made him even better looking. He dropped his voice and bowed with a flourish, as if realizing he'd not greeted her properly.

She tried not to roll her eyes and bit back an order for him to go away.

Seamus extended his hand, obviously wanting to offer her a customary kiss on the knuckles and Alana shuddered for reasons other than his dooming repetition.

She didn't want his lips on her, but she couldn't be outwardly rude, especially considering what he'd gotten from her thoughts. She needed to come up with a plausible explanation.

Quickly.

So, he'd go away.

Because of their difference in station, Xander couldn't save her, either. He'd come closer to chaperone, as was appropriate as her bodyguard, but he wouldn't interfere unless her life was in danger.

Alana slid shaking fingers into the Irish prince's grip, and he lavished her knuckles with several presses of soft lips. When he licked her, she yanked back, but Seamus chuckled, his eyes gleaming.

I should slap him.

She couldn't cause a scene at the ball. Her father had warned her that morning. He'd invaded her rooms and even promised to watch her. It'd be more like him to have spies reporting back to him, but no matter; she needed to be on her best behavior.

Alana inhaled and released her breath slowly. Twice. Clenched her jaw and forced a curt nod. "Good evening, Your Highness."

He looked even more amused.

Wretch.

Xander's gaze shot daggers at Seamus. Her cousin must've caught sight of the bastard's slimy tongue on her.

"Are you enjoying the feast, Sir Xander?" the prince asked. "King Fillan is so very generous." He tossed the half-eaten Sùbh fruit from one hand to the other, then threw it down on the table she sat at. His tone was conversational, normal.

Alana swallowed. She'd expected him to repeat his question for the third time. Why was he holding back now? He had to be scheming.

Her cousin narrowed his eyes but nodded. He too,

was covered from head to foot in finery. Instead of his normal hunter-green chest-plate, Xander wore one made of gold, embossed with the Scottish Court's Seal. His silver epaulets denoted his place in the royal guard, and as her protector.

His trews were also gold, making the platinum hue of his thick warrior braid even more fitting, as if it was an accessory. At his waist, he wore a decorative golden-hilted dirk, but her cousin was as deadly with the smaller blade as his oversized broad sword.

"Ah, never a man of many words," Seamus mused. His vibrant eyes settled on her. "Care to dance, Your Highness?"

Her gut shouted something like, *no way in Five Hells,* but she reached for manners and stood from her chair. Alana inclined her head and offered a hand. "As you wish, Your Highness." She was proud of herself for not lying and telling him she'd be fond of dancing with him.

The prince's eyes glinted with obvious desire and bile rose in her throat. He gave her a leering onceover and she fought the urge to fidget in her lavish royal purple gown. It had an open back and a low-cut bodice. Her shoulders were exposed as well, and she wished she was covered to her neck with yards of fabric.

The front of the dress was decorated with large multi-hued purple feathers that didn't quite hide her cleavage. It was gorgeous, and she'd loved the design from the moment the seamstresses had brought it to her especially for the ball, but now Alana felt naked. Regretted not choosing something with more coverage.

Seamus had never hidden his want of her, but now that he'd invaded her thoughts, it was worse somehow. More repulsing.

Xander growled low but quickly disguised the noise by clearing his throat. At least he was still protective, even if he remained upset with her.

If the prince noticed, he chose to ignore her cousin.

"I'll be here when you return," her bodyguard said.

Alana threw him a nod and slipped her hand to the Irish prince's elbow, trying not to quiver against his side. She didn't want to be anywhere near him, let alone *in* his arms on the dance floor.

Equally undesirable, because of the gown's open back, he would likely be touching her exposed skin. She shivered and gooseflesh rose on her forearms.

"You're stunning, as always." Seamus' smooth voice should've been a compliment, but she wanted to break their physical contact and retreat. "Purple is certainly your color, my dear princess."

She wanted to shout at him that she wasn't his *anything but* managed to reach for decorum. "Thank you." Alana took another fortifying breath with the statement and willed herself to calm.

There was no way someone as calculating as the Irish prince was going to let go of what he'd overheard in her mind. He was biding his time.

But for what purpose?

He placed his hand at the small of her back and hauled her into his chest when they'd selected a spot with a multitude of other couples.

It took everything Alana was made of to let him

maintain the hold, as his fingers did indeed brush her bare flesh above her waist. Her spine tingled up and down, as if her body was attempting to dispel his large hand on its own.

"MacLeod. 'Tis a human surname, is it not?"

Alex's name with an Irish inflection gritted over her senses, and she fought a wince. "What?"

Something akin to irritation crossed those pale green eyes. "Princess, you've never been a good liar."

They swayed with the movement of the slow love ballad the best Scottish Fae bards were singing from the raised dais. They used magic to enhance their voices and the tempo, deeper male and higher female blending perfectly.

Alana fought the urge to shove Seamus away. "I don't know what you're referring to."

He smirked, then whirled her around as the dance steps required. "Thoughts do not lie, even though you're shutting me out now."

"Again, Your Highness, I think you're mistaken...I do not know of what you speak. *Humans?* You should watch what you say. 'Tis forbidden to speak of such things." Her heart kicked up.

Seamus wasn't going to believe anything she said, and Alana couldn't panic.

His laughter surrounded them, as if she'd said something amusing and the prince was delighted. "I'm going to enjoy owning you, Princess Alana."

Anger surged in her veins, as if she was a candle being lit, and the wick traversed her form. "How *dare* you speak to me as such?"

He gripped her waist and swung her around as a part of their dance.

Her slippers left the floor, and she was too stunned to do anything but hold on.

"Keep your voice down, and keep dancing," the prince said in a light tone, as if chiding a child. "Unless you want…others…to enter our conversation."

Alana's eyes darted around the vast room, landing on her father and King Ciaran, Seamus' father. Both leaders stood together and watched them dancing, and *both* wore pleased expressions.

She shuddered and fought the sensation of spiders crawling over her where the prince was touching her. Too much of his palms and fingers were on her skin. The gown couldn't protect her. "Put me down," she pushed out through clenched teeth.

"Keep dancing or I'll tell King Fillan of your Alex MacLeod." Seamus' words were bright, as if he'd imparted some very good news.

Do not react, Alana chanted. "I don't know of whom you speak," she repeated.

His chuckle spoke for how much he *didn't* believe her.

She thrust away the encroaching terror and reached for her wits, then whispered the first memory-scatter spellword that popped into her head.

Seamus laughed again.

She gritted her teeth.

The Irish prince set her to her feet and reached for something around his neck. He revealed a red-stoned medallion that was glowing. "Spells don't work on me."

Alana swallowed for the hundredth time in lieu of vomiting on him. Didn't bother trying to deny what she'd attempted.

"As royalty yourself, sweet princess, I would think you'd have one of these, too." He tucked the jewel out of view again and gathered her back to him for the last steps of the dance.

She didn't answer; didn't have anything to say.

True fear wasn't something she was familiar with, and she didn't like the feeling as it prickled all over her skin.

What am I going to do now?

She couldn't stop shaking.

Alana trembled so hard her teeth rattled. The bastard Irish prince had released her with a parting, *"I'll come to you, my sweet."* She hadn't said a word about Alex—denied knowledge of what Seamus kept remarking on, but he only continued to laugh and call her a bad liar.

He'd caressed her cheeks while she'd stood frozen and silent.

She'd gagged as her dinner made another threat to expel itself from her churning stomach and fled the first chance she'd gotten. She needed some air...or something.

The winged Fae Warriors guarding the huge doors of the great hall both inclined their heads as she passed.

Alana felt, rather than heard Xander's footsteps

behind her, and his familiar scent of leather and sage tickled her nose. It was mixed with a hint of armor oil today, but it wasn't bad. At least the pleasantness of her cousin's presence helped chase away Seamus' negative aura a bit. Bile receded and she was able to ground herself some.

"How bad is it?" The Warrior's voice was low and serious, right above her ear.

When she didn't answer him or stop walking down the wide corridor, he grabbed her arm.

She tried to whirl on him, but he tightened his grip. Their eyes met and she bit her bottom lip.

"Nay, Your Highness, not here," Xander whispered. "You can't be gone from the celebration for long, and you can't be seen upset. The king will worry." He said the last words for public benefit.

What he'd meant was that her father would send someone to find her. They'd *both* likely be punished if that happened.

Alana didn't want to cause her cousin any more grief.

He swept her up into his arms and they slid into the nearest sitting room.

Her eyes landed on a couple entwined, but they'd interrupted before the tryst could escalate to joining their bodies fully; they were still mostly clothed.

The male, a short-haired blond nobleman tore his mouth off a redheaded courtier's large exposed breast. He looked irritated, until his eyes landed on them. The lordling—because he couldn't be out of his twenties— hastily climbed off his lover and bowed. "Your

Highness. Sir Xander."

"Find another room," her cousin growled. "Learn how to lock a door while you're at it."

The lass scrambled up, tucking her bare breasts away and adjusting her bodice. Fae were generally not ashamed of nudity on display, but her pale skin lit up, her cheeks flaring the same color as her hair. She straightened her deep pink gown and bowed. She was no older than the lordling.

Alana couldn't help but think of Alex and being close to him like that. She hadn't gone far enough with him on the beach that day, but she'd ached to do so. She wanted to bury her face against Xander. Nobles didn't need to see her close to tears.

"I hope all is well," the pretty redhead whispered, then the couple joined hands and left the room.

Her bodyguard set her down on a fluffy bronze sofa—opposite the one the lovers had been on—and locked the door with magic. Its blue glow receded around the decorative gold plate and handle, holding her attention before he took a seat next to her.

"What did that bastard say to you?" Xander demanded.

"Nothing." She kept her eyes busy by surveying the room.

The large hearth was lit, and a friendly fire was bright and warm. Purple, pink and orange sweetwoods burned, filling the room with the saccharine scents of baking treats.

The lumber was the finest their realm had to offer. Her father had procured all varieties and colors of sweetwoods from all over the Fae Realm for Beltane. He had to impress his guests, after all.

The flames danced in the colors of each wood, their enticing aroma filling the room, and good enough to make her want dessert.

Xander frowned. "What happened? You usually don't agree to dance with him, no matter how much he begs."

Alana's stomach somersaulted again. "I had to."

"Then *'nothing'* isn't quite correct, is it, lass?"

She startled at his gentle tone and inappropriate address.

Her cousin hadn't called her that in a long time. Maybe he'd forgiven her. Too bad this time just made her hurt because it reminded her of Alex.

His gaze was soft, concerned, but she didn't want to be honest with him about her interaction with Prince Seamus.

She was *embarrassed* that he'd gotten one over on her. Especially considering how dangerous her…situation…was.

"I heard him ask who the laird was, Alana. He said Alex MacLeod's name. So just tell me what we're dealing with."

"I didn't tell him a thing."

Xander sighed. "To an onlooker, it appeared that you and the *prince* very much enjoyed your time together. It also didn't escape my notice that your father *and* his were very pleased. Don't get yourself into a position you can't reverse." He'd been polite, obviously avoiding the word *betrothal*.

"Oh Goddess, I *am* going to lose my dinner."

Her cousin smirked.

"He said he'd enjoy *owning* me."

Amusement dissipated and rage darted across his eyes. Xander's jaw was set and hard, his mouth a flat line. "What?" He exercised his arsenal of Fae curses.

"I tried to use a memory spell, but he wears an anti-magic medallion. And I have a feeling it's a good one, also spelled against removal from his body, if against his will. He wouldn't flaunt it, otherwise."

Her cousin shot to his feet and started to pace, his wings tremoring. He cursed some more.

"Relax, he doesn't know anything." Alana's gut roiled. Instinct told her his knowing *'nothing'* wouldn't be the case for very long.

Ireland had Faery Stones, too. The prince couldn't use the Stones in the Field of Light to get to the Human Realm—undetected anyway, and he wouldn't be able to get permission—but he could use his own. Where they'd place him in the Human Realm was a mystery, but Ireland and Scotland were only a *blink* away from each other.

Alex was the leader of his clan. A nobleman in the Human Realm. It wouldn't take much of an inquiry to discover *everything*.

Alana blinked tears away and watched her best friend jerk back and forth on the shiny floor. The tile in the sitting room was even finer than what was in her rooms.

The furniture was of the most comfortable King Fillan's palace had to offer. The room's décor had been done in rich metals, all the upholstery was bronze, gold and copper.

The heavy drapes on both floor-to-ceiling windows matched. The pieces were also coordinated with embossed and engraved filigrees on their backs, arms, and legs, so fine it was a wonder anyone was brave enough to sit.

Three couches, four high-back chairs, and even the tables all complimented each other. The tone was welcoming and wasn't *that* a jest around this place.

"Why are you crying?" Xander whispered.

"I don't know," she wailed. Alana swiped at her cheeks, but more tears just graced her skin.

"What are your plans?" He whirled and stared her down from where he stood. He stopped pacing, but his gaze singed.

"What d'you mean?"

"What does *Prince Seamus* want?"

Dread rolled over her form, making her shake from head to toe again, despite the fact she was sitting, and her cousin had said the scoundrel's name and honorific as anything but respectful.

"I don't know." Her answer was low, and quivered as much as she did.

"Well, you damn sure had better find out."

chapter eight

"Do ye want ta tell me why yer takin' vigils down a' tha beach every morn?"

Duncan's deep voice yanked him from his gloom, and Alex looked up, meeting his brother's blue eyes.

"Nay." The word came out on a sigh, and he dropped the parchment Hamish had asked him to read. He reclined in the carved chair at his desk. The wood hit his shoulder blades and he pressed harder, reveling in the discomfort. Alex rocked the chair off the stone floor a few times before letting it land with a *thump* that resounded in the room.

His twin shut the door quietly and stepped away from the frame. He ran his hand through his long dark locks. "Shall I restate? Order ye ta reveal all?"

Alex arched an eyebrow. "Ye? *Order* me? I'm yer laird."

Duncan scoffed. He was the only member of their clan who could get away with such disrespect. "Ye shared a womb wit' me a' fore ye were *my laird.*"

He narrowed his eyes, weighing his options.

Did he want to argue with his twin?

Or should he tell him about Alana?

Could they get into a brawl?

Alex might enjoy some pounding fists. He

should've gone out to the yard to spar with their men that morning. Needed a workout.

"Och, now I *ken* there's somethin' wrong wit' ye. Ye've nothin' ta say about what I jus' said? I thought a' least ye'd *try* ta knock me on my arse."

Alex snorted. Duncan could always read him well enough to seem as if he'd taken thoughts right out of his head. "Dinnae be worth tha effort."

His twin laughed and took a seat he'd not been invited into. When their gazes brushed, concern chased Duncan's mirth away. "What's goin' on, brother?"

"Nothin' of yer concern."

Something akin to hurt flashed across the face that matched his.

Alex winced. Aye, they'd always shared everything. Neither had to say it. "I'm sorry." He sighed again. "'Tis nothin' I care ta discuss."

"Are ye well, then?"

I wouldn't go that far.

"I dinnae plan on fadin' away."

"'Tis a lass, dinnae?"

He froze.

Duncan slapped his forearm; Alex jumped and cursed. "I knew it! Alex MacLeod, tied in knots o'er a lass! Who is she? Why tha beach? Are ye havin' a clandestine tryst?"

Alex groaned. "'Tis none of yer concern, as I've said."

His twin's excitement rolled over him, turning to frustration and annoyance when it hit his chest. Duncan was just like the rest of his family.

Meddlers. The lot of 'em.

"She's no' a MacDonald, is she?" His brother scowled. "Da dinnae—"

He cast his eyes to the ceiling. Wouldn't look at a lass from their rival clan if she showed up at Dunvegan naked, ready and begging. "Nay. She dinnae be a MacDonald."

"Weel then, who *is* she?"

You wouldn't believe me if I told you.

"No one." The lie burned its way down his throat, into his belly until the bile rose back up. Alex swallowed.

Denying Alana *hurt*.

She was so far from '*no one*' he didn't have the appropriate words—even if he'd *wanted* to tell his twin about her. It didn't matter that he'd only seen her twice. Or that it'd been a fortnight since he'd held her. Kissed her.

Alana was still fresh in his mind, in his dreams.

In his heart?

She said goodbye.

Alex couldn't—wouldn't—accept that he'd never see her again.

So, he couldn't give up his morning rides down at the beach. He hoped—prayed—he'd find her again.

They'd had lengthy conversations in his nightly dreams, as well as made love for hours. He longed for another opportunity to do both with her. Explore that little burst when they touched.

The dreams felt so *real*. Like they were memories...visions. As if the answers to his questions were real, not something his mind's eye had just filled in.

"Then why d'ye look as if yer gonna retch?"

Again, Duncan's words were spot on, and Alex wanted to shout, swear, and make him go away. If he was to come clean, where could he even begin?

"Leave off, will ye?" he barked.

"Is she wed or somethin'?" Duncan's eyes widened.

He didn't want to answer his nosy brother. He inhaled and shook his head. Alex should call him on his inquiry, really. Duncan knew him better than to ask if he'd touch a married woman. He *wouldn't*. Neither of them would, despite his twin's womanizing ways.

"Then...what 'tis the problem? Da would certainly welcome ye marryin'."

Marrying?

Alex wasn't ready for that. Maybe not even with Alana...

She's not human. She's Fae. As a matter of fact, she's a princess.

He couldn't *say* any of that. "Do ye believe in tha Fae?" Alex cursed the blurt when it tumbled out.

Confusion drew his twin's brow tight. "Fae? Whate'er fer? Now, brother, ye *are* worryin' me."

"Remember tha legend Da always tol' us when we were abed an' wee?"

"Aye, I know it weel."

"Weel..." Alex shook his head. "Ah, ne'er ye mind. 'Tis foolish."

"Alex?" Duncan studied him as if he'd lost his

mind now, and he fought the urge to shift in the chair.

Don't tell him one word.

"I dinnae be sure 'tis just a legend."

God's blood, really?

Where had his fortitude gone?

Silence reigned.

His brother's eyes were so wide the whites showed around blue irises. "I need ta call Malcolm Beaton from *Mamaidh's* chambers."

"What?" Alex croaked.

"Although, I dinnae be sure he can help. Does he examine heads? Tha insides, I mean. I think ye must've hit yers on somethin'." His brother didn't crack a smile until he finished speaking.

He threw a punch his twin dodged.

Duncan broke into a deep chuckle.

"Sod off," Alex mumbled, but the laughter didn't subside.

"Ah, come now. 'Tis amusin'."

"At my expense, as always."

Duncan's expression sobered again. "Alex, yer worryin' me somethin' fierce. Why tha Fae? Why would ye think 'tis anathin' but an ol' tale?"

"How did collectin' the rents go?" he asked, needing a distraction.

"Nay. Ye dinnae fool me like a laddie. Tell me what's goin' on."

Alex took a breath and shook his head. "I need yer full accountin' of what ye brought home. Beasties as well as coin."

His brother narrowed his eyes. "Cormac already

gave tha list ta Hamish. 'Tis sittin' right there, in front a' ye."

Alex's gaze shot to where Duncan had pointed and heat exploded at the back of his neck, creeping upward. He shifted on his chair and avoided looking up. He was probably bright red and couldn't remember the last time he'd blushed. *That* was the scroll he'd been reading and obviously not comprehending. "Thank ye," he muttered.

"Alex MacLeod." His name was full of warning.

Did he want to heed it?

"Ye dinnae believe me if I tol' ye." His earlier thought fell out of his mouth at a whisper.

Duncan regarded him solemnly. Reclined in the chair and crossed his arms over his chest. "Let *me* be tha judge a' tha'."

"I'm tryin' ta decide if I've gone mad."

His brother cocked his head to one side. "Go on..."

"I *did* meet a lass. I've no' seen her fer a fortnight."

"Why?"

"I've been askin' myself tha' every day. Did I dream her up?" The last part was a muse Alex hadn't meant to say aloud.

His brother shifted, making his long hair dance. He didn't speak; probably sensing Alex needed a moment to gather his thoughts, like he had since they were wee.

No one knew him better than Duncan.

Alex was closer to no one either, not even Janet or their father. If he confided in anyone about Alana, it made sense it was his twin. "I asked ye abou' tha Fae because tha's what—*who*—she is. I met a Fae Princess named Alana."

She'd dreamt of Alex. Dreams that consisted of long walks on the beach, conversations she'd never gotten the chance to have with him and holding his hand.

Then there was the lovemaking. Of course, he'd touched her when they'd last been together, but in her fantasy, he'd tasted and mapped every inch of her *naked* skin. She'd even ridden him while he'd guided her, held her, and helped them both to completion.

Alana knew what his kiss was like, but her mind, her desires, had filled in the rest and she'd woken in bed a sweaty pulsing mess, so aroused she'd seared from it. The resulting disappointment crashing over her because it was just a dream made her sob.

Fae magic was vast and varied, and of course some got visions. Premonitions of the past, the future, even empathic insights when touching people.

She'd never had a vision.

Of all her magic, she'd not been graced by the Goddess with that power. So how could the dreams be more like memories that hadn't happened?

The way Alex had kissed her, caressed her, taken her…it felt so *real.*

Even the pleasant ache at her core was what she'd imagined it would feel like when she was no longer a virgin.

Alana ached to see him again.

The risk is too great.

Besides, she'd have to figure out yet another way to access the Faery Stones. They were spelled against stealth magic, so she'd have to be even cleverer than before. An explosion in the woods wouldn't work twice. When she'd done that, her invisibility spell had dissipated the moment she'd stepped onto the dais that held the Stones. No one could get closer under disguise.

Xander was still irritated with her.

Now she also had Seamus to contend with. Her cousin was angry about that, too.

It *was* all her fault.

Alana had a hard time keeping these logical, rational thoughts at the forefront in her brain. What she needed to do and what she *wanted* to do had vastly separated from each other.

"Alex…" she whispered.

She needed to forget the human laird and figure a way to keep the Irish prince away.

The problem was her heart wasn't in *that* plan.

When she'd told her cousin she believed Alex was for her, it'd been the truth. Emotion smacked into her chest and spread wide, making her double over and grab her middle. She *couldn't* forget Alex. It just wasn't *possible.*

Could that confirm that they were indeed fated?

"Alana, what's wrong?"

Xander's voice pulled her from her internal chaos.

She looked up to find him standing in the doorway of her sleeping room, a food tray in his strong grip. The covered bowl had steam wafting from it, but she was afraid to eat, even if her stomach was growling, and she did like a good morning porridge.

"I need to see Alex," she blurted.

Her cousin entered the room sighing. He closed his eyes and his chest rose and fell, as if he'd taken a deep breath. He said a spellword, and the tray grew thick legs as he set it down over her lap and took a seat on the edge of her bed.

Alana would've teased him about being a handmaiden and bringing her sustenance to break her fast in bed, but she needed to prepare herself for the argument she'd rather avoid.

Keeping herself busy with food was a good plan for the time being, so she lifted the lid from her porridge and inhaled. The aroma of roasted grains and honey hit her senses and she was able to smile.

She glanced over the plate next to the large bowl. There were a variety of sweets, all iced or buttered, and looking as good as the sweetwoods burning in her hearth smelled. "Hmmm. You're spoiling me this morning."

"Not me. Gwynna prepared your meal, and she…"

Alana grinned at the way Xander trailed off and averted his gaze. "Likes *you*," she said. "She also knows since I'm being punished, Audra and Lenya aren't caring for my needs. She probably figured she'd see *you* this lovely morn." She hadn't seen her two favorite handmaidens in almost a month.

Her cousin cleared his throat. "Aye, she's fond of me."

"Xander!" She giggled when he still wouldn't look

at her.

He wouldn't confirm—he never did—but he must've taken the maid as a lover. Xander had always chided her that it wasn't proper for them to discuss his bedmates, but her cousin was handsome and honorable. And...male. He no doubt *'had needs'* like the men she'd dallied with always touted.

She suspected he didn't sleep alone a lot. Besides, he was a bit of a hypocrite, because as her bodyguard, he had no choice but to know about *her* bedmates if and when she took a lover.

He'd known the men she'd dabbled with, but she'd never brought anyone back to her rooms anyway.

If Xander didn't like the man, Fae noble or not, he wouldn't get close to her. She hadn't been involved with any man her cousin hadn't approved of...except Alex.

Her heart slid to her stomach and her appetite slipped away, along with her amusement. She gripped her spoon so tightly her fingers protested. "I need to see him, Xander."

The apple of his throat bobbed when their eyes met. He didn't speak.

"I know 'tis foolish, and dangerous, and now even worse with Seamus involved, but..."

"You've been miserable."

Alana startled. Hadn't expected him to say that. "Aye, I have been."

The stupid Irish prince still hadn't clarified what he wanted from her, so she'd been on edge, as well, waiting for his promised torture.

King Ciaran had departed for his own lands the

day after the feast, as had the majority of the members from the other Fae Courts, but Seamus remained in Scotland as her father's honored guest.

Being confined had its merits. At least she hadn't had to *see* him. Then again, without eyes on him, Alana didn't know what he was up to, either.

Xander's exhalation had her finding his gaze again.

"You're not going to admonish me?" she whispered.

"There's no use. You've said everything already. It *is* foolish. And more dangerous than it was before."

"But?"

"I have an idea."

"To…help me?"

"Aye, of course."

Alana sputtered and set the spoon down. "'*Of course?*' After everything?" He'd been so angry with her. So against going to the Human Realm in the first place. Righteously so. He'd been lashed *ten* times. Had called her a fool when she'd been honest with how she felt about Alex, too.

Xander held her gaze, but she didn't like that his expression was resigned more than supportive or eager. "Have I not always been there for you?"

"Aye, but—"

"Alana, if I do not help you, you will still pursue this on your own, is that not true?"

"Probably." She pursed her lips so she wouldn't give into a smile.

"I would rather know what's going on than have to explain why I didn't catch you sneaking around."

Alana laughed — couldn't help it.

Annoyance flashed in her cousin's eyes.

She schooled her expression. "I'm sorry."

"You are not!" he returned quickly, but one corner of his mouth shot up.

"So…what's your idea?"

chapter nine

"**Y**ou disguise yourself as a Warrior and we go on a *'secret mission'*."

Alana blinked. "Really?"

Her cousin nodded as if he didn't see or sense her shock.

"Since when do *you*, my rule-following bodyguard, my conscience most of the time, *willingly* break commands, orders…decrees?"

Xander smirked. "When I have a plan 'twill work."

She bit into a fruit pastry and moaned as the flavor burst in her mouth, then darted her tongue out to catch a renegade icing drop. "This is so good. I *love* Gwynna. If you haven't taken her as a lover, you should."

He cast his eyes to the ceiling. "So, you don't want to hear my plan?"

Her heart skipped.

Alex.

"Of course, I do."

Xander launched into a tale of a faked proclamation and orders that wouldn't be questioned by the half-Wing of guards at the Faery Stones. They would tell them of their *'secret mission'* and flash the scroll. Swear that the king and Captain Daegus had commanded silence from all with the knowledge of them crossing realms.

It would be easy enough to disguise Alana with a

glamour spell. They could even make her appear as a winged Fae Warrior, but from one of the other Courts. She shouldn't be required to speak but had a passable Irish accent if the need arose. The spell itself would make her sound male.

The fact it was common knowledge the Crown Prince of Ireland was still at Scottish Court would help their cause; allay thoughts of it being odd that there was an Irish Fae Warrior with Xander.

As her personal royal bodyguard, her cousin was privy to things his brethren were not—which also fed credibility to a clandestine assignation from the king.

Her mouth hung open when he stopped speaking.

Amusement darted across his face, and she gave a slight smile. Perhaps he'd forgiven her after all.

He tugged on his warrior braid and shook his head. "I have no idea why I'm mad enough to entertain this, honestly."

"Because you love me."

"Aye, unfortunately you're right. I do."

Alana arched an eyebrow. "Unfortunately?"

Xander gave her a long look and didn't answer.

He didn't have to. Their relationship caused him nothing but hardship lately—if not most of the time—and she loved *him* for staying by her side. Was he a lesser man, or Warrior, he could've asked for reassignment. He'd vowed to protect her with his life, so perhaps pride in his word had made the decision for him.

Somehow, that idea hurt; she didn't want that to be the root of his loyalty to her.

"Why *are* you…willing, Xander?" Teasing, blood ties, and worries aside, Alana wanted to know. He hadn't believed her when she'd mentioned fate.

"I did some digging."

"About what?"

"Your human's many times removed Fae Princess grandmother."

"And?" Her gut tightened and she fidgeted as she waited for him to explain. Her spoon *clinked* against the ceramic bowl, and despite the porridge's thickness, it sloshed against its confines.

"Eirini knew of the tale and directed me to the *one* scroll in the whole library with her name."

"She *was* a princess, then?"

Her cousin nodded. "There was a reference to a Princess Sima being banished for unspeakable acts. Of course, the *'crimes'* weren't detailed with the punishments, a sure sign of royal embarrassment. It was a long time ago, about six hundred years. No one remains alive that could confirm or deny what little is there."

"That's it?" Alana's pulse pounded in her temples.

"Well, you know how old Eirini likes to gossip. And she's very good at her duties." He took a breath and didn't give her a chance to respond. "She found a few vague mentions about a rebel runaway princess from that time period. But she said her suspicions were confirmed on the royal name ledgers and family trees, because Princess Sima was wiped from all official records. There's no mention or confirmation of her birthright. Odd, considering she was the heir, like you.

To support this, she never rose to be queen. A prince—most likely Sima's first cousin—ascended after the king who had to be her father, died. No record of any other children, so the throne went to the next blood relation in line."

"She got pregnant and fled to be with her laird," she whispered.

"So, Eirini suspects."

"She told you that? You didn't tell her you were asking for me, did you?"

Xander flashed another smirk. "I didn't. But she knows your fascination with Fae history well enough, so even if she guessed I was researching for you, she wouldn't go anywhere of import with that knowledge. She does miss you, though. Told me to tell you to come see her."

Alana smiled. The librarian had always proved discreet before. "So, you believe Alex's clan legend is true?"

"There is merit in what I discovered. And you said he feels magic. Evidently even diluted Fae blood means something."

She blew out a breath. "If that's what's happening. I just know…" she swallowed, "what I feel." She put her hand over her heart.

Her cousin offered a curt nod.

"Do you…believe me, Xander? Do you believe Alex is my fate?"

He sighed. "I don't know, Alana."

Sadness rolled over her, but she'd have to accept what he could offer…for now. "You'll take me to see him?" she asked, voice just above a whisper.

Xander sighed again. "Aye, I suppose I will."

She tried to tamp down her excitement but busied her hands by moving the tray from her lap and throwing her arms around her cousin. "Thank you so much! You won't regret it."

He chuckled and patted her hands. "Calm yourself, Your Highness." He flattened his mouth when he looked at her. "I *already* regret it."

Some of Alana's joy dimmed. "Please don't, Xander. If it were you, *I* would support you no matter what."

Silence descended, but then he nodded. "I know you would. Which is why I'm doing this."

"When do we go?"

Her cousin sighed for the third time and gestured with his hand. "When you're ready."

She screeched like a lassie, then slapped her hand over her mouth when Xander winced.

"Finish breaking your fast. I shall step out and make excuses to Rannick as to why I'm escorting you from your rooms."

"Father said I could go out," she reminded him.

"Aye, but your movements are to be restricted and recorded, so we have to tell him something credible."

Alana rolled her eyes. "The market?"

Xander nodded. "That should suffice. There'll be enough people there you wouldn't necessarily be spotted easily if anyone is questioned about seeing you. Just have an excuse prepared for why you failed to purchase anything."

She giggled. "I'm the princess. I'm picky."

He shook his head and she grinned.

She hadn't seen him so normal with her since before their first journey to the Human Realm, and she wanted to cling to it. Alana had her cousin's grudging support regarding the object of her desire, and she was going to take that for now, until she could convince her bodyguard Alex was her fate and gain his true approval.

Alex couldn't give up his daily rides. So much so, he'd deigned to make them two times a day instead of just the early hours of the morn. He was now seeking the beach in the afternoon, too.

He couldn't risk missing his princess, after all.

It'd been over three weeks since he'd seen her, but no amount of reminding himself time did nothing, but creep forward would let him accept he *wouldn't* see her again.

He *refused* to believe she was gone for good, even though defeat would settle low and dominate his body and mood alike when he went home emptyhanded each evening of his quest.

Alex had even sought the method of magical travel that brought her to the Isle of Skye — the Faery Stones — to no avail. He'd tracked the path she always took on the beach but found *no traces*.

Then again, he didn't know *what* he was looking for; he was just driven to find *her*. So perhaps he'd passed them a dozen times and not known it.

No matter how he examined things, he *should* go home. To Dunvegan with the rest of the MacLeods. Stay home.

He'd accused himself of being a coward and running from his clan. Recited every reason his actions were nothing but foolish. However, Alex couldn't stop calling for his stallion to be readied and taking off when the need in his gut—and perhaps his heart—arose.

When confronted by anyone, he'd just stated he would address his duties as *he* saw fit and that he hadn't failed at anything yet.

Except finding Alana. That little tidbit he had to keep to himself, of course.

As laird, Alex refused to be questioned. So far, his hollering and bluster had worked, but knowing his family, it wouldn't last.

Last eve, his mother had questioned him about his *'secret lass'* when he'd visited her. Alex had wanted to murder Duncan on the spot for his big mouth, but his twin had just grinned and kissed their mother's pale hand, then openly dared him to tell her about Alana.

It was quite the wonder since he had nothing to say to his twin. Duncan had openly disbelieved his claims about the princess, yet he was trying to torture Alex in front of their mother?

What was he supposed to do?

He'd *had* to speak.

Alex had wished their father was still angry with his twin and had banished him from the castle—hell, the isle—for tupping too many maids.

They had family on Lewis, after all. Maybe the

laird, their cousin, could use his troublesome brother. Duncan was good for collecting the rents, soldiering, and manual labor, after all.

Then their mother had smiled.

He had to swallow hard—then and now—and he hadn't been able to help himself from launching into a tale about Alana.

Most of what Alex had told her had been true—save that she was a Fae Princess—and when his mother had held a light carefree expression on her face, his eyes had smarted.

Afterward, he'd only wanted to maim his brother instead of killing him.

He hadn't seen their mother look happy like that in a long time. Her hazel eyes had glowed, and she'd even had pink on her cheeks that wasn't fever induced. Her light brown hair hadn't looked so limp.

She'd had a coughing fit that had his pulse thundering when Alex had been done with his recital, but the previous joy on her face had been worth revealing a little of his princess.

He and his brother had exchanged worried looks, but Lady Caitriona had stopped Duncan from retrieving Malcolm Beaton and asked for some water, which his twin had scrambled to get.

Alex had been grateful their da wasn't in the room at the time; he wouldn't have obeyed regarding not fetching the healer.

They'd managed to talk the retired laird into bathing and getting something to eat—something their father did less and less regularly, the sicker his wife got.

Iain had lost weight and his dark hair was graying more and more.

Lady Caitriona didn't like that anymore than Alex or his siblings. She didn't want her husband to abandon caring for himself for her sake. She hadn't wanted him to step down from being the laird, either, but her protests hadn't swayed his decision.

That just made Alex feel more guilty for wanting to flee.

He'd been given responsibilities his father had *entrusted* to him, and he'd rather be down on the beach, searching for a renegade princess he couldn't possibly have for keeps anyway.

"Alex!"

His name from the familiar voice made his heart skip and yanked him from the melancholy musings about his family.

Am I imagining her?

Had he been missing her so long he'd dreamed Alana up?

Was he *that* desperate?

He startled on Bán's wide back and his eyes landed precisely on *her,* as if instinct. Alex frowned. Her guard was right behind her, and he tried not to hate that she wasn't alone. His body mourned. He'd be unable to hold her, kiss her, if they had no privacy.

Alana jogged up to his horse before he could dismount. "I knew you'd be here!" She smiled, and it made his gut quiver. She was dressed head to foot in three or four different shades of purple again, like she'd been every time he'd seen her.

Her hair was braided in a thick plait today instead of loose, but little flaxen flyaways framed her pretty face as she peered up at him. The style made her look even more like her oversized protector. Her visage was bright, and those intriguing eyes twinkled.

Forcing a nod, Alex slid down Bán's side and landed beside her in the rocky sand. His hands itched to touch her, but for the sake of her cousin, he kept them at his sides instead of cupping her face. "Aye, lass. I dinnae chance no' seein' ye if ye came."

Alana threw her arms around his neck and pushed to her toes to press her mouth to his.

He swallowed surprise and wrapped her in an embrace, leaning down to match her height. The fine material of her royal purple cloak distracted him for a second, but he got down to the business of kissing his lass — especially when her seeking tongue demanded entry in his mouth.

Her taste exploded and Alex groaned. It was the same summer berries and sweet wine, but somehow better, sharper. Need settled low in his groin; his cock and bollocks ached.

Alana buried her fingers in his short hair and kissed him harder.

Until her bodyguard cleared his throat.

Alex reluctantly parted their fused lips and shot the tall man a glance.

Xander had his arms crossed over a broad muscular chest and his eyes were narrowed. His thick plait swayed when he tilted his head, glaring.

"Sorry," Alana whispered, looking over her

shoulder at the fair-haired man, but she didn't seem apologetic, and she didn't loosen her hold on Alex.

Self-preservation told him he should move her away and prepare a defense, but he didn't want to tear his eyes from the princess who'd just kissed away his coherent thought.

Gorgeous was too weak a word.

Air was a foreign concept, and his lungs constricted, so *breathtaking* was more valid.

Her cheeks were flushed pink to her ears, and the little wisps of hair dancing around her face demanded his caress as much as her lips called to him to taste them again.

Alana's body was still close to his—and it was a damn good thing, because if her bodyguard noticed his obvious erection, he'd likely try to lop it off, and Alex desired to keep his tender bits.

Get yourself together. Now.

He was going to need his wits.

Too bad they were still very much *below* his belt. His need wasn't concerned with her cousin's presence. However, his brain reminded him the man carried a huge sword, likely the match in size to his claymore.

Alana didn't look bothered by Xander's being there, either.

That was bad for his efforts to clear the passionate haze from his head.

She pressed her forehead to his chest. "I missed you so much." Her voice wavered as if she was about to sob, so he *couldn't* release her.

Alex squeezed her against him with an uneasy

glimpse at the warrior not ten feet from them.

Alana looked up and he fell into her violet eyes. They were indeed misty, and his heart stuttered.

It wouldn't have mattered if an army marched down the beach toward him. He couldn't look away from his princess. "I feared I'd ne'er see ye again." The truth breeched his lips and they sighed at the same time.

"You weren't supposed to. But Alex...I couldn't stay away."

"Thank Jesu," he whispered.

She flashed another brilliant smile that made focusing on anything other than *her* a serious challenge. "Come, let us walk together."

He nodded numbly with one last look at her guard.

"Don't worry about my cousin, he's not as mean as he looks." Alana winked.

Xander grunted but didn't uncross his arms even as he took a step toward them, obviously intending to follow.

Alex hollered at himself again, but his senses were still off, and he struggled with getting his libido under control.

It was surreal, wasn't it?

As if he'd willed her into appearing.

One kiss wasn't nearly enough.

If her cousin wasn't there, he would've stripped her trews down to finish what they'd started up on the ridge the last time he'd seen her. Perhaps it was for the better that the oversized man was present, as much as his cock hated the idea.

Alana left his side to stroke Bán's neck, and his

horse nickered, bumping her hand for more affection. "He's beautiful. What's he called?"

"Bán." Alex cleared his throat and made a go for his stallion's reins, brushing the thick gray mane out of the way.

"But he's not *all* white, is he?" Alana's mouth curved up again.

"Ye speak Gaelic?"

"Human Gaelic isn't so different from Fae, really. Most of our words are close, or even the same." She said what he could recognize as '*hello, how are you?*' but the tone and some of the inflection was off. "Could you make out what I said?"

He nodded. "I'm weel, how're ye?"

Alana grinned and he couldn't help but return it. "See? Not so different."

The cheerful look on her pretty face turned his brain to mush, and Alex had to concentrate to speak. "Well, aye, my horse was named for his hide's color, but when he was wee, his mane and tail were white, as weel." He pushed words out about his beloved mount, but he didn't care to discuss the animal.

She reached for his hand. "Let us walk. Show me your isle."

They talked about everything. Laughed together. Questioned each other about everything human, and everything Fae.

Alana had a bright curious mind and all the knowledge Alex had didn't seem to satisfy her. In that, she seemed innocent, but he couldn't call her naïve or childlike. Her beauty stunned him as much as the shot of energy when she put her hand on his arm so he could escort her.

The more her countenance displayed obvious excitement about mundane day-to-day clan life, the more his heart cantered. He wanted to mention his dreams, but her cousin followed their path, and took part in the conversation when Alana forced him to.

Alex respected him a notch for the distance he tried to keep to give them an air of privacy, but he wasn't foolish enough to believe the man couldn't hear everything that was said—another reason to hold his tongue on what he'd done to the princess in his sleep.

She told him of her realm—things of magic and wonder he couldn't fathom being true, although Alex believed every word. Even about the orange and blue grass, and pink and purple trees.

His princess explained that her cousin was her sworn personal guard, and he was a renowned Fae *winged* Warrior.

He didn't have his wings in the Human Realm, but she swore his magic and skills were still unparalleled. Alana stated there was less magic in Alex's realm, which made the place undesirable for most Fae, and was the reason Xander had no wings.

Actual wings were hard to imagine, let alone a man flying, but when her cousin grunted and looked away from her praise, Alex had to smirk.

The affection they had for each other was obvious—there was no doubt the man saw her as more than a mere charge, and the princess felt the same. They resembled each other enough to be siblings, and he could tell they cared about each other as such, as well.

Alana explained that they'd grown up together, and been educated together, so it was only natural they'd stayed together when he'd finished his training as a Warrior and sworn himself to her.

Alex found it hard to tell her his mother was very ill, especially when her eyes watered for a woman she didn't know, but he made his way through it, explaining how he'd ended up being the laird and telling her of his da, Duncan and Janet. He talked about his family and his clan, as well as their proud stronghold, their castle.

Morning melted into late afternoon, and he didn't want her to leave — *ever*.

He wanted to sweep her into his arms, steal her away to Dunvegan and keep her forever. Alex didn't care that he hadn't eaten since dawn, and his stomach was rumbling demands for food.

Alana squeezed his hand as if she could read his mind, and he slipped into those unusual eyes again. His gut shouted what she'd say before she opened her mouth.

"I…need to go. We've been here a long time."

He swallowed a sigh and looked at her cousin. Offered him a nod. "Thank ye fer bringin' her back ta me."

She smiled and pulled his hand to her mouth, kissing his knuckles. "He couldn't keep me away."

Xander snorted and averted his gaze.

"Contention a' tween ye?" he whispered.

Alana nodded "'Tis dangerous…for me…us…to come here."

Instinct shouted that there was something she *wasn't* saying, but he released a breath and tried to stave off the sorrow threatening to consume him.

She's leaving me again.

Alex cupped her face and tugged her chin up so she had to meet his eyes. "I dinnae want ye ta go."

Alana swallowed.

His need to kiss her burned, but he wouldn't tempt a wager with Xander.

"I do not want to go, believe me. But...I must."

"Fer good?"

She closed her eyes and the raw emotion she was trying to hide was just about slayed Alex. "It...should be."

"But it dinnae?"

"I can make no vow to you, this day or any other." When she met his gaze, her violet orbs were filled with tears she was trying hard not to shed. One slid down her cheek, and he thumbed it away.

"I shall make a vow ta *ye*, Yer Highness." He kept his voice low, serious.

Alana startled in his grip but made no move to break their physical contact. "Alex—"

"I *will* see ye again. I dinnae accept anathin' less."

She whimpered, then slid her arms around his neck and tugged him down to her mouth.

Alex didn't deny her—wouldn't have been able to—but he kept the brush of their lips soft, tender and short, for her cousin's sake. If he kissed her like she'd kissed him earlier, it'd just be more of a lure to steal her away. He didn't need another erection he couldn't use, either.

Xander had respected him; he owed him the same.

Even so, pulling away stabbed him in the gut—and maybe higher, in his heart.

"I don't know *if*, let alone when," Alana whispered.

More tears spilled, and he wiped them away as they appeared. "Dinnae worry, lass. I shall find ye."

When her protector beckoned, she put her hand in his.

Alex watched until they'd disappeared from sight, his grip so tight on Bán's reins his knuckles burned.

If he had to stalk the beach every moment of every day, he *would* see her again.

chapter ten

The knock on the door gave her pause. Rannick wouldn't announce his advent like that, and neither would her cousin.

Alana opened the thick carved panel, half-expecting to see the oversized man-at-arms, but her heart hit her gut like a brick when her eyes met a pair of very green ones.

"Good day, Your Highness." Seamus bowed with his normal flourish and flashed his dimples.

Her gaze swung over to Rannick, who was watching the prince with barely contained annoyance.

In the very least, everyone at Scottish Court agreed on their dislike of the Irish prince. The only person who *liked* him was her father. That said a great deal about the king's judge of character.

"Your Highness," the big guard said. "The king has given leave for His Highness to visit you."

She nodded, because she couldn't blurt that she had no desire to see Seamus at all, let alone admit him to her private sanctuary.

Damn that stupid dance!

It didn't surprise her that her father would try to nurture what he thought he'd observed when she'd danced with the wretched prince at the ball.

After the Beltane celebration, the king had relaxed Alana's confinement, but only a tad, and probably *because* of Seamus. Her father likely wanted to encourage her to court the Irish imp.

She was permitted out, but had a curfew, and Rannick was still at her door. Her movements were still to be reported and tracked, as when Xander had taken her to the Human Realm the previous day under the guise of their secret mission.

Her cousin's plan had worked flawlessly, including his reporting to the oversized man-at-arms that they were going to market.

Two different guards had replaced Rannick overnight—as if the king feared that time was the most common for her to sneak out. Little did her father know, she preferred to leave her rooms in the morning. Especially if she intended to sneak to the Human Realm.

Xander could still come and go as he pleased and brought most of her meals himself. Alana hadn't seen her handmaidens since her initial punishment and lockdown, and suspected her father assumed she would feel deprived without them.

She didn't; it was easier to keep things private if she only interacted with her cousin. Even trusted servants like Audra and Lenya sometimes had waggling tongues. Much too dangerous, considering her Alex situation.

The appearance of the stupid prince washed away all the positive feelings that'd been floating around her since she'd seen her laird and spent the hours, she had with him. Kissing him, touching him, and holding his hand. However, caution reminded Alana to guard her mind—block Alex from her thoughts.

Until she could get rid of her *'visitor'*, anyway.

"Good day, Prince Seamus," she forced words out, and tried to ensure her face was a mask of pleasantness that was the opposite of what her insides felt like when she looked at him. She glanced at Rannick. "Where's my cousin?"

"Sir Xander should be here shortly. I received word he was delayed by Captain Daegus."

Perfect.

Alana would have to endure the prince *alone.*

She said her mind-blocking spellword again for good measure. "Very well," she gritted out, then tightened her jaw to keep the unladylike curse inside her mouth.

"I'm so very happy to see you and have been looking forward to our visit all morning." Although Seamus' words were friendly, there was a gleam in the lousy royal's eyes that made her heart leap to her throat.

What do you want?

She wanted to demand, but instead watched him warily and held her tongue. For now. Alana rubbed her arm, wishing she'd donned a simpler dress.

Like the one she'd worn to the ball, this gown had her shoulders and neck bare, with intricate flowers sewn into the low-cut bodice. It was purple, as she wore little else, but the shade was lilac, one of the few of that hue in her collection.

Lavish gowns had always been her weakness, and Fae maidens weren't too shy to show some skin—most of the time. Open backs and shoulders, as well as strapless and revealing bodices were the current style.

The prince swept into her rooms and Rannick threw her a sympathetic look as he closed the door.

She wanted to ask him to step inside, but it wasn't proper. If he was Xander, she could get away with requesting a chaperone, but the man-at-arms' rank wasn't high enough to merit it. At least he wouldn't assume she and the Irish prince were lovers.

Alana shuddered, almost gagged, and tried not to openly glare.

The scoundrel had taken over her favorite chaise, and she considered burning it when he left.

His back was straight, and he had one leg crossed over the other, with one of his hands resting on his top knee. Like the night of the ball, he was dressed elegantly in green, and his doublet brought out the stunning color of his eyes. His wavy hair was bound at the back of his neck, and his trews were striped two hues of green, one light and one dark. They were disgustingly tight, like always.

She smirked at his feminine posture and straightened her shoulders.

"Have a seat, my dear princess. After all, this is your abode. I must say, this is a very nice sitting room."

Alana ignored the compliment. "Nay. You shan't be staying long."

He smiled. It could've been a nice gesture, but there was too much smugness in it. Without breaking eye contact, Seamus made himself more comfortable on her lounger. He reclined, lying back and putting his shoulder into the plush upholstery, pitching his powerful chest toward her. Like he was there to stay.

I really need to burn it now.

Apprehension crawled up from her toes. His visit had a purpose, even if he denied it, and it wouldn't be good.

Xander had told her to find out what the prince wanted from her. Whether or not she wanted to, instinct told her she was about to. Alana inhaled, tapping into her empathic powers and telling herself to be calm and strong.

No matter how relaxed he appeared, the prince's sharp eyes betrayed his intentions.

She wouldn't like whatever he had to say.

"I can't stop thinking about the ball, and how lovely it was to dance with you, sweet princess."

"What do you *want*, Seamus?" she demanded. Impatience got the best of her, but she couldn't regret her near-shout.

"You."

Revulsion roiled her gut. "That's *never* going to happen."

He let out a rich peal of laughter that at any other time would've been as appealing as his full-dimpled grin.

If he wasn't who he was. If it wasn't mocking, too.

"Ah, but that's where you're *wrong*, my dear princess."

Alana let the shudder of anger pass over her shoulders, down her spine and into her limbs until she could breathe again. Her fingers twitched and she talked herself in to relaxing her tight fists, too. She'd fling magic at him — if it wasn't for his damn medallion.

"I'm *not* sleeping with you."

Seamus laughed again. "Oh, Your Highness, I want *more* than that."

She swallowed as her rage blanched and her stomach churned with the ensuing fright. "Wh-wh-what?" Alana *hated* that she'd shown weakness in front of him, especially when the stutter resulted in a slow evil smile spreading over the Irish prince's full mouth.

"You'll have to *pay* for my silence."

"With what?" There was no use denying Alex again. Seamus hadn't believed her at the ball, and he certainly hadn't changed his mind about her lie now. His laughter had said as much. She just needed to keep him from *more* knowledge about her laird.

Somehow.

"Your hand."

"Nay. Not if you were the last Fae Prince in *all* the lands. I'd marry a gelded *human* before I'd wed *you*."

Seamus didn't bat an eye at her hard fast refusal or the insult. "I don't require your heart, or even your body, beyond consummation, and perhaps once or twice for an heir. I need your signature on the sealed agreement. Then when your father passes on, I'll be the king of Scotland and Ireland's Fae Realms. As agreed in our marriage contract, of course."

Alana blinked.

Ambition?

The womanizing scoundrel had this kind of ambition? As scheming as Seamus could be, she'd never seen *that* coming. Not to mention, her father wasn't an old man by Fae standards. He probably had one hundred years left, if not more.

Was the Irish prince willing to wait for his dual throne, or did he have nefarious plans?

Alana wasn't overly fond of her father, but he *was* her king, and the rightful ruler of the Scottish Fae. He was a decent king, and the people respected—if feared—him. *She* was supposed to be queen after him.

Seamus had chased her for years, but she'd always assumed it was for the mere physical conquest, so he could brag he'd been with her. Even more so if he'd taken her maidenhead. It wasn't uncommon for him to vocalize the noble lovers he'd had, and of course, he flaunted his skill between the sheets.

She tried not to gag.

Alex's blue eyes popped into her head. She quickly reinforced her mind-block spell again. Her heart skipped, then cantered.

Why was it when the word *marriage* danced by her thoughts, the human laird came to mind?

That was more than just forbidden. It was…unthinkable.

Impossible.

Despite the same supposedly happening in his family history. Princess Sima had gotten her man. She'd been lucky, hadn't she?

Stop thinking about him.

Alex's smile disobeyed, appearing as real as it had yesterday on the beaches of Skye. She ached for him and prayed to the Goddess Seamus wouldn't discover it.

"I won't do it." Alana crossed her arms and looked down her nose at the stupid prince.

Another slow malicious smile spread over his too-full lips.

She swallowed.

Why does he look so pleased?

She tried to brace herself for anything he could possibly say next.

"Alex MacLeod."

It took everything within her to not reveal her shock. Alana stood her ground five feet from her enemy and tried to hold herself together. Project even more calm over her form. She pleaded to the Goddess he hadn't just picked up her thoughts, despite her spell being repeated thrice. "I've already told you—"

"Laird of his clan." He continued as if she'd not spoken. "Lives in a castle called Dunvegan, on what's called the Isle of Skye. I believe the humans call the islands the Hebrides. The Western Isles? He's a tad young for you, sweet princess." Seamus *tsked* and waggled his finger.

Her heart stopped.

Do. Not. React.

"My, my." The Irish bastard rose from her chaise and took two steps toward her, but Alana slid backwards. "What's wrong, *Princess*? Why've you gone so pale? I didn't figure out your little secret, did I?" His eyes went wide, and he put his hand to his chest, as if he was sincerely apologizing. Or playing innocent.

Alana considered retching on his fancy shoes.

Where was Xander when she needed him?

When she still couldn't muster words, Seamus covered his mouth with a hand in mock-surprise. "Oh, I suppose I *did* figure it out!" He stepped forward again, and she barely dodged him this time.

Tremors started in Alana's shoulders, and she sucked her cheek in and bit down. What she said next would make or break this situation.

Too bad she didn't have a clue *what* to say.

Her heart dipped low and stayed there; she couldn't stop shaking.

The prince backed her up to the wall next to her sleeping room's door. His big body blocked her in, and he slid his arms on either side of her, planting his palms flat alongside her head, but he didn't touch her.

Yet.

His eyes vowed he would.

"Oh, my dear princess, you smell so good." Seamus inhaled with exaggeration, leaning in and leering. "You don't have to say a word about the human, Your Highness. I can read you like a book, even though your mind is like a vault right now. Just know, if I don't get what I want, I *shall* go to King Fillan with what I've discovered."

Alana clenched her jaw as his threat—no, promise—washed over her. She was more worried about his proximity at the moment. "Step back, or I shall scream."

He smiled. "I like screamers. Surely, you've heard how the courtiers praise me." He pitched his hips into her, and an erection was evident.

She stilled and swallowed again. He wouldn't—

"Step away from the princess, Your Highness." The voice was a hard order.

Alana gasped and did her best to peer around her captor. Her gaze collided with Xander's, and he had his hand on the hilt of his broadsword.

Seamus froze, but still wore a smile.

She slunk away from him when he released her, but she stayed against the wall, so it would hold her up. She had to resist the urge to dart behind her cousin and grip his waist.

Cower. Hide.

He could not, but she wished Xander could run him through.

"I'm sorry, Sir Xander, I think you misunderstand."

"I don't think I do, Your Highness." Although her cousin's voice was even, the honorific was more of a sneer.

"I was given leave by King Fillan to visit my betrothed."

Xander's eyes shot to her when she didn't immediately protest. Both his eyebrows arched high. "I was unaware—"

Alana cleared her throat. "There's nothing to *be* aware of. I've refused Prince Seamus."

Seamus reached to caress her cheek, but she yanked away. "Oh, you will relent, my dear sweet princess. I've no doubt about *that*. Then we can continue what we started here."

Her cousin narrowed his eyes. His sword inched up, as if he'd pull it, instead of securing it wholly within the scabbard. "You should leave, Your Highness." Again, Xander's tone was close to forbidden for addressing a royal, but Alana would shout praise at her cousin before she'd ever chide him.

He could curse at Seamus aloud and she'd cheer him on.

The Irish prince didn't argue. Perhaps he felt her protector *would* harm him.

Plus, if Alana reported his untoward behavior, Seamus could be punished, despite her father's fondness of him. No man could put their hands—or bodies—on a woman who didn't wish it, especially the Crown Princess. He risked falling out of the king's favor.

The stupid prince had the knowledge of Alex to hang over her head.

Alana couldn't say a word.

He was smart enough to know that.

She wished she could order her cousin to geld him.

When Seamus sauntered out of her sitting room and the door shut, she slid to the shiny marble floor, unable to come away from the wall. Her bottom hit with a *thump* that wobbled her even more.

Xander rushed to her and pulled her to her feet. "What did he do to you?"

She swallowed again—couldn't speak.

"Alana." Her cousin shook her shoulders.

She collapsed against his chest and wrapped her arms around his neck. The sob bubbled up and she couldn't stop it. She could feel the tremors of his wings. His concern washed over her magic, making her limbs tingle.

"Alana." Now her cousin's deep voice held alarm,

but he squeezed her against him.

Alana lifted her head and met his eyes, but her vision blurred. "He...he... Nothing." She hiccupped. "Trapped me against the wall. Didn't even try to kiss me, but he was aroused."

Xander blew out a breath. He scowled and muttered something about relieving the prince of his bollocks. It would've made her smile at any other time. "Why, by the Goddess, would he ever think you'd agree to *marry* him?"

She crushed her eyes shut and fought through big shuddering breaths. "Because he knows everything, Xander. *Everything* about Alex."

chapter eleven

▶▶ "So, I suppose now we know what he wants." Xander's gaze was grave, and he flexed his powerful jaw. His wings quivered with barely contained ire, catching the light, and bouncing off the different colors. Irritation rolled off him, and he ignored her gesture to sit in the overstuffed chair across from her.

Alana shuddered. "Me."

"Nay." He tugged on his braid and threw it over his shoulder. "I will never allow it."

"*I* will never allow it, but he said he will take the knowledge of Alex to my father if I do not sign a betrothal contract. He told me he wants to rule Scotland and Ireland."

"Does he plan to assassinate your father?" Her cousin cocked his head to one side.

She blinked. "I contemplated that."

Xander scoffed. "Seamus isn't smart enough to accomplish that."

"We can't be confident he wouldn't try. He discovered every detail about Alex. He either had to go himself or send someone to the Human Realm." Alana's heart ached for her human laird.

A trip to see him just tripled—if not more—in risk. *Perhaps I won't ever see him again.*

"He didn't go himself. He's not been absent from Court. He's been so far up your father's arse, vying for favors, the king's throat must itch."

She managed a small laugh but didn't say anything. Couldn't stop thinking of the man she craved in another realm.

"Stop thinking about Alex MacLeod. You have a tragedy to avert. *He* only complicates it."

Alana scowled. "First of all, get out of my head. Secondly, *how* can you read my mind? I said my mind-block spell."

Xander smirked. "I can't read your thoughts right now. I wagered correctly, is all. Your expression told me everything I needed to know. You need to get a hold of *that*. If I can read you, so can other people, despite your mind being closed. You probably handed information to Seamus without meaning to." He tapped his forehead and relented on the seat, perching on the arm of the chair. He flexed his wings.

Heat rushed her cheeks, and she fidgeted on the sofa. Alana wouldn't point out that the stupid prince *had* remarked about reading her, mentioning when she'd gone pale.

She sat in her cousin's normal place because she couldn't bring herself to sit on her chaise. Maybe wouldn't ever sit on it again.

I should burn it.

Her cousin's slight mirth melted into a scowl.

"What is it?" she asked.

"Speaking of thoughts, I did not like what *your laird* was thinking about *you* yesterday."

Alana straightened. "What was he thinking?" Her stomach somersaulted. She told herself not to look eager, but her body pitched on the edge of the plush cushion beneath her.

"He wants you, Alana. With an intensity that scares me."

Of course, it wasn't a surprise he wanted her. Alex had told her as much, and she wanted him, too.

She'd felt his arousal yesterday, as well as when they'd first kissed up on the ridge. Her need equaled his, but she wasn't about to confess that to her protector. She swallowed. "I told you we're fated, cousin."

Xander's mouth set in a hard line. "Doomed, is what you are."

"I know." She closed her eyes. Her voice broke with a half-sob. "If we weren't before, we certainly are now." Her heart churned in her gut. That realization lanced like a physical injury.

"You being with the laird was *always* doomed, Alana." This was said softly, as if his volume could soften the blow of his words.

It didn't work; just made her ache more. She fought the urge to rock on the sofa and clutch her stomach.

"I hate that I don't *dislike* the laird."

"You don't?" Alana swiped her cheeks and pinned her cousin with a stare. She sat back into the plushness of her seat, missing her chaise. She needed the distraction from her agony, but she didn't want to be too hopeful.

Her cousin's approval now wouldn't fix the problem.

Xander sighed and cast his eyes to the ceiling. "I saw other things in his mind. He doesn't have a clue how to guard his thoughts. He's a good, honorable man. Loves his family and his clan, and wants to do right by them, even though he's overwhelmed by responsibility. He hasn't been the laird for more than a few months. Alex MacLeod is very young, Your Highness."

The honorific was a chide, but she ignored it and nodded. "I know how old he is. I don't care, and neither does fate."

Her cousin flexed his jaw but didn't respond. He looked away, as if he had to gather his thoughts.

Alana had never been able to read minds, but she wished she could at the moment, to tell what he was thinking. Xander was usually frank with her, but was there something he wasn't saying right now?

It didn't *really* matter; nothing could distract her from the human laird.

Alex.

Alana wanted to dissolve into a pile of sobs. "What in Five Hells am I supposed to do?"

Xander didn't flinch at her harsh, unladylike language. "For the safety of all involved, for now, I think you have to tell Seamus what he wants to hear."

She gasped. "You mean—"

He leveled her with a serious violet stare. "Aye. Tell the bastard you'll marry him."

The claymore slammed into his, and it took too

long for Alex to regroup. He was about to fall on his arse.

Duncan laughed as he stumbled about the bailey. His brother released him, which made his unsteady gait even worse, reversing his momentum.

Alex refused to concede to the ground rushing up and shot his arms wide until he regained his balance. Like he'd been a laddie imitating birds and pretending to fly. He sucked back a curse and glared at his twin, but the rascal beat him to speech.

"Yer rusty, brother."

Damn, he wanted to wipe that smirk off the face that matched his. He'd had nothing to say to his brother since the day Alex had tried to tell him about Alana. When he'd admitted that the lass consuming his thoughts was a Fae princess, Duncan had laughed so hard he'd cried.

His twin had slapped his plaid-covered thigh and had wiped his eyes dry only to further his mirth by accusing him of going mad.

Alex had tried to convince him he'd spoken only the truth, but that only amused his twin even more. He hadn't spoken more than a few words to him in over a week—since that conversation in his ledger room. He'd been forced to interact with Duncan in front of their mother, for her benefit, but even that had been strained, and his twin had acted oblivious, of course.

He'd accepted the challenge of a spar today with the sole purpose if kicking his arse, leaving him bruised. A bump on the head from the hilt of his sword had merit, too. Maybe a little bloody?

The surrounding men — a mixture of clansmen and MacLeod men-at-arms, murmured. Some watched, and some were also sparring.

Alex and Duncan were used to an audience when they were on the fighting yard, due to who they were as much as their skills with the weapons.

Dunvegan loomed behind them, a long shadow cast over the grounds. It was a sunny, breezy spring morning, but there was still a bite to the air that could cause shivers and dry the sweat they'd worked up.

Thank Jesus they were on the opposite side of the large courtyard where the lasses were beating tapestries and rugs clean. The wind carried feminine chatter their way, but they were still out of sight.

Alex had no need for female concern or attention. "I dinnae be rusty. Yer no' playin' fair." He prayed his statement hadn't sounded like a petulant, untrained lad.

"Fair? In a fight?" Duncan scoffed as he circled him, obviously trying to hone in on another perfectly mounted strike.

Truth be told, Alex would rather retreat inside than finish the match, even at the risk of being accused of weakness.

He didn't want to be out with the men. He didn't want to *look* at his brother or be forced to talk to him.

He didn't believe me.

Duncan had always been the closest person to him. To be thought a fool by his twin, or that he'd been jesting, let alone that he'd gone mad, had more bite than Alex wanted to admit.

They weren't lads at play any longer. He'd needed

his brother to listen, to believe him. Perhaps to solidify he wasn't actually going mad.

Obviously, he couldn't focus on swordplay anymore than he could Hamish's endless scrolls demanding decisions. He just wanted to say *aye* to them all, but he couldn't empty MacLeod coffers, either. He needed to study the requests, be smart, and see what was truly *needed.*

Alex just wanted everyone — including his pesky twin — to leave him the hell alone. If Duncan had tried to apologize, it would've gone a long way toward forgiveness, but not only had he *not*, his brother acted as if he didn't see his ire — and hurt — toward him.

To worsen his mood, Alex had missed his ride on the beach that morning, instead giving in to the requirements of his position at his steward's behest. He was trying to talk himself out of panicking that he'd missed her presence.

Alana would come to him if she'd been able to sneak into his realm, would she not? She knew where he resided. Or would she sit on the ridge where they'd kissed and wait for him, ultimately to no avail?

Give up when he wasn't there, and go back to her realm?

After the hours they'd spent together the previous week, he was even more obsessed with the Fae princess than before. He'd gotten a real taste of her as a person — not to mention those two kisses in front of her cousin.

She was even more delightful than he'd originally assessed, and he *craved* her.

Which was worse? Not seeing her for days — maybe

weeks at a time—or having to hear Duncan's yammering about her not being real? About him being mad?

Then there was the charge that he wasn't being truthful because she belonged to someone else—or worse, really *was* a MacDonald and Alex was trying to hide it with a jest about a myth.

'*Prove it,*' his brother had commanded.

Alex growled and rushed forward, pushing Duncan back when their weapons *clanged.*

"Ah, there's my brother." His twin backed up and circled again, beckoning with a flat palm. "Come a' me."

"Dinnae stick out what ye dinnae wanna risk losin'."

Duncan smirked. "Dinnae make threats ye dinnae see ta tha end."

Alex narrowed his eyes and made an unsuccessful strike—his brother was able to slide out of the way. He cursed again and tossed his sword from one hand to the other, then re-gripped it and glared before trailing closer again.

"What has ye in such a foul mood, brother?"

Of course, he has no idea I'm still upset with him.

Alex didn't answer, just kept loping around his brother. Staring. Trying to intimidate him.

They were equal in strength and physical breadth—they were identical twins after all. In addition to that, they'd been trained with the sword from the same age and were well matched in skill.

Who won their bouts tended to switch off, but Duncan was always more bothered by that than Alex ever had been.

Their clansmen often wagered over who would win and how long the streak would last. Of course, his brother would never bet against himself. Betting against his laird, on the other hand, made for a worthy brag when Duncan managed to beat Alex.

"Methinks ye need a good tumble."

Alex tried not to pause his movements or show a reaction to the jibe. It probably wasn't untrue. He *was* wound pretty tight. His erotic princess dreams hadn't decreased. If anything, they were more intense, more frequent since the last time he'd seen her. Touched her. Kissed her and held her hand as they'd walked and conversed on the beaches of Skye.

The nightly torments still seemed too real to be mere dreams. Perhaps he should discuss them with her next time he saw her.

She was magically inclined after all, maybe they were actually communicating somehow?

Aye, I need a tumble. With Alana.

No other lover would do.

The longer Alex remained silent, the more Duncan looked torn between amusement and concern.

He preferred being laughed at; had no desire for another *I-don't-believe-your-lass-is-a-Fae-princess* conversation with his brother.

"Somethin's botherin' ye." His twin waited; lowered his claymore.

You didn't believe me.

"Nay, nothin's botherin' me."

"Alex, whate'er 'tis, can be remedied, dinnae?"

Apologize to me.

"Raise yer sword! Are ye ou' here ta fight, or ta natter like a lass?" Alex growled back.

Duncan smirked, but something passed in his eyes that said *he* was bothered Alex wasn't opening his mouth to confess all.

"Duncan, I dinnae wan—"

His brother invaded his space and grabbed his forearm. "'Tis the lass?"

Despite his low volume, Alex frowned and let his eyes dart about the bailey to see if anyone was looking their way. He had no desire for explanations if his brother had been overheard.

All the men were sparring, and no one seemed to be observing the laird and his twin quipping more than knocking swords.

"Jesu, *'tis* tha lass!" his brother exclaimed when he'd failed to answer.

"Keep yer voice down," he barked.

"What fer?"

Alex sighed and sheathed his sword. "I've duties ta attend ta."

Duncan stopped him from turning to go with a stronger grip. "I'm concerned abou' ye, brother."

"Dinnae ye mean, *'my laird'*?"

"Ye can bluster all ye want, but dinnae work. Tell me."

"Tell ye *what*?" Alex's inquiry had been too loud. A shout that made him want to wince.

I tried to tell you, and you didn't believe me. He wouldn't say the words.

His brother would demand a real confrontation, and he didn't have energy or desire for it.

"Whate'er 'tis, a' course." Duncan was reasonable. Even. Calm.

He wanted to yell again and shove him away.

Usually, Duncan was the one with irrational bursts of temper, not *him*. The idea was sobering, and Alex straightened his shoulders and told himself to breathe.

"My laird?" The question was wrapped in amusement and flared his anger all over again.

"Sod off, Duncan MacLeod."

He broke the hold his twin had on his arm and whirled away, ignoring his twin's wide eyes and arched eyebrows, along with the way he'd reared back as if Alex had punched him.

chapter twelve

alana's hand shook as she made a fist and hollered at herself to knock on Seamus' guest suite door. It'd taken all evening, the next morning, and into the afternoon until she'd worked up the nerve to do what had to be done.

Get it over with.

It mattered not that she never intended to follow through with the arrangement. She didn't want to agree, let alone sign something binding.

When she closed her eyes, she only saw—and yearned for—a certain pair of sapphire ones, and guilt swirled in her gut. Every once in a while, it jumped up and took a bite of her heart, leaving her shaking. Fighting sobs.

It'd taken hours to gather her wits even after she'd resigned herself that her cousin was right.

At least Xander hadn't lectured her anymore. He seemed to recognize how hard this was for her. Besides, he too despised Seamus.

Relenting to the stupid prince's demands—even if they really were for naught, and she *had* to keep reminding herself of that—was like losing a battle that would never sit right in her mouth, let alone her cousin's.

Xander had promised to help her figure out a

plan—for *everything.*

Too bad her whole body still ached for Alex, and Alana felt like she was betraying him by agreeing to sign a parchment that would declare Seamus as her betrothed.

Nausea roiled her gut. Bile rose and what little food she'd forced down at midday threatened to spill onto the corridor floor.

She jumped when her cousin put a hand on her trembling arm. Alana swallowed, but the distraction had helped, and she clamped down her urge to retch.

"I'll come with you. I can chaperone. Decorum will keep him from asking me to leave." Xander's voice was right above her ear.

"Nay. I shall handle this."

He offered a curt nod, but squeezed her wrist when she went to move away from him. "You scream if he so much as—"

"I will, but he won't do that today. He's getting what he wants." She gulped.

"I'll be right here, waiting for you." Xander planted his feet, flexed his wings and locked his jaw. He inclined his head once more and crossed his arms over his green armor. The hilt of his sword brushed one palm.

At least he was ready for anything and *would* save her—if she needed it.

Alana nodded. Couldn't find her voice. With one last fortifying look at her cousin, she swept into the room without waiting for Seamus to call out after she'd knocked.

The wretched Irish Prince was lounging on the

oversized bed instead of in the sitting room, and wearing nothing but a diaphanous green robe covering his arms and shoulders, but the rest of the material was lying at his sides on the plush mattress.

Completely open.

His green eyes went from surprised to smug much too fast for her liking, and he made no efforts to cover himself. If anything, when Alana looked at him, the bastard preened.

Her urge to vomit was reborn, despite the vast expanse of defined muscles on display. His body *should* be pleasing to the eye, but this was Seamus, so it was *not*.

She avoided looking at his manhood, which she'd had the unfortunate opportunity to notice was a hard length, standing at attention. He was aroused.

Had she caught him about to touch himself? Or was he awaiting a lover?

Alana shuddered, but that seemed to please him more.

"Do you like what you see, dear princess?"

She rolled her eyes and didn't honor him with a response, but his answering smirk said that was what he'd expected—or desired.

Seamus smiled, flashing his dimples and sat up. His hard pectoral muscles flexed, and his abdominals rippled with his movements. "I was lying here, thinking of you, my sweet princess. See what you do to me?" He had the nerve to gesture to his erection.

Was he about to stroke himself?

Alana scoffed. Wanted to demand he cover up, but

that would let him know his nudity bothered her, and *that* was the last thing she wanted to admit.

Like most Fae, she usually had no qualms about naked flesh—and *he* needed to assume she was comfortable with all that bare skin; immune to his good looks would be even better.

She strode forward but kept her body out of grabbing distance. Alana didn't believe he'd try to snatch her to him, but the memory of being pinned by his big form was at the back of her mind.

His anti-magic medallion was still in place at his neck, gleaming red in the light as if the deep stone dared her to try a spell.

"Not talkative today, are we?" The prince cocked his head to one side and shifted the dark waves of his hair.

His looks were wasted on him, but the fact she could *see* his beauty just irritated her. Alana wanted to picture him as shriveled and ugly as he really was.

She took a breath. There was no reason to dance around the Acana tree. "You get your way, Seamus."

For now, until I can figure a way out.

Alana resisted the urge to scowl. "I'll sign a contract, but 'tis *betrothal* only. 'Twill be worded that it can be ended at *my* behest." She narrowed her eyes at the triumph on his visage.

He could be so handsome if he wasn't such an awful person.

"Nay."

"Nay?" Her heart thumped. She planted her hands on her hips and straightened her shoulders.

"When you sign a parchment for *me*, 'twill be seen through. We *will* wed."

Alana sucked down a calming breath when she'd rather scream at him, but Seamus would enjoy that too much. "Don't forget, we have our fathers to contend with. As you know, most royal betrothals are at least two years long. *You* may decide on a great many things, but not that. Both *kings* will have a say. And I will plead with my father that I have one, too. That *I* can say when." It would do little good with King Fillan, but Seamus didn't need to know that.

The prince wrung his hands, and his indignation rolled off her empathic magic.

It was the first time she'd managed to make him angry, and even though it was a result of mostly the truth, Alana held back a smile. "Something wrong?" she asked in her brightest tone.

Her father would want to negotiate with the Irish King, and Fae lived a long time. Especially in nobility, let alone royalty, long betrothals were common, some longer than the two years she'd cited. Her dowry wasn't set in stone. The king would want to release as little wealth as possible.

King Fillan had been betrothed for five years before he'd married her mother—and although noble, the queen had not been born a princess. He was a greedy man and would take all he could wheedle from Ireland for Alana's hand.

Even if she'd *wanted* to marry Seamus, the terms of *when* weren't really up to her. No doubt her father would exercise *all* his rights and level all the power he could.

There was no love in these types of arrangements. Royal marriages were for alliances, and King Fillan had had his eye on an agreement with Ireland since she was wee.

He'd be delighted that she appeared to *want* to marry Seamus. Perhaps so much so that he *would* let her make decisions regarding the wedding—not that she'd tell the idiot prince that.

"*I* am in control." Seamus thumbed his bare chest.

Ah, she'd hit a nerve by pointing out what King Ciaran must hold over his head. He was a prince, *not* the king. He'd always been arrogant, but so was his father. They probably clashed about such things. That was possibly why he had no apparent desire to go home — trying to scheme for Alana aside, of course.

She wanted to grin but managed not to. She could handle his petty emotions but needed to watch herself. He could still go to her father about Alex, even if he did get his way.

"*Here* 'tis how it 'twill work," Seamus mocked her, but she told herself not to react.

"And how is that?" Alana tried to make it sound like a quip, as if she was unconcerned, but her voice had too much of a hard edge, and his expression told her they'd both recognized it.

"You *will* sign the contract, and I will *not* be designated as only your royal consort, but as *king* along your side...when the time comes, of course. Provided...our fathers agree."

She narrowed her eyes. Instinct flared. There was

more left unsaid. Mayhap he *did* have evil plans for her father.

Could she voice concerns to King Fillan to get out of this mess?

Alana would have to have proof. She'd have to watch him—or have him watched. "Of course," she made herself echo.

"I shall indicate the same for you, concerning Ireland. My father will not disagree."

Don't offer me any favors.

She cleared her throat. "I would expect nothing less."

Seamus nodded, as if the little concession was out of his sense of generosity. Even if he didn't truly have the power to make such a designation, despite his confidence King Ciaran would agree.

The bastard.

"We shall marry, and you shall provide me with heirs."

Alana trembled and had to talk her shoulders into remaining upright. She stood taller.

"I won't make you get rid of your human."

"What?" she blurted. She fought the urge to slap her hand over her mouth. So far, she'd denied every reference to Alex. She cursed her inability to hide her shock.

"I don't expect you to remain faithful to me, so long as you regard me with the same…understanding…and employ discretion."

She blinked.

What a scoundrel.

Seamus was the worst. Taking a lover, or lovers, before being wed was one thing, but marriage in the Fae Realm expected monogamy. All contracts spoke to as much, as well as all outside dalliances being outlawed, and were punishable by the king if the injured spouse presented evidence.

Society, nobles and peasants alike, lived by these rules. On the occasion a third—or more—bed partner was desired, all parties had to agree, and it was generally a joint effort, not one person taking a new lover. They even had designated mediators for such instances, if the married couple desired.

Alana would die before she'd give herself to him. If she hadn't been sure about that before, she was now. "Oh, well then how could you ensure your *heirs* are *yours* indeed, my dear prince?"

He chuckled, and she wanted to vomit at the charming twinkle in his emerald eyes. "I do not worry on it much. My rival isn't worthy."

He means Alex.

So he didn't even care if she was innocent. Probably assumed she and Alex were already lovers. Somehow that made her detest him even more. Alana opened her mouth to speak, but Seamus beat her to it.

"If you disappear for more than a day, I shall tell my father-by-marriage that I'm being cuckolded by a human. I will, of course, be properly appalled and wounded that you would seek a dalliance after our betrothal or marriage. With a *human*, no less. What an embarrassment for the Scottish Court and King Fillan."

"Seamus—"

He held his hand up. "I'm not finished, my sweet princess."

Alana glared.

"*I* will lead the army not only to wipe out your beloved, but his *whole* clan. The walls of Dunvegan would be easily breeched by Fae weapons even in a realm that is not ours and where magic is diminished." He sat taller, and his green eyes were like hard emeralds.

Ice crawled down her spine at his even, serious tone. She swallowed and her insides wobbled.

"You know your father as I do. His bloodthirstiness has no end, especially where *humans* are concerned."

"Seamus—"

"Every. Last. Wee. MacLeod."

No matter how Alana told herself not to show a reaction, it didn't stop how she jolted on her feet by his bed. Her frigid flush went across her chest, down her limbs to her toes and she gritted her teeth so they wouldn't chatter. So, she didn't sway or fall over.

She wanted to reach out and steady herself, but the bedpost was the closest solid object, and she wouldn't touch it or show that kind of weakness in front of the bastard. Or risk getting closer to him.

Alana wanted to claw his eyes out when a slow evil smile spread on his lips.

"You and I have come to an understanding." The prince's voice was smug, and he reclined into his many pillows. His body reeked of arrogance and triumph. Not to mention, he was still very exposed.

"I-I-I..." She cleared her throat and tried again,

clenching her fists at her sides so she didn't attack him. "Haven't said anything." Her words still came out cracked and Alana fought a wince.

"You don't have to. It's not open for negotiation." Seamus beamed, then leaned forward, as if to impart a secret. "Oh, and it extends to however long it takes until you call me husband, and even *after* that. I don't care if you keep your human, but *I* shall have you as well. As *mine*. *My* wife, *my* queen. Something the laird will never have."

Do not cry, beg, or kill him. Act indifferent.

Alana cleared her throat again, tilted her chin up and reached for an expression of haughtiness. "Very well. I shall tell my father I wish to marry you." She had to swallow so she wouldn't vomit. "Just ensure that *you* employ the same discretion you expect of me when it comes to trysts." She thumbed her chest. "If not, be assured *I* can also act more than appropriately *injured* that you would *dare* be unfaithful to me. As you so aptly pointed out, my father has a tendency toward bloodthirstiness, and being a Crown Prince won't save you if you harm Da's wee lassie's tender feelings."

That was laughable, really. Her father wouldn't give a dungeon rat's shite if her feelings were hurt. He would, however, kill any man who dared violate a contract with him, and Prince Seamus *would* be no exception.

She took a breath and looked away from the scoundrel, then turned on her heel and left the room without a word, scowling at his parting laughter.

Somehow, even though her reasons were valid—to

protect Alex—and she had no intention of actually marrying Seamus, Alana had never sunk lower in her life. Her heart resided in her gut with no hope of returning to where it belonged. Her whole body *hurt*.

After opening the door, she fell into Xander, unable to hold back her sobs.

Thank the Goddess her cousin caught her up and carried her off before anyone could spot them.

chapter thirteen

"'Tis done." The pleased smile on her father's face only made her feel more morose.

Actually, make that hopeless. Desperate.

Alana wanted Alex.

Now.

The swirling guilt plunged her to feeling ten times worse and made it rather difficult to plaster a smile on her face for her audience.

Irish and Scottish scribes, royal bodyguards, Seamus, her father and his, were all in the lavish throne room King Fillan used when he was trying to be most impressive.

King Ciaran had *blinked* back to Scotland for the momentous occasion.

It'd been two days since she'd agreed to this subterfuge, and Alana had regretted it every *second* since leaving the stupid prince's guest suite.

"Our children will marry!" the Irish King exclaimed. He patted her father on the back and the two royals exchanged overly satisfied smiles.

Like they'd each won a huge bene over each other.

They hadn't started the marriage contract negotiations just yet—this one was merely betrothal, declaring they would enter talks of a permanent bond and alliance—so they *both* probably had grand plans to pull the wool over their opponent.

Her father's violet eyes—a match for her own—positively sparkled. His hair, also the same pale blonde of her own, was gathered in a neat tail bound with the finest leather at the back of his neck and reached down to his waist. Of course, he looked younger than his one hundred odd years, and he was a big man like her cousin.

In years past, he'd been known as a fierce warrior king, but the less he battled, the more his midsection had filled out. That didn't seem to dim female attention. Most women thought him handsome, and he'd had no shortage of lovers since her mother's passing, despite the weight gain. His personality still boomed, but he was too cruel. Always had been. Ruthlessness was ingrained.

Seamus caught her eye and winked as his father shook his hand.

She told herself she could *not* glare at either of them.

Like her, the Irish Prince resembled his sire, including the dimples, except King Ciaran had blue eyes instead of green. He was tall, but didn't have as much muscle as his son, so he was slim. He was older than King Fillan by many years. His ebony locks had long since been mixed with gray. He'd been a young King of Ireland when Alana's grandsire still reigned over the Scottish Fae Court, before her birth.

Also like her, Seamus' mother had long since passed, but at least the Irish queen hadn't had to grieve over what a useless rake her son was.

Xander's gaze was serene as her eyes rested on him, but there was no hiding the slight quake in his iridescent wings or the white knuckled grip he had from time to time on his sword's hilt.

Alana had already seen him release the hold and square his shoulders a few times—as if he'd caught himself doing so and thought it better to seem indifferent.

After all, his status really didn't give him the right to an opinion as to whom she'd marry. Nor would he want anyone to know he was less than pleased about the forced agreement.

For now.

She reinforced her mind-block spell. None of her present company—save the stupid prince—could discover her true feelings on the matter at hand, either.

"Daughter, I am so proud of you."

She sucked back a cringe and ordered herself to meet King Fillan's eyes.

Proud of me?

That was certainly a first.

"Thank you, your Majesty," she whispered and curtseyed, as decorum dictated. Alana tried not to startle when her father cupped her cheeks and urged her to look up at him again. She couldn't remember the last time he'd touched her. The hold didn't hurt, but she wanted to squirm, nonetheless.

His smile was genuine—and rare, which just turned her stomach even more. "Thank *you*, and your fine prince for initiating an alliance I am most pleased will *finally* be in place."

She could feel Seamus beam at her side and wanted to retch on his fancy shoes.

"I am pleased my dear sweet princess will have me." The scoundrel bowed, his voice and manner humble.

Bile burned her throat and Alana fought through her urges.

King Ciaran said something that made the men laugh and the scribes grin, but their deep voices faded in and out as the opulent room spun.

Glinting jewels became streaks of light in her line of sight. She wobbled on her feet to a chorus of "Your Highness!" but her vision darkened, and blackness crept in on her.

Alana lost control of her body and cringed, expecting the hard marble to greet her behind.

Instead, she was enclosed against a wall of muscled chest by two solid arms. "It appears my lovely betrothed is overwrought from all the excitement."

She groaned. Didn't want to open her eyes.

Would've have preferred bruises from the floor to his embrace.

She was in Seamus' arms. Insects crawled down her spine and gooseflesh pebbled her arms. She needed to hold it together for show.

Where's Xander?

"My dear, are you well?" Her father's voice held concern—and didn't *that* make her want to look at him to see if it was real.

She put her hand to her forehead, shuttering her

gaze. "Perhaps my prince is correct, and I should lie down."

"Shall I call a healer?" one of the scribes asked.

"Nay, nay. I shall be fine. Xander."

Her cousin was stopped by a headshake and wide smile from her stupid *betrothed*. "Nay, Sir Xander, I've got her. I shall see her to her suite."

Please don't.

"You can put me down. I can go on my own."

Seamus laughed and she wanted to glare.

Xander gave a helpless half-shrug when their gazes brushed, and his wings jerked, betraying his irritation despite his expression.

Damn Seamus!

"Don't be silly, *my love*, I've got you."

Alana *really* wanted to vomit now. Would he put her down if she covered his chest in half-digested breakfast? "Very well," she gritted out. It sounded as weak as she felt, and not because she'd worked herself up so much, she'd almost passed out.

She didn't want to accept the guilt and negativity that'd caused her lightheadedness, but being in Seamus' arms made it worse, even if it wasn't *her* choice. Nausea was a live, writhing thing in her gut.

"Do feel better, daughter, you must attend your betrothal feast."

Of course, because King Fillan wouldn't be able to stand the gossip if she didn't.

Appearances, appearances.

"Of course, your Majesty. I'm sure I'll be better after a lie-down."

Other male voices murmured well-wishes, but they all faded as the idiot prince carried her from the vast room, her cousin on his heels.

She waited until late into the night.

Alana needed to ensure the celebration from her betrothal feast had died down, and that all guests had gone home or were tucked into their borrowed beds.

Not to mention her father, her betrothed, *and* her cousin.

Luckily for her, the king and Seamus had gotten quite inebriated in the great hall. Even if her father hadn't retired alone, he would have hours of sleeping off the drink in his future.

This time, she was leaving Xander behind, so she hoped he was curled up with Gwynna and not the least bit concerned with her.

"Speaking of beds—" she whispered to her empty room.

Alana said a spellword and her blankets lifted, as if covering someone, and the shape of a female form lying on its side appeared, complete with a blonde head on her pillows.

It was just an illusion; if someone went to touch it, their hand would go straight through, but it *did* resemble her perfectly.

She smiled at her handiwork and conjured her purple mantle. The silky material settled over her body of its own accord, and she tugged the hood up, tucking her hair inside before knotting the ties at her neck to keep it in place.

Alana needed to be quick and quiet and would use her Irish Fae Warrior glamour-spelled figure when she got to the Field of Light.

She could only pray to the Goddess the scheme would work without Xander. She already had a sealed scroll in her possession, and she tucked it into the pocket of her trews.

The journey through the tunnels was stealthy and silent, and this time she relished the earthy scent surrounding her because it meant she was close to freedom. Normally the musky odor bothered her senses, but not tonight. She wanted to cling to it with both hands.

When Alana spilled out into the forest, she ran away from her home until her chest was tight. Couldn't risk *blinking* so close to the palace.

Being the warrior king he was, her father was paranoid, and had mages on duty at all hours, in addition to his multitude of men-at-arms. Their orders were to sense magical threats. Her teleporting power wasn't nefarious, but it would be detectable.

Forested areas thickened and thinned as she ran through a few clearings, then more wooded areas, but she had to stop when her lungs burned.

There were commoner settlements high above in some of the trees, so she needed to push past them as well. The older and larger the tree, the more likelihood it contained a home, and there were a cluster of villages in the vast groves that surrounded the palace, complete with their brightly painted round doors and wide porches.

Alana couldn't afford for *anyone* to see her.

She leaned heavily on a big, blue-barked Sùbh tree, panting to catch her breath. She looked around, but this copse was thick, and the canopy blocked the light of the moon, so it was too dark for her eyes to penetrate much.

Insects called to each other, but there was no movement she could sense. Even the woodland creatures were in their beds.

She could smell the sweet round fruit hanging overhead and her stomach rumbled. She hadn't managed more than a bite at the betrothal feast. She'd been in knots, and if she *had* eaten, she would've thrown up all over the great hall.

Even though Alana had had witnesses to her almost-fainting spell that morning, her father would never have accepted such embarrassment, or believed she was actually ill.

When Xander had escorted her to the great hall for the feast, after her sobbing fit—she hadn't gotten a wink of rest when she'd tried to nap—King Fillan had done little else than nod and compliment her lavish gown.

He hadn't asked if she was well, but King Ciaran had. As far as her father was concerned, she'd done one good deed, and he had no more need of her—until she raised his ire again. Undoubtedly, she would, she always did.

Alana had donned the same dress she'd worn to the Beltane celebration, at the risk of all the courtiers gossiping about its reappearance after so recently being worn.

They *would* talk. She didn't care.

It'd been too much of a challenge not to look as miserable as she felt as she'd endured *hours* of unwanted conversation and congratulations, not to mention dancing with all the lords. Concentrating on looking passably happy had made her not the least bit worried about nattering ladies.

She'd had to survive a spin on the floor with her *betrothed,* too. Worse, it'd been a slow love ballad that'd had her stomach again poised to empty. Seamus had held her close and put his hands in less than polite places. Alana shuddered, trying to banish the memory.

One glance up told her the heavy pink orbs were ripe. The artificial weather was warm and lush enough to encourage the trees to a year-round harvest. Perhaps that was the *one* good thing about it.

She muttered a summoning spellword and heard a *snap*, then put her palm out. Firm but juicy flesh smacked into Alana's hand, and she dug in without peeling it.

"Hmmm." Tangy flavor exploded on her tongue, and she reminded herself to chew before taking two more huge, unprincesslike bites.

She devoured the whole thing, seeds, and all, and then another, even bigger than the first. She was tempted to eat more but didn't have time. Needed to get moving, couldn't risk being gone all night, and she only had three—four at most—hours until the sun was up.

Alana would need to be back in her own bed before the palace awoke. Rannick had taken to greeting her every morning, earlier than Xander brought her breakfast.

Although now that she was betrothed, her father had removed all restrictions, so she *could* leave her suite and break her fast in the great hall if she so chose. She wouldn't want to see Seamus, so her rooms remained the better option. Stay hidden and *away* from him.

She ran into a clearing and glanced around. The whirling colors of the magic stones that made up the palace gave off a glow in the night brighter than the moonlight but were barely visible on the horizon. Alana was far enough away to *blink*.

She took a deep breath, squared her shoulders, and concentrated on her destination. She pictured the dais holding the Faery Stones and closed her eyes. Then she *blinked* to the woods at the edge of the Field of Light.

Alana peeked through the trees, spotting Fae Warriors. There were two on the dais, and two patrolling a path through the blue and orange grasses of the Field of Light. They walked side-by-side, as a pair. She could hear the low hum of their deep voices, but she couldn't make out what they were saying from her current distance. She didn't see the remaining two guards who should be on duty right now.

Why're they missing?

She hid only feet from where the treeline ended and the long orange and blue grasses of the Field truly began, tucked behind a maroon-barked Acana tree, not far from the area she'd caused the explosion the first time she'd snuck to see Alex without Xander. The charred underbrush remained, marking the spot black;

it hadn't been enough time to grow over.

I can't tarry here forever.

Alana tilted her head back on the tree and patted the bark on either side of her, reveling in the rough feel under her palms. Her heart jumped at the thought of seeing Alex again.

Holding his hand, hugging him. Definitely kissing him.

She had no illusions about this trip. If—*when*—she found him, she'd do all of that, and more.

Alana would give herself to him if he'd have her.

Guilt churned her stomach, souring the two Sùbh fruits she'd eaten, despite how good they'd tasted. She needed to tell Alex about Seamus. It *should* be the first thing out of her mouth.

Not just because of what she'd had to agree to, but because it was *him*—and his clan—that could be the victim of Fae revenge.

Death sentences for all the MacLeods.

Because of me.

She crushed her eyes shut and inhaled. Perhaps she should go back. Return to her suite and get back in bed.

If she actually stayed away from him, Seamus couldn't hurt Alex and the MacLeods. The Irish wretch wouldn't have a reason to, right?

He wouldn't have anything to hold over her head. Then she could break the betrothal. Her father would be angry—but Alana wasn't really going to marry Seamus, so it was only a matter of time until she tapped into King Fillan's rage regarding the Irish prince anyway.

She'd have to make it look like Seamus' fault; that

was the only way she'd avoid the king's wrath. With the prince's appetite for the lasses, combined with his *requirement* to be faithful to her, it was a real possibility Alana could get out of the betrothal validly, and get back at the bastard at the same time. Maybe she'd even be able to muster some tears for her father's benefit.

It was the only way to save herself *and* Alex.

She'd have to run the plan by Xander in the morning.

With Seamus' threat—no, vow—hanging over her, she really *should* go back to the palace.

Was she being foolish, or worse, selfish in her desire to see the human laird?

Nay, he's my fate.

Was he really?

Was there a way to find out for sure, or should she blindly follow her heart?

Alana frowned as the negative emotions jumped up and bit into her again. She panted through a wave of nausea and let the Acana tree take her weight as she reclined into it completely.

The urge to retch was becoming too common, haunting her. She'd never had a weak constitution.

Rough bark bit at her shoulders through her mantle, but it grounded her in a way, and she clutched at the tree as she wobbled against it.

Stay here, go home, or go to the Human Realm?

What was the *right* thing to do?

She pushed off the tree and squared her shoulders. "Nay. I need to see Alex."

Everything would melt away if Alana saw her laird.

chapter fourteen

*a*lex, come to me. I need to see you.

The words were a whisper in his mind, and he jarred awake. It took him moments that felt like hours to orient, despite familiar surroundings. He was in his bed, in the laird's chambers. In his home, Dunvegan.

Alex sat up, throwing the plaid and furs off his sweaty body. He put a palm to his bare chest. His heart was hammering. He was hot, skin clammy.

Why was he overheated?

His bollocks ached, answering him. His shaft was hard and heavy, pulsing as if beckoning his hand.

The dream.

He'd been with Alana again.

Exhaling slowly, he closed his eyes as visions of carnal things floated across his mind. His princess, stripping. Kissing him. Touching him. Mounting him. Taking him into her lithe body. They moved together, hands all over each other. Lips, too.

They hadn't been in his rooms. Or his bed.

Where *had* they been?

Everything except *her* was fuzzy.

Alex, if you can hear me, come to me.

He jerked and his bedframe creaked.

Her voice was loud and clear, as sure as if she'd

whispered in his ear.

"Alana?"

Please. I need you.

Alex slipped from his bed and looked around the room. The fire had been banked hours before, but embers winked from the hearth. He shivered, but he wasn't cold.

He grabbed a leine from his trunk and tugged it over his head, then wrapped his plaid around his waist and belted it on.

"Alana?" he repeated. He swept the room, looking everywhere, even under the desk and behind the thick drapes.

I need to be with you, Alex.

She wasn't in his suite.

Panic inched up from his gut. Not that he'd finally lost his mind—as it probably should—but that she'd be gone before he could find her. That he'd dreamt her up only to miss seeing her.

Need burned a path from his pelvis to his throat and Alex was torn between the very opposite feelings. But it helped him inhale and calm.

He glanced at the closed window. The angle of the moonlight leaking inside told him it was late—the middle of the night.

"The beach!"

She's down there.

Waiting for him on the ridge where he'd first kissed her.

At the current hour, he was mad indeed to consider going out alone, and on foot—because he'd not want to alert anyone to his jaunt—but he *had* to go.

Alex stomped into his boots and grabbed his sword, dashing to the double doors of the laird's chamber—where he made himself stop and *breathe*.

He needed to be stealthy and alert no one. His parents were right next door. The Lady of the Castle's rooms adjoined his, and even shared a door on the inside.

Iain had moved into the room, even though it was smaller than the laird's, when his wife had first taken ill. Alex had tried to refuse to take his father's former private space and been unsuccessful, then had moved out of his childhood quarters soon after.

He stared at the thick wooden panel from his spot near the main entrance to his suite.

All quiet.

No sound was coming from the room where his parents slept.

Alex wasn't inept at sneaking out of the castle—had done so many a time to meet a lass in the stables for a tryst in years past, but that was all *before* he'd become the laird.

He'd not want questions from his family—or his clansmen if he encountered anyone. His father was a notoriously light sleeper, and with the man so close, he had to be extra careful with every footfall.

Barely breathing, he made it out of the room, down the stairs, through the great hall, and waited until the night guards were on the other side of the embattlement before sneaking through the gates.

Alex kept his back plastered to Dunvegan as much

as possible—the men-at-arms were high above, and it was their duty to detect threats. Their roving patrols of the wall made the whole area easily visible—even at night.

Although their laird stealing off into the darkness wasn't a danger to those within the castle walls, it *was* certainly another root of those questions he wanted to avoid.

He couldn't straighten to his full height until he was well away from the stronghold. He thanked God for the long untamed grasses and small hills between the castle and the beach.

When Alex could smell the waters, he ran. The ridge came into sight in the light of the moon, and his heart stuttered.

She was indeed up there, looking toward him as if she'd known he'd come to her. "Alex!"

He skidded to a halt, bent at the waist with his hands planted on his knees. He wasn't out of breath, exactly, but his heart cantered so hard he was dizzy.

Alana scampered down the incline as if she did so every day, and her body collided with his. She threw her arms around him, hugging him so tight it took his breath all over again.

Alex barely had time to catch her up and keep them from both tumbling to the rocky ground. "Alana. Lass." He inhaled her aroma, familiar and overwhelming at the same time. Floral and wild, mixed with the scent of the moving waters of the sea. "Alana, Alana," he chanted.

She pulled back and pinned him with that violet stare. "Alex." His princess exhaled audibly. "Alex. I knew you'd hear me. I knew you'd come."

"Always, lass. Always."

They strolled in a companionable silence by the moonlight, but like the first moment he'd spotted her and she'd yelled his name, Alex still wasn't convinced he wasn't dreaming.

The waves were calm tonight as they slapped the beach, the repetitive sound washing even more peace over him as they walked.

Had she really been calling him?

Why couldn't he find his voice to ask?

Alana had said something about him *hearing* her, and he could find out what that meant, if he could stop staring and *ask*.

Alex grabbed her hand and entwined their fingers because he couldn't *not* touch her. The familiar spark shot up his arm and he swallowed.

She flashed a grin that had his heart pattering again.

"I really did fear I'd ne'er see ye again," he whispered.

Sadness darted across her ethereal face, visible despite the darkness of the night. The moon was high and full. "I...I really shouldn't have come back. It's too dangerous." Alana paused as if she'd say more but didn't.

Like the last time she'd come to him with her cousin. When they'd languished in each other's company for hours that felt like days.

What was she *not* telling him?

His gut told him pushing her would get him

nowhere. He brought their joined hands to his mouth and kissed her knuckles. "I'm glad ye did."

Alana nodded. "I know I said goodbye. That I could make no promises to you. It's still true. But…I…had to come back."

Rightness settled over Alex like he hadn't felt since he'd met her, then lost her. All three times. "This feels like 'tis supposed ta happen."

She made a noise that sounded like a half whimper, half laugh.

"Alana?" he whispered. When he looked down into her eyes, they were misty.

His princess had her free hand over her mouth, as if holding back a sob.

"Is somethin' wrong?"

Alana shook her head but didn't speak.

"If ye dinnae tell me, lass, I—"

She tugged her hand free and launched herself at him.

He caught her up and chuckled, but the sound was lost with the frantic press of her lips against his. Alex didn't hesitate to meet her seeking tongue, pushing his way into her mouth as she did the same to him. He let her deepen their kiss as they clutched at each other.

She wrapped her arms around his neck, and he hiked her higher, until Alana wrapped her legs around his waist.

He couldn't get close enough. Couldn't hold her tight enough. 'Twas a foolish *foolish* thought, but he didn't want to let her go. *Ever.*

"I need to be with you," Alana breathed into their

kiss.

"Lass—" All sorts of words formed in his brain, but there was a disconnect with his mouth. He didn't want to waste time or statements. Wanted to agree with her wholeheartedly. However, they were on the beach, out in the open at night—it was cold, too—and he couldn't exactly take her back to Dunvegan.

His brother may know of her, but Alex wanted to avoid questions from the rest of his family and clan. Come morning, he'd certainly have to explain the lass in his bed, let alone a beauty such as her.

He could sneak her in through the kitchens, but there would be no solution for hiding her when the sun rose. His parents so close to his rooms were another problem entirely.

"I know a place we can go," Alana said, as if she'd read his mind. She loosened her hold around him, and he set her to her feet.

She slid down his body, and the soft push of her breasts into his chest made Alex's insides quiver and his cock jump. His princess took his hand, and led him down the beach, away from the ridge where they'd first kissed.

He didn't argue. Didn't care where she took him; his sole concern was *Alana.*

Kissing her. Touching her. Taking her.

Their gazes met. Emotions that didn't make sense stared back at him. A part of him wanted to question what he was seeing, and the other part reveled in it. Alex's pulse skipped, his heart bounded off his ribs, and it was difficult to look away from her, especially when she put her hand on his arm.

She wasn't close enough.

He needed more.

"Alex?" she whispered.

"I dinnae ken how ta explain any of this. But I *need* ye, lass. Like I need my next breath."

Alana swallowed and he wanted to kiss her throat. "I know, Alex. I feel the same way."

"Take me where ye will."

She laughed, and the charming grin curving her kiss-swollen lips was almost his undoing. "I was hoping you'd take *me*, actually."

His half-mast erection tingled, the friction against the wool of his plaid worsening, torturing with every step they took. "Aye, I've tha' in mind." The thickness of his voice made the jest fall off a bit, but Alex didn't care, because the sultry look in her eyes only made him harder, until his whole body was begging. "Just hope dinnae be far."

"Nay, 'tis not."

The refined edge to her words was distracting since it was so different than his own—reminding him of her station—but it didn't dim Alex's desire.

Alana pulled him around a large boulder, until they stood in front of the tall wall of an incline, with what appeared to be a crack dividing the cliff-face. It widened as it came down into the rocky sandy ground. "We're here," she announced.

"Where is *here*?"

"Remember I told you about the Faery Stones? The portal to come to this realm is born of their magic.

They're housed inside. It doesn't look like much, but 'tis a cave within. We'll be safe. No one will bother us." She moved toward the split in the cliff.

Although the entrance was cave-like, it wasn't very wide. Even her slender form blocked his view, and Alex would have to duck, possibly turn sideways to fit through it.

He let her go into the fissure first, but his protective instincts protested. She'd said it was safe, but he couldn't *know* that until he could see inside.

Indeed, the cavity opened up into a cavern, and once they were under the cover of it he was able to straighten. The ceiling was low, though. If he reached up, he could touch it. Alex relaxed a tad when nothing jumped out at them.

A glow in his periphery—along with a low hum—took his attention, and his gaze shot to the left. Five crystals sat atop five natural-looking rock-like formations, in a semi-circle shape that looked too perfect to be an accident. They were lit from the inside, an almost throbbing radiance, and in turn, illuminated the cave.

Alex gasped.

Alana took his hand and led him closer. "Behold, the Faery Stones."

His mouth was dry for reasons other than his urgent libido. "Magic," he breathed.

She nodded. "They bring me to you."

"Then I'm fond of 'em."

Her smile was brilliant, and she threaded her arms around his middle, squeezing him tight.

Alex returned her embrace, but let his eyes scan the cave. It wasn't overly large, but it wasn't tiny, and the natural floor was littered with starkly white sand, much different than what was outside on the pebble-ridden beach.

The area was well lit by the Faery Stones. More light than the moon had offered them.

"Magic," he repeated. "To see it…'tis different than hearin' of it."

"I know, and I'll tell you anything you want to know…later."

"Later?"

"Aye. I cannot stay long, and right now, I want you, Alex MacLeod."

He gulped.

Again, her words were forward, but he wanted her, too. It mattered not that they didn't really know each other. That they'd seen each other three times, besides tonight.

What was between them felt natural. *Right.*

Alex didn't like the idea of her leaving again, but he'd deal with that…*later,* as she'd said.

Now, he was going to *take* her.

He cupped her face and claimed her mouth.

Alana was right with him, kissing him back deeply and enthusiastically. She twined her tongue with his as she pushed for control.

He groaned against her lips and hauled her closer. His cock pounded, pleasantly trapped against her stomach, but he needed so much more.

She mewled a protest when he ended their kiss and

rested his forehead against hers.

Alex had to pant to breathe and needed a minute before he could speak. "I want ye, lass."

"Aye," Alana whispered.

"Undress," he ordered.

The smile she flashed as she broke their physical contact was erotic and made his erection strain even more against his plaid.

She shimmied out of her purple trews, and the crystals behind her offered all the light he needed to see every inch of her body. Her light purple leine fell mid-thigh, obscuring what he wanted to see most, but it was only a matter of time, and Alex could do with some calming of his impatience.

Or so he was trying to convince himself as he shifted in his boots and resisted the urge to rip her clothing from her lithe form.

Alana's long hair was loose, swaying around her hips with her movements, and he couldn't wait to bury his hands in it.

"Lass," he groaned.

She cocked her head to one side and paused. "Somethin' wrong, Alex?"

He growled and darted forward—couldn't help it. "Dinnae tease me."

There was a gleam in her violet eyes. "Tease you?" This was a fair imitation of innocence, but just because she was a virgin didn't mean Alana didn't know *exactly* what she was doing to him.

He framed her cheeks, tugged up, and took her mouth again.

She moaned and opened for him, pressing her body close, and slipping her arms around him.

Alex slid his hands over her shoulders and down her back. When he reached the bottom of her leine, his fingertips brushed bare warm flesh and he stilled. Her arse was perfect, and he needed more. He cupped her, kneading, caressing until she wobbled in his arms.

"Alex…" She pushed his name into their kiss, and the wanton plea made his cock pulse, his bollocks tingle like he was about to climax.

He nibbled on her mouth, dipping his tongue inside the warm recesses again to play with hers.

Alana whimpered and kissed him back, but her hands were busy at his belt, tugging at it. When she had it open, he backed up and caught the falling plaid.

"We can lie on this." Alex formed a makeshift blanket with his garment, but it was narrow. He would lay in the sand before he forced her to do so.

Next time, he'd remember to bring a blanket.

Her eyes were low, as if *she* was trying to see past his leine, which also fell mid-thigh, concealing his straining manhood — at least for the moment. "I want to touch you," she whispered.

He shivered, despite the unmanliness of it. "An' I ye, believe me." Alex shucked his tunic and watched it fall to the sand next to his plaid.

Her gasp had him meeting her eyes, but then she was on him — her hands all over his body. Alana buried fingertips in his chest hair, dragging her other hand lower, through the dark springy curls dividing his abdominal muscles, and then swept her palm beneath his bollocks.

Alex jumped and a curse fell from his mouth.

She stilled. "Alex?"

He grabbed her wrist and kissed her knuckles. "Lass—"

Her cheeks pinked. "I'm sorry, I just wanted to touch you. I didn't know how it would feel."

"What?" The word came out a croak.

"Your...hair. Fae don't have hair on their bodies. Just on our heads. See?" She lifted her leine, revealing a bare, glistening sex.

Alex swallowed for the hundredth time. Told himself it was rude to stare at the tempting slit of her womanhood, but his eyes wouldn't move from the apex of her thighs. "Take...take...off yer leine."

Alana obeyed. She slipped out of her boots, and he took time to do the same, although his whole body was tremoring as if *he* was the innocent.

She was flawless, from the curve of her bottom to her slightly rounded hips, slender waist and the soft part of her belly. Her breasts were perfect, too. High and tight, neither too large, nor too small. Dusky nipples were peaked, begging for his lips and fingers.

Whether that was due to the cool humid air in the cave, or her arousal, he couldn't know, but Alex needed a moment. If he touched her now, he was going to orgasm before he ever slid inside her.

He'd never wanted a woman like he did Alana. Combusted from the inside out.

Alex ordered himself to look away from her bare sex over and over again. He wanted to get his tongue there, too. Instinct said she'd taste as good as she smelled. "How…how does it feel?" he asked to distract himself.

She wrinkled her nose, and it was adorable. "Well, umm…rough. But not bad…" Her cheeks stained a deeper crimson and he chuckled.

"'Tis fine, lass. Men tend ta be…hairy. Human ones, anaway."

Alana bit her bottom lip and he groaned. With the forwardness he was coming to crave, as well as admire, she closed the distance to him and circled her hand around his hard shaft.

Alex couldn't suck back a moan, and he closed his eyes as she explored him.

"Is…this all right, Alex?"

"Aye," he croaked.

"I don't want to hurt you." She left his cock bobbing to caress his chest. "Your body is so hard. Beautiful."

His thoughts scattered; his blood ran hot on its way to a rolling boil. He should answer her, tell her he was flattered, she thought so, but he couldn't form words. Every touch notched him higher, until his head spun, and he hollered at himself to hold it together.

He'd had lovers before; this…situation…shouldn't be any different, should it?

Except…it *was*.

She was.

Not because she was Fae or a princess.

"Alex? Are you well, love?"

He blinked at the endearment, and their gazes

locked. If it was possible, she'd gone even redder. "Aye. Come lie wit' me." Instead of addressing the word she shouldn't feel enough *for* him to *call* him, he gripped her wrist and pulled her down with him on the plaid that was still warm from his body.

Alana snuggled into Alex as soon as her shoulders touched the familiar MacLeod pattern, but a shudder traveled her slender frame he couldn't help but feel.

"Lass, are *ye* well?"

"I am." She smiled and it made his gut jump.

"I dinnae hurt ye."

Her expression softened and she caressed his stubbled cheek as Alana gazed up at him. "Oh, I know. The first time will likely cause pain, but that's not *your* fault. I still want it to be…you. I still want *you* and no other."

Alex had to swallow. Heat kissed his neck and cheeks. He needed to tell her he was honored, and he wanted her, too, but his words had journeyed afar.

He'd not been with an innocent since he'd been innocent himself. He and the blacksmith's daughter had discovered each other when she'd been seven and ten to his fifteen summers, but he'd not felt an iota for the dark-haired beauty of what he did for the Fae Princess lying naked on his plaid against him.

Which makes no sense.

He'd known Sorcha since they'd been wee.

He'd met Alana four times, including tonight.

Instead of trying to speak again, Alex let his eyes trail her perfect body one more time.

She had one knee bent, and she was open to him,

not shy as her arms lay at her sides, leaving her breasts and sex on display. "Alex, touch me."

Tremors chased each other down his spine and his hands lowered to her supple skin of their own accord, as if he was compelled to obey, but damn, he burned to do so anyway.

Alex cupped and kneaded her perfect globes, thumbing her nipples until a whimper drew his attention to her mouth.

She licked her lips, making the pink skin glisten and shove him beyond temptation.

He lowered himself onto her, his chest brushing hers as he sank his mouth over hers and his pelvis claimed hers, his erection trapped between them.

Alana kissed him back and snaked her arms around his neck. She trembled, but when he pulled back, she wore a grin. "Your hair...it tickles."

He smiled and spread a trail of kisses down her neck across her collarbone and chest, circling his tongue around her nipple before sucking her into his mouth.

His princess gasped and buried her hands in his hair. She tugged, but he didn't care.

Alex continued to kiss his way to her belly, laving her navel until she giggled, but he didn't want her to laugh, he wanted her to beg for more, so he moved downward.

His tongue met his fingers at the same time, as he parted her silky hairless folds, and he couldn't help his groan at the dual feelings under his lips and hand. She was hot and already wet.

Alana breathed his name and tightened her hold on

his locks.

The sting felt good, urging him on as he licked up and down her sex, lapping at her moisture, and the smooth feel of her most tender flesh.

He'd been right about her flavor. Alex couldn't get enough as her essence coated his tongue, and he gently pulled the sensitive cluster of nerves at the top of her sex into his mouth.

Alana screamed and arched her hips, pushing into him.

He cupped her bottom and urged her higher, even closer, but quickly slipped one hand back between her legs so he could touch her as he tasted her.

Alex slid two fingers inside her and her inner muscles clutched him with a surprising fierceness, but he maintained ginger thrusts, very aware that her tightness was due to the barrier he would no doubt feel if he pushed all the way forward. He didn't want to hurt her with hand or manhood; he just wanted his princess to shatter in his arms.

"More, Alex, I need..."

Of course, he would obey any command. He grinned up at her, but stilled when he took in the passion on display.

Her head was thrown back, chin jutting up. Her long flaxen tresses were spread in every direction. Alana was flushed pink from head to toe, and so pure in her abandon.

It was going to unman him.

Not just now, but *forever*.

Alex had never seen a more gorgeous sight.

When she pinned him with those violet eyes—likely because he'd stopped his ministrations—they were half-lidded and hazy, making him groan again.

"Alex," she whimpered.

"Jesu, lass," he breathed, he couldn't help it. He shot up her body, the demand to taste her mouth, hold her, have every inch of her under every inch of him was too much to resist.

He needed to claim her. *Now.*

They kissed until he couldn't breathe. Her breasts were flattened into his chest, and they grappled at each other, holds not lasting long because they were both writhing and rocking, imitating lovemaking, but he'd not joined their bodies yet.

Alana tore her mouth from his. "Now, Alex. *Now.* You're driving me mad. I need you inside me."

Alex stilled, and their eyes locked. "Are ye sure? Yer ready? I'd wanted ye ta come first."

She shook her head, those incredible eyes wide. "Aye, I'm sure. I've had pleasure before, but I haven't had *you* before."

He quivered and shifted above her. "I need ye."

"Have me."

Breathe, just breathe. You need to breathe.

Alex kept the chant up as he gripped himself and guided his erection to her gleaming sex. She was swollen and ready, and looking at her made his desire settle even lower, the flames scorching hotter. His bollocks pulsed.

Alana grabbed his forearms, as if she knew she'd have to brace herself, but he'd still do his best not to hurt her.

They both watched as he sank into her slowly, inch by inch, until he had to close his eyes because the tight hold rocked him to his soul, and he wanted to drive forward and mark her, take her maidenhead hard and quickly, so there would be no question of who she belonged to.

Mine.

The bolt of lightning he always associated with her at first touch traversed his limbs; made his heart skip and settle in his gut, urging him on.

This time, he didn't question what it was or what it meant.

It only solidified that the princess in his arms was all *his.*

Alex would never let her go.

Chapter Fifteen

Alana gasped and winced as Alex shoved forward the last inch, breeching the barrier of her virginity. Sharp pain took all her attention and made her head tip. Tears blurred her vision.

She'd been warned it would hurt but hadn't expected such a bite. She sucked a breath and steadied herself by meeting his vivid blue eyes.

Moments passed and he hovered above her.

They didn't speak.

Her sex clenched and quivered, but it wasn't a demand of pain like first penetration.

Her sweet lover, who'd been so gentle with her so far, groaned and whispered a curse.

She flexed her hands on his forearms and tried not to break his skin with her nails. She wanted the discomfort to pass so he'd make love to her.

"Alana," Alex croaked. "Are ye… Do ye wanna stop? We can stop, lass."

He was seated deep inside her, his pelvis covering hers as his muscled chest hovered over her torso. He held his back and buttocks stiff, his powerful legs between hers, but Alana wanted him closer.

His nipples brushed hers when he inhaled and his scratchy chest hair tickled her skin, which caused gooseflesh, but that only made her want him more.

"Nay. I want you inside me."

"I am."

She blinked away the moisture at the corners of her eyes, and smiled when he dipped down to kiss her forehead and cheeks before a tender press of his lips on hers. Alana caressed his cheek, reveling in the stubble under her palm. She'd not meant to call him *love* earlier, but she'd *meant* it.

That shouldn't make sense, but it *did*, just like the shock of what'd felt like magic when Alex had first pushed all the way inside her.

She'd felt *that* as sure as the hurt of him tearing her maidenhead away.

We are *fated*.

Alana had her answer.

"Can you…move, Alex? I want to make love to you."

He closed his sapphire eyes and made a noise in his throat. "I dinnae want ta hurt ye."

Alana cupped his face and made him look at her. "The sting is gone, love. I want to feel you take me. Fully."

"Alana—" His expression was tight, pained. Alex was holding himself back.

"Kiss me, Alex. Show me pleasure."

He'd already given her ecstasy with his mouth, even though he'd stopped before she could climax. It didn't matter. She still wanted *all* of him.

With a groan, Alex obeyed, dipping down so their mouths could meet, and he thrust forward at the same time.

The friction of his first few thrusts had more discomfort than positive sensation, but Alana concentrated on his mouth slanting against hers, the feel of his warm body moving over hers, and the feather-softness of his hair under her fingertips.

She was with Alex, the only man she'd ever wanted to give herself to.

Alex.

Her human laird.

Alex.

Her fate.

Other words floated around in the back of her mind, but she couldn't let herself think them, let alone *say* them. Even if they *were* fated, the depths of Alana's feelings for a man she barely knew were alarming, and not something she could voice — or put life to even in her own head.

She slid her hands over his shoulders and down his back. He felt so good beneath her fingertips. Rough, hot and smooth all at the same time, perfection against her whole form.

Pleasure slid into her and spread wide as Alex kept driving forward, kissing and touching her as they found a rhythm, and Alana gripped his muscled rear end to encourage him.

She tilted her hips and he fell even deeper, groaning against their current kiss as she started to move with him, under him.

He took them higher and higher, until her body tightened on the brink of climax, and restlessness shot as low as her desire when she needed Alex to go faster.

"Lass, I dinnae...I—"

"Alex," Alana breathed. "Come with me. Come for me."

He let out a growl that was more like a plea and buried his face in her neck. Alex's back stiffened and they held each other tight as his erection jerked inside her.

Alana gasped when her core clenched and relaxed as they both found release.

Alex's lips caressed under her chin, kissing her overheated skin, and she smiled as they both panted. His weight covered her completely, but she didn't care.

Alana craved him on top of her, from the springy hair on his legs that tickled hers, to the dark curls on his chest that shot awareness all over her breasts as he breathed against her.

He was *perfect*.

Alex was *hers*.

They both shivered as his softening manhood slipped from her body, but she felt the loss and wanted to banish it.

They were still together.

I'm fine.

Alex propped himself above her on his elbow. "Alana...tha' was..."

"Heavenly. Everything I've ever wished."

Her lover averted his gaze until she whispered his name.

"I dinnae wanna hurt ye, lass."

Alana ran her fingers through his short dark hair. "It was wonderful, love. I mean it. Thank you for being gentle and caring, but it was unnecessary. And next time, it won't hurt at all." Alana winked.

The apple of his throat bobbed. "Next time?"

She giggled and pressed a hard fast kiss to his mouth. "Of course. You don't think I'll walk away, now that I've had you?"

He shook his head but wore a charming smirk. "The things ye say, lass."

She stilled. "Is that bad?"

Alex flashed a lopsided grin. "Nay, a' course no'."

"So, you want me again?"

He chuckled, and that grin went wider as he squeezed her against him. "A' course, lass. I dinnae let ye walk away, either so 'tis a good thing ye dinnae want ta."

Alex was so handsome, her insides wobbled.

Sadness closed in on her, and Alana didn't want to let it chase their banter away.

How could she stay away from him?

Hadn't she decided they were indeed fated?

Selfish. Foolish. Careless.

The words looped her head and Alana wanted to shove them away. She was with her laird, her Alex, and it was too soon for reality to encroach.

"Lass? Somethin's wrong."

Statement. Not question.

How to answer him?

Alex had a right to know about Seamus and her betrothal, but she couldn't bring herself to tell him.

"I'm…fine. I'm here with you."

She wasn't fine. She wanted to cry.

"Ye have ta go, dinnae ye?" Alex whispered.

His face was lined, no proof he'd been laughing and smiling just moments before, and the somberness made Alana ache all over, despite the fact his warm body still covered hers, despite that they were still touching; they were still together.

"I do. Soon." It wasn't why devastation was crashing in on her, but it was convenient, and true, nonetheless.

"I dinnae want ye ta."

Alana sniffled. "I don't want to. But I'll be expected in the morning." She couldn't tell him more than that, even though she *should.*

He sighed and rested his forehead against hers. "Aye, as will I, as much as I'd like ta stay here. With ye, always."

Alana fled in tears. She didn't even tell Alex she'd had to use a spell so he wouldn't remember where the cave or the Faery Stones were.

He'd remember *her,* their time together, so that was what mattered, right?

She didn't regret giving herself to him, but she shouldn't have. Walking away from him now would be impossible, so she couldn't solve her Seamus problem by having nothing dangling over her head.

Why are you so weak?

If we're fated, I'm not weak.

Posing and answering questions to and from

herself didn't do anything but spin her into more chaos. Tears flowed freely as she ran through the tunnels on the way back to her rooms. Alana tried not to stomp up the winding staircase that led to her hearth.

She'd walked with him to the slit-like entrance of the cave and left him on the beach outside of it. He'd asked her not to leave, then kissed her until her toes curled and vowed, he'd never let her go.

Her elation that Alex was just as determined to hold onto her made things worse, didn't it?

I…can't let you go, either.

Alana hadn't waited to see his no doubt confused expression after she'd said the spell. To Alex, she would've just vanished. She didn't want to hurt him, but she'd already broken rules—*so many rules*—by telling him who she was, by showing him the Faery Stones…by being intimate with him. It'd be better for them both if he only remembered *her*, not the cave or the portal.

Xander wasn't going to be pleased that she'd sneaked off again, even if she didn't confess what she'd done with the laird.

No matter her skill had improved at getting by the guard undetected—both leaving the realm and returning to the Field of Light. Her cousin wouldn't see it as positive, even if the smallest part of her was proud of herself.

Would she tell him she was no longer innocent?

He was far from stupid, so Xander would likely take one look at her and guess it. They'd never made a habit of discussing bedmates in detail—as he'd declared it inappropriate—and Alana wanted to cling to that, bark how it was none of his concern, even though he'd argue.

Despite the affirmative things her cousin had recognized in Alex, Xander had never agreed they were fated. He wouldn't approve of her in Alex's bed, for all the reasons that were, in fact, *correct.*

She winced. Didn't want to destroy the memory of her time in the human laird's arms. Her cousin would say what he would; Alana couldn't erase what she'd done with Alex—even if she'd wanted to. She most certainly did *not.*

I'll cherish tonight forever.

She would've even if it hadn't been her first time.

Her rooms were blessedly empty when she slipped past the hearth and closed the heavy portal with a spellword. Alana glanced at her bed and said another to make her fake form dissipate. She watched her bedding lower to the mattress as if deflated.

She'd half-expected Xander to be sitting on her bed, arms crossed, and anger written all over his handsome face. Like he'd sense her fleeing presence. She could actually put off dealing with him until the morning.

Thank the Goddess.

Light slowly bleeding past her heavy drapes told her she didn't have that long to wait after all. Dawn was upon her, so she'd fled the Human Realm just in time.

Regret Alana had had to leave Alex mixed with worries about Seamus and settled in her belly as if she'd eaten rocks. She gulped and swallowed a sob inching up from her throat. She didn't want to cry anymore. Or feel desperation crowding her gut...her head, her heart.

It was her new unwanted constant.

She'd put herself in this situation, and now she was even more ensconced.

"Fool. You're a fool." Alana's voice startled her, and she jumped.

Xander would no doubt agree.

Her head piped up and scolded her for going back to Alex, no matter how tightly knotted the Irish prince had her. Her heart disagreed vehemently, citing fate, of course.

Selfish.

Alana sank onto the edge of her bed and cradled her face. Was she the only person mad enough to have an internal argument?

Or was she only mad because the whole thing was on repeat, it'd become so common.

Was she really as selfish as her mind accused the organ that thundered for only the human laird?

"Aye," she whispered.

Alana didn't bother agonizing over what she should do next, because her internal turmoil made her unqualified to make the decision.

chapter sixteen

lex whistled as he looked over the latest scrolls Hamish needed him to review and sign yay or nay. His world was…lighter.

Since Alana.

It mattered not he that hadn't seen his princess for five days. He'd kissed her, held her, taken her innocence, and being with a lass had *never* been like that before.

She was *perfect*.

If only he could've stayed with her…brought her back to Dunvegan.

He'd see her again. It couldn't be any other way.

Alex had dreamt of her nightly, just like before; visions real enough to be memories, and somehow it kept him going, focused on her, as much as his duties.

He'd hold her again. Kiss her again.

Take her again.

Fae princess or not, he wasn't letting her go. Alana belonged to him now.

She'd come to him when she could. His heart told him as much.

He didn't even chide himself for the hovering emotions that were much too deep for the time he'd known Alana. Feelings that didn't make sense…but just *were*.

Alex smiled and dipped his pen in the inkwell on

his desk so he could scrawl his name on the proper line. He'd already finished with all the records from Duncan's collecting of the rents, organizing them by coin or other tithes received, like livestock and physical goods. His da would be proud, and the cranky steward could relax.

He chuckled. Perhaps Hamish couldn't be put at ease no matter what. The man had always been wound tight, set in his ways, since he and his brother were wee laddies. He'd only seen the man smile a handful of times. A glower was the steward's most common facial expression.

The sound of a male throat clearing had Alex glancing to his ajar ledger room door and wishing he'd closed it all the way.

His twin filled the frame, one dark eyebrow arched in his direction. "Are ye laughin'?"

Alex scowled. "Go away."

He still hadn't forgiven Duncan for his disbelief regarding Alana, nor had they really settled it. Even after the passing time, his brother hadn't tried to apologize, and neither of them had brought up the subject of his continued rides on the beach, or his lass.

They were on an *only-speaking-when-he-had-to* basis, meaning, when they had witnesses. Alex had been avoiding his twin, although pounding his face in or some hand-to-hand combat on the fighting yard had merit. He didn't dare put a sword up against him; he feared the temptation of running him through.

"Why? Am I intrudin' on ye, my laird?" His brother smirked.

Instead of repeating his order, Alex snorted. "Oh, a'course no', my *dear* brother, come in, come in. 'Tis nothin', no'withstandin' duties ta keep ye busy, I'm sure."

His twin chuckled as he entered the room and closed the door. "I dinnae help but notice…yer mood…'tis much improved. Makes a man…curious, s'all."

Alex frowned when Duncan dragged a chair to the side of his desk and planted his arse in it, but then again, he *was* close enough to punch. Maybe he'd exercise his fist in his brother's face after all, since he'd chosen his seat as such. "Ye know wha' they say regardin' curiosity and felines, dinnae? Aye, tha same goes fer twin brothers."

Duncan threw his head back and bellowed a laugh. "Mayhap I was wrong abou' yer improved visage."

Of course, you haven't a clue.

Alex grunted, and tried to concentrate on Hamish's last request, but his brother's eyes were dead set on him; he could feel them as sure as Alana's magic. He tried not to fidget in his chair.

"Alex?"

"What?" he barked.

When he met Duncan's gaze, his twin tilted his head to one side, making his long hair shift. Then he sighed. "I'm tired a' pretendin' I dinnae know yer cross wit' me."

He reared his head up. "Oh?"

"An' I'm tired a' pretendin' I dinnae know why."

Alex narrowed his eyes. "Ye had me thinkin' ye

really were daft."

His brother chuckled again and shook his head. "I dinnae be."

"Weel?"

"I'm sorry."

"Fer what?" He kept his voice even and ignored how his stomach pitched. Did he really need someone to know about Alana that badly?

Believe she was who she claimed to be?

Aye, so he might convince himself he wasn't about to wake from a dream where she wasn't real.

"Fer laughin' when ye said yer lass was a Fae princess, and fer accusin' ye of hidin' a MacDonald lover." Duncan scowled when he named the neighboring rival clan.

Silence descended because Alex didn't know what to say. He didn't feel like thanking him *or* talking about Alana.

Would his brother believe him this time—*really* believe him—if he could manage more than a nod?

"Ye dinnae believe me," he whispered finally. "Do ye now?"

Duncan stared—studied him, really. "I dinnae ken."

Alex appreciated the dose of honesty—maybe. "I spoke true, I swear 'tis true." His voice came out as a low cracked murmur instead of the vow he intended, but his brother only nodded, as if he could finally accept the truth.

More silence, then his twin looked thoughtful. "How can the Fae be real?" He blinked, as if to clear his blue eyes.

"Da has been tellin' us tales of the faeries for years—"

"Aye, but as ye say, *tales*. No truer than tha banshee tha' would come after us if we mistreated a lass."

Alex smirked. That particular story was courtesy of their mother.

What could he say?

He didn't know how to explain how he just *knew* Alana had spoken the truth from the moment she'd told him who she was.

He'd felt it in his gut.

"I tol' her of our clan history," he said.

"Meanin'?"

"Tha' Da believes we're part Fae."

Duncan snorted and shook his head. "Ye dinnae believe tha'? I ne'er have. *Ye* ne'er have. No' even Janey—"

"Maybe 'tis true," Alex blurted.

His brother's mouth snapped shut. He reclined in the chair and crossed his arms over his broad chest. "Alex—"

"Alana *is* Fae. I've seen her magic."

Duncan leaned in, planting his palms on the edge of Alex's desk. "Magic?"

"Aye. She called me ta her with mere thought."

His twin narrowed his eyes. "Are ye sure ye dinnae dream it up?"

Alex shook his head. "Nay. She summoned me ta tha' beach."

"An' then?"

Heat flared over the back of his neck and settled in his cheeks. He prayed he wasn't bright red like a lass of three and ten. Alex fought a fidget on the chair and studied the parchment he'd been ignoring since his twin's advent.

The words were a blur he couldn't focus on.

When he finally met Duncan's gaze, his brother's eyes were dancing, and he wore a knowing smirk.

"What?" he barked. He didn't want to order him to sod off, although he should, but that would confirm Duncan's assumptions as much as a confession.

Alex had never been open about his infrequent dalliances, the opposite of his brother in both experience as well as directness about being with a lass. It was none of Duncan's business that he'd made love to Alana in the beach cave. He wasn't ashamed of what'd happened, but he didn't want to share it with anyone, even the one he'd shared a womb with.

Alana was special.

She's mine.

"I said nary a word," his brother quipped.

Alex narrowed his eyes. "Keep it as such."

Duncan beamed. "How…how…is—"

"What?" Alex leaned back, wary of what his twin was trying to say.

"Tuppin' a Fae—"

He clocked his brother in the shoulder with a quick fist. He'd diverted from his plan to punch his jaw only to avoid questions from their father. He couldn't leave a mark on Duncan and explain it away.

Maybe he should offer to spar on the fighting yard

after all. His twin wouldn't say no.

His brother rocked back in the chair, rubbing his biceps, and cursing in Gaelic as well as English. "Jesu, brother! Ye hit me!"

"Ye need ta watch yer mouth," Alex growled. He braced himself for retaliation, but his brother didn't hit him; Duncan threw his head back and laughed.

"Ye've got it bad, my laird." He shook his head, making his long dark locks dance.

He straightened. That was the last thing he'd expected him to say. He didn't want to confirm or deny, but the words were probably true.

Alex *did* have it bad for Alana.

Duncan caught his eye and grinned. "So, when do I get ta meet yer princess, then?"

She was in Heaven again, in the human realm. The cave of the Faery Stones had become the keeper of their tryst's secret over the following weeks after the night—it was a month today, actually—since she'd given him her innocence, but Alana didn't care where they were, as long as she was in Alex's arms.

They'd made love twice, and her core ached pleasantly. Afterwards, they'd lain in each other's arms, talking about everything and nothing, and she'd smiled so much her face hurt. Laughed, too. Being with him chased all her misery away.

She'd taken every chance she shouldn't have come to him again. Xander had grudgingly acknowledged she could safely travel between realms and remain uncaught when she'd admitted coming to see Alex that night.

Her cousin also seemed to take it in stride, she was no longer a maid. Hadn't threatened to kill her laird as she'd worried. Telling him what'd happened seemed natural, and her bodyguard hadn't said much.

He hadn't interfered further—although he'd refused to swear, he'd let her do as she pleased wholly. Xander had only accompanied her twice more, and the two men she cared about most seemed to have a tolerance, if not an appreciation, for each other. It wasn't the affection she desired, but Alana would take it for now. They weren't so different, and had the potential to be great friends, but the Warrior wasn't open to that.

Seamus had been extra annoying, under the guise of being an attentive betrothed, so she'd had to be more cautious, but couldn't stop sneaking off to be with Alex.

The prince had constantly placed himself at her side, trying to touch her, and calling her his love publicly. She'd become adept at sneaking away from him, too. Alana couldn't guarantee he hadn't had her followed, even though she hadn't sensed anything.

The dangers were still there, of course. They wouldn't disappear until the betrothal contract did, but she was still too selfish to stop seeing her lover. Guilt over that only bothered her a little bit. Being with him solved that, too, even if it wasn't permanent.

For now.

Her laird seemed to delight in making her laugh. His sapphire eyes twinkled, and his face lit up. He'd told her he'd been dreaming of her, and she'd admitted the same. Alex had explained the detailed nature of their conversations and lovemaking in his dreams, and had asked if it could be real; magic.

She'd never gotten visions, and told him so, but the question *was* in the back of her mind. *Her* dreams of him had also been vivid, as clear as memories, although real lovemaking was better.

Alana might seek the library for research when she was able. She'd have to be discreet, and would have to avoid scrolls on fated mates, even though she burned to read every recorded word.

If they *were* fated, it might explain the joint dreams, but it would be difficult to confirm.

We are fated.

She could accept nothing else.

Alana regretted every piece of clothing she donned and did so slowly. Their time together today needed to end, and she didn't want to leave the cave; go back to reality in her realm with no Alex.

Especially since she was to dine with Seamus and their fathers for evening meal.

She still hadn't found the words to tell her laird about her betrothal. Guilt again churned her stomach, chasing away the residual sated feeling in her limbs and heart from making love with him.

I need to tell him.

Alana straightened her shoulders and watched him tighten his belt. The plaid he was wrapped in was longer in the back and she noticed it sway with his movements. The pattern of Clan MacLeod was appealing with its rich dark colors. It stopped below his knees in the front and didn't hide his muscled legs.

The play of Alex's thick arms caught her attention and made her remember being wrapped against his chest. He sheathed his sword and glanced at her, wearing a smile.

She gnawed her bottom lip and searched for the right way to say what she needed to. Nothing came. Alana kneaded the material of her cloak in a white-knuckled grip, instead of slipping it on. Nerves tightened her gut.

"If ye make me ferget this place, how will I know when ye come ta me? I dinnae be able ta live on the beach." Amusement rippled in his eyes.

Her heart skipped and she clung to the distraction of his inquiry.

She'd finally told him of the spell she'd cast each time she'd left, so he couldn't reveal the location of the Faery Stones, even by accident.

Alex had confessed to not contemplating the *where* of their trysts and had only focused on her when he remembered their times together.

That caused a smile—earlier and now.

That morning he'd been riding and had caught sight of her up on the ridge, so she'd not needed to call him with her mind like the night she'd given him her innocence. Most of the other times they'd met had been previously agreed upon more than happenstance, always at that same ridge, at night, relieving the need to call him from his bed.

Alana cleared her throat. "I'll call to you."

"Like you did a' fore?"

She nodded. "Aye."

If she didn't have a connection to the person she was trying to call, it didn't always work. She and Alex were lovers. It mattered not that he wasn't Fae. It was easier to show him again, rather than explain the magic, so she spoke to him with her mind.

Alex, can you hear me?

He blinked and stilled. "I…think so."

I'm speaking to you with my mind. You won't be able to answer me, but can you hear me?

"'Tis unsettlin'. I hear yer voice, but yer lips…dinnae move."

She grinned. "You heard me clearly?"

"As if…weel, yer standin' beside me already, but 'twas as if ye were whisperin' in my ear."

Alana giggled and darted to him, pushing to her toes to press her mouth to his.

Alex flashed a grin that made her insides wobble and dipped his head down for more.

She gladly moved back into his body, let him deepen the kiss and wrap his arms around her. Like always, desire shot low and hot, spreading downward until her core throbbed, her thighs trembled, and her knees went weak. How could she want—*need*—this man so much? She'd already had him inside her twice today.

"Hmmm, lass." Alex nibbled at her mouth as he kissed her, his stubble brushing her cheeks, but it only made her flare hotter for him. He was already hard for her, his erection pressing into her belly.

"Alex, I should go…" Alana panted into his lips,

sparing a glance toward the glowing Faery Stones. As much as she didn't want to. As much as she wanted him to part her from her trews, touch her, and push inside her again.

He groaned but ended the kiss. Her laird was always respectful. That just made her want him even more.

I love you.

The words played at the tip of her tongue, but she swallowed them away. She shoved at the sorrow that came with them. Until she figured out what to do about the Irish prince and her unwanted betrothal...the deadly vows...she wasn't free to love Alex.

She'd *never* be free, unless she walked away from the Fae Realm—her future throne—and she would in a heartbeat, but Seamus would also do as promised, report them to King Fillan and lead Fae Warriors to raze the MacLeods.

Alana couldn't let that happen.

Running wouldn't solve her problem.

Her situation wasn't Alex's fault—let alone his clan's. She couldn't be responsible for their deaths. She was chained to Seamus...for now.

Xander wanted to kill him, but they couldn't risk that.

Her laird would likely—and righteously—be upset she was promised to another, although she'd never even kissed the prince, and would vomit on him before she did so.

Alana had given herself to Alex in love.

She might not have recognized it their first time,

but it was the truth. However, Alex aside, she'd still never lay with Seamus. She didn't think he'd try to rape her, but that doubt played in the back of her mind from when he'd held her against the wall in her suite. If he tried that again, he might seal his own fate—Xander would kill him without delay. Perhaps get away with it, too.

"Alana, what's wrong?"

Her heart skipped. "Nothing. Why, love?"

Alex paused, like he often did when she referred to him with the endearment. "Ye've gone stiff, an' if 'tis due ta yer need of me, I agree, but I fear 'tis somethin' else."

She smiled. He knew her too well. "I do want you. So much. But I cannot stay any longer. There's so much I want to tell you." Alana tried not to wince as her last statement hit. She'd not meant to blurt that bit of honesty.

"Then do so, lass." His voice was low. "If ye want."

Mixed emotions swirled around her. He really was *perfect*. "You never push me, Alex. I need that. Thank you."

"Ye dinnae unburden yer mind, can ye?"

She blinked tears away, shaking her head. "Nay, I cannot."

His jaw flexed, but her laird nodded.

Alana closed her eyes and took a breath. How she wished she could tell him everything. Would it make things better or worse?

Despite his youth, he was a strong man, and had his pride. He'd be angry and hurt, but the truth could help them, could it not?

Nay, he cannot help with matters of the Fae.

His blue eyes bored into her as she hedged in his arms.

"I need to go, Alex," she whispered.

His handsome countenance fell, but then her lover schooled his expression. Alex nodded again but squeezed her tight against his chest instead of releasing her. "One day, I shall no' let ye go, *mò chridhe*."

Her vision blurred and she tried to smile. He'd spoken in human Gaelic, but the endearment wasn't so different from Fae, and meant, *'my heart'*. He was *her* heart, too. "And I love you for that."

Alex froze and gripped her shoulders almost painfully. "What did ye say?"

Alana flushed to her toes and inhaled. Her mouth had run away from her…again. Blurting seemed to be a new talent, as if she'd picked up a new power. Too bad it wasn't one she wanted.

He shook her gently when she didn't answer. "Alana, what did ye say ta me?" Hope and wonder from him rolled over her empathic powers, and her heart missed a beat.

She couldn't keep her feelings from him. Had been foolish to try. "Oh, Alex, I love you. I love you so much it hurts. I shouldn't love you, but I do. I just—"

His mouth crashed down on hers and she didn't hesitate to meet his kiss. Alana opened for him without delay, letting her laird control things as she slanted her lips against his. Alex branded her as he kissed her harder, and she clung to his thick arms so she wouldn't slide to the white sand of the cave on her rear end. Her legs threatened to dump her.

The humid air danced around them, helping the desire that slicked over her form. Her sex ached, pulsing with a begging edge for his as he hauled her even closer, flattening her breasts against his chest.

His huge hands were all over her back and bottom, but fingers soon brushed her overheated damp flesh as Alex shoved her leine up and pushed at her trews, trying to move them over one hip without loosening her belt.

Alana wanted to lose herself in him, in them moving together, screaming their climax at the same time, like they had earlier.

Abruptly, he tugged away from their kiss, making her head spin and she struggled to focus on his face.

"I love ye, too. Jesu, how I've waited ta say tha' ta ye. I tol' myself 'twas too soon. I tol' myself it dinnae make sense." He tossed his head back and laughed, making Alana want to bury her hands in his short dark hair.

Elation, relief and *love* washed over her magic, and she shivered in his grip. "Alex—"

"I love ye," he repeated. "Did ye hear me? I love ye, Princess Alana of tha Fae Realm."

Tears scalded her cheeks as the words piled against her lips and pushed. She wanted to tell him *everything*.

He *loved* her, which fulfilled her wildest dreams.

Why did it make her feel so *guilty*?

It was what she'd *wanted* more than anything. *Needed*, more than air.

"I heard you," she whispered.

Alex studied her, and his bright grin fell off a tad. "Somethin's wrong."

She wished for the passionate haze of his kiss but inhaled instead and forced a nod. "Aye. There's so much I need to tell you. So much I need to explain." Alana swallowed—twice.

When his dread hit her magic, she wanted to pull away, open the portal, and bolt.

"Go on." It was a command, but his voice wavered.

She crushed her eyes shut because she didn't have the bollocks—as Xander would say—to look at the man she loved when she pushed the words from her mouth. "The truth is, I'm betrothed."

chapter seventeen

"The truth is, I'm betrothed." The sentence was like one of Duncan's low gut shots when they'd had a tussle, or maybe worse.

Like a fatal stab wound to the heart with a poison-tipped sword.

Alex reeled. Released Alana and stumbled back until he hit the natural wall of the cave—away from the radiance of the Faery Stones.

"Wait. Alex, let me explain."

There was no need for her to clarify.

She was a Fae Princess. Never his, despite giving him her innocence.

Despite telling him she loved him.

Despite *him* telling her he loved her.

"Alex, please." Tears streamed down her gorgeous face, making her alabaster skin glow in the soft magic light from the crystals.

Each one just about killed him, but Alex was dying anyway, every breath a dagger slicing off another piece of his heart.

Alana reached for him, but he jerked away, only to receive a sharp pain in his shoulder blade from the rough surface behind him.

"Alex!"

He wanted to flee, but when he turned to go, his

vision tilted, and he tripped over his feet. He went down hard, his bare knees landing in the bleached sand. Agony shot into his wrists from where he'd braced himself on his palms, and white-hot streaks went into his thighs, making him twitch.

"Alex, I'm sorry, are you all right?" Alana's purple boots appeared in his line of sight, but he didn't have the guts to look up at her. "I didn't mean to make you fall, but I *need* you to listen to me."

Alex pitched back on his haunches, and his thighs barked another protest. "Ye made me fall?"

She bit her plump bottom lip and gave a small nod. "I used magic. To stop you from leaving me."

His gut roiled, and when he should be angry, he only found pain. A black hole where his heart used to be.

"I love you. I really do. Please believe me."

He made tight fists and planted them on his aching thighs. "Ye…lied ta me."

Her violet eyes downcast for a moment before meeting his. "I didn't, really."

Alex growled. "A lie of omission…'tis still a lie."

Alana's beautiful face flared pink, but it wasn't from the passion they'd shared. "I…need you to listen. Please…will you listen?"

"Will ye release me?"

"I'm not holding you there."

"Nay, but ye dinnae let me leave this place, will ye?"

Again, she wouldn't meet his gaze. "I would prefer not to handle this as such." Her voice wavered, and her mouth wobbled.

More tears rolled down her cheeks and Alex's resolve warred with his agony. Something inside him snapped; he couldn't let her suffer. He muttered curses under his breath in Gaelic, then ridiculed himself for being weak. "Alana-lass, come ta me." He pushed to his rear end and his lover squatted beside him. Even if he wasn't fond of the notion at the moment, he *did* love her. He'd called her *mò chridhe*, and damn if that wasn't true, too. She made his heart sing.

S'pose I owe her a listen.

"Aye, I believe ye love me," Alex whispered.

Her shoulders shook, but Alana didn't move any closer. Nor did she look at him. "I *do*. I didn't mean for it to happen. I never should've come here." She finally met his gaze. "But I don't regret *you*, Alex. I couldn't. Ever." She took big shuddering breaths that were his undoing.

Alex hauled her onto his lap and rubbed her back. He inhaled her scent—which was really a mixture of his own and hers, as well as their lovemaking. The humidity of the cave left it hanging in the air, but it wasn't unpleasant. "I dinnae regret ye, either. I love ye, lass." He didn't mean to repeat his feelings for her.

She belongs to another.

"I don't."

"What?"

"Belong to another."

Damn, he'd said that aloud. He cursed again, at the way his gut quivered when she'd spoken. "Ye said ye were betrothed—"

"Aye, but I could never *belong* to him. And I don't intend to marry him. I didn't even before I agreed to sign the contract."

Alex frowned and tried not to react to her imploring gaze. Her violet eyes said so much more than her words. Alana *did* love him. He'd never doubted that. "Explain, *mò chridhe*." He swallowed and pushed away the confusion.

She made a noise in her throat, and more tears rolled down her cheeks. "I'm still your heart?" Her question was a whisper, and her voice trembled as much as her slender form, even though he held her securely against him.

With a sigh, he leaned forward to kiss her forehead. "Aye, lass. Minutes passin' dinnae change tha'. I dinnae think anythin' could. I love ye."

Alana flashed a tremulous smile and sucked in an audible breath. "My betrothed is an Irish prince named Seamus, and he's a bastard."

Alex smirked at her unladylike descriptive, but his amusement quickly flipped to rage when she launched into a tale of deadly threats and forced agreements. He didn't give a shite that his life had been endangered, but he did have a pang about his clan. However, he couldn't end things with his princess because of that.

Selfish? Aye.

They'd have to figure something out. There was no other choice.

He wouldn't let Alana leave him.

The more his love spoke about the royal bastard, the more he wanted to run him through, and not only because he'd wheedled her into agreeing to give him her hand.

Alex was glad that her cousin and protector, Xander agreed, but too bad neither seemed to be able to affect the outcome—yet. "Ye dinnae wed him," he growled.

"I wouldn't even if I didn't love you. I've been avoiding his pursuit for years."

He wiped her tears away and cupped her face. He kissed her softly and Alana snuggled into him. "Marry me instead."

Alana blinked and shock washed over her. "Wh-wh-what?" She stilled against his hard chest and wanted to look away from his intense blue gaze but couldn't.

"Marry me instead," her laird repeated. His voice was even. Calm. Grounded. Alex gripped her shoulders to hold her steady, but she needed that.

How could he sound so sure, when she'd just crushed him?

She felt it with her magic, as well as saw it written all over his face.

He'd tried to run from her.

Alana still felt guilty for using the spellword that'd made him fall, but she couldn't let him go. Then or now. "Alex, I—"

Her lover cupped her cheeks and ran the pad of his thumb over her kiss-swollen bottom lip, sending a tremor down her spine. "*Ye* are tha lass I want ta spend tha rest a' my life with."

"What? After everything I just told you? You—"

"I want ye by my side always. *I* want ta wed ye, Alana. Not some bastard, Irish prince or no'. I shall no' let him have ye. I shall no' let any other man have ye. Ye are *mine*."

His thick brogue rolled over her and her heart skipped, then cantered. "Oh, Alex—"

He kissed her hard and fast. "I tell ye I love ye, and yer surprised by tha'? After everthin' we've shared?" Alex's whisper was a tease and a chide at the same time and had a smile tugging at her mouth while her heart plummeted to her knees.

Alana wanted him again. *Needed* him.

She should've left already. Surely the time she was supposed to have met Xander had come and gone. They were lucky her cousin hadn't opened the Stones and barged into the cave. He would've likely caught them making love. Her bodyguard had cautioned her to keep her visit short, and it'd been hours.

"I love you," she said.

"And I ye." Alex grinned and it made her mush, head to toes, chasing away all the Seamus-induced misery.

It wouldn't last—she still had no answer—but at least she'd been honest with her laird. He'd not only listened to her; he'd shared mutual anger at what a wretch the prince was.

Then he'd asked her to marry him?

Alana swallowed.

He'd been so hurt, but able to forgive her so quickly? Declare *he* wanted her for the rest of his life?

Alex loves me. He wants to marry me.

He'd been able to see past what she'd had to do *for* him.

Goddess, he's too perfect for me.

"I dinnae be loose wit' my favors, Yer Highness." Alex's teasing voice wrenched her attention back to his handsome face.

She cocked her head to one side and watched her long hair brush the bare skin of his forearm. 'Twas a shame they were dressed. "You're not?" She bit back a grin.

"Nay." Alex arched a dark eyebrow. "Meanin' ye dinnae have me over and over and *no'* keep me."

Alana giggled. "So, if I don't marry you, you'll reject me? Tell me I cannot have you again?"

He nodded, but his mouth rippled as if he was trying not to smile.

"I cannot change your mind?"

He mock-glared and shook his head.

"Even if I do this..." She wiggled in his lap and pressed her breasts into him until she felt his body's response.

Alex was hard, and she wanted him again.

Her gorgeous lover gasped and color spread across his high cheekbones as he tried to fight his desire. "Nay..." he croaked.

Alana scooted away, until she was sitting on the sand next to him, off his powerful thighs. "If you insist."

His sapphire eyes went wide, and he tugged her

back to him, urging her mouth to his.

She didn't refuse him; she couldn't.

Alex kissed her with the familiar skill that made her heart skip and her body ache with desire, but then he pulled away, and his eyes bored into her. "Ye dinnae answer me, lass."

It's impossible, isn't it?

Not just because of Seamus and his threats. She'd live much longer than him. Would have to watch him grow old...die.

Her heart skipped. Alana could see no other man as her husband. Fae prince or nobleman alike held no interest—or her heart—like the MacLeod laird.

She thought of Princess Sima being wiped from the royal records because she'd fled the Fae to be with Alex's ancestor.

Would that happen to her?

Did she care?

Princess Sima got her man.

All those years, all the potential lovers, and Alana had waited for a human to take her innocence. She'd never let a Fae man's sex between her legs, no matter how hot his kisses and touches had been. None of those would-be lovers had ever come close to making her feel like Alex did.

Caution screamed in her mind. The Irish prince was nothing to trifle with. The bastard meant the vows he'd made. Not to mention, her father had formally recognized her betrothal to Seamus. The contract was signed, and he was negotiating the marriage portion with the Irish king.

She needed to tell Alex *nay*; reiterate the dangers of them being together.

It *was* a weight lifted that he knew about Seamus.

There's no solution yet.

Alana's heart galloped as hard as the racing thoughts and fears.

She loved this man. This human laird.

If she and Alex were fated, would the Goddess not save them from Seamus?

Or Alex's God?

She didn't want to fear the answer, so she let it be and took a breath. It was supposed to calm her so she could answer him, but it made her head spin. "Aye, Alex, I want nothing more than to marry you and be by your side forever."

Triumph darted across his face, and he looked so hopeful it made her shake beside him.

"Truly?"

Alana bit her bottom lip. "It won't be easy. I'm trapped..."

"Ye ease me, Alana."

Tears blurred her vision again and he wiped the moisture from her cheeks for the third time—or was it the hundredth?

How could he melt her with words that weren't exactly tender endearments? He did, even without a touch, but that helped, too.

"You ease me, too. Like no one ever has. But—"

Alex put two fingers at her lips. "Dinnae worry. 'Twill work itself out."

Alana shook her head and grabbed his hand. "You

don't understand—"

He narrowed his eyes and fierceness glittered across his expression. "I *do* understand. Ye tol' me weel what 'tis at stake. My family. My clan."

"Your lives."

He pinned her to him. "I dinnae be afraid ta fight, Alana."

Her breath evaporated and her chest ached. "Nay. Alex. I will *not* let anything happen to you and your people because of me."

Alex cupped her cheeks and stared into her eyes.

Alana swallowed again.

"I love ye. *Ye* are worth tha fight."

She didn't know what to say, so she shivered in his arms and met his kiss when her love dipped his head down to claim her mouth again.

chapter eighteen

lana avoided Seamus' gaze as she tried to make herself eat the food on her jewel-encrusted plate, instead of just shoving it around while the two kings and her vile *betrothed* carried on lively conversation. There was too much *come-hither* in those emerald depths, and a smugness in the Irish prince's expression that made her blood boil.

What does he know?

Or what did he *think* he knew?

Her mind-shields were in full force, so it wasn't possible he'd gleaned where she'd been all day — at least not from *her*.

The three deep voices went on while she played the dutiful speak-when-spoken-to princess. Alana sucked back a sigh, forcing herself to chew and swallow a piece of meat. After the afternoon of energetic lovemaking with Alex, she really *did* need to eat.

Xander hadn't been surprised about the declarations of love exchanged, but his concern had dimmed her excitement. He hadn't shouted a denial when she'd told him Alex had asked for her hand, but he *had* expressed relief that she'd told the human laird about her Seamus-predicament.

She'd demanded to know why her cousin felt that way, since he wasn't exactly encouraging her to be with Alex permanently. Her Warrior protector only asserted it was the right thing to do. Xander hadn't given judgment—or comment—that she'd told the human laird she *would* marry him.

Unfortunately, her cousin could also offer no advice relieving the impossibility of the situation. So, she still had no answer on *how* she could marry Alex.

Other than run away and doom the MacLeods, of course.

"Wouldn't you agree, Your Highness?" King Ciaran's blue eyes—so different from a certain laird's despite the similar hue—were friendly as they gazed at her, but his bushy brows quickly melted together with concern when Alana failed to answer.

Her father cleared his throat, then three sets of eyes were fixed on her.

She tried not to fidget. The back of her neck was hot, and her tongue heavy, glued to the roof of her mouth. What had Seamus' father asked?

Shite.

Alana pulled a word from Alex's repertoire. Should she agree? She had no idea to *what*, and it would likely cause issues later.

"Alana?" Her name on her father's lips was just short of a demand.

"I'm sorry, Majesties, what was that?" Alana made her voice just above a whisper and averted her gaze. Embarrassment edged in closely, eager to eat her alive.

Seamus laughed—too loudly—and patted her shoulder as if she was his pet.

Her face flamed again, but she didn't dare look up or she'd glare at him.

"My love was daydreaming again. I'm sorry, Father, Your Majesty." He nodded to both kings. "My sweet princess speaks of little else but our wedding, and no doubt it has her overtaxed. I'm sure she was contemplating tapestry and flower placement, not to mention fine gowns."

She clutched the meat knife under the table on her lap to restrain herself from stabbing him, and plastered on a smile then nodded demurely for her father, more than for Seamus'. "Of course. I was contemplating my wedding." The words came out through gritted teeth, so Alana held her breath to see if they'd be accepted.

King Ciaran patted her hand—the one *not* clutching a weapon—and wore a smile of indulgence. As if she was so silly a female that his son's words made perfect sense.

She *really* wanted to stab the prince.

Seamus winked.

Alana had to concentrate not to narrow her eyes. He was up to something, but she didn't want to guess what. It didn't bode well for her. The prince enjoyed riling her when she couldn't respond, so it was best to play the stupid oblivious female anyway. Even if it made her angry.

Her father knew she was too clever to be convinced, but it appeared for the sake of the Irish King he would play along, too.

She prayed to the Goddess she wasn't in for a lecture, later. Nothing was worth a summons to King Fillan's private ledger room, or worse, a public shaming he was so fond of from his high perch of a royal seat in his throne room.

Seamus' gaze didn't waver for the rest of the horrid meal. He studied her, with eyes like bright green slits. He kept his arm around her shoulders, but not consistently touching her.

The prince rested his arm on the back of her chair, gripping the carved ball that was atop the right spindle from time to time.

It didn't escape her peripheral vision that his grasp was white-knuckled, and whenever his arm brushed her, Alana couldn't help but jump. Her gown was fancy and off-shoulder, so he touched her skin, even though his long sleeve spared her from touching his. The inches of fine fabric didn't allow her to feel protected from his touch. No amount of material would ever be enough.

Alana's stomach churned.

Something had happened.

The prince had changed from the teasing—annoying—and smug too-attentive betrothed. Something had melted him into anger. She could feel his emotions through her magic, as well as his proximity.

What did I do to upset him?

Seamus had declared she could keep Alex, as long as she was discreet—and she had been, so even if he'd guessed where she'd been, why would that raise his ire?

All evening he'd stared as if he had a secret and was pleased with himself. Why now was he subtly glaring, as if *she* was keeping something from *him*?

As much as she was curious, Alana dreaded the look in his eye.

What the hell is wrong?

Seamus escorted her from her father's private dining chamber with a too-tight grip on her elbow. His stride, which was much longer than hers, had her practically running to keep up.

"Seamus, you're hurting me!"

Where's Xander?

A desperate sweep of the corridor didn't produce her cousin, nor did her betrothed stop dragging her.

"Seamus!" She struggled in his grip, but he held her tighter and urged her faster. She was tempted to use a blast-spell on him, but his medallion would protect him. Alana wasn't fond of the idea of backfired magic hitting her—even if it *would* get her free. Pain and scorch marks weren't worth it. "I'm going to scream."

Her *betrothed* remained undeterred, failed to slow or answer.

When they made it to her chambers, Rannick narrowed his eyes on them immediately. No doubt the big guard noticed her clipped gait and the hold on her arm. "Your Highness?"

"Open the door, guard," Seamus barked.

The man-at-arms glared and flexed his grip on the hilt of one of his two oversized swords.

Alana wished she could order him to free it and lop the prince's hand off.

When Seamus growled, ice slid down her spine. She'd never heard him speak to castle staff or men-at-arms that way, and she wasn't keen on being alone with him. Anger radiated from his aura, staining it a menacing crimson. She didn't even have to concentrate to make it visible.

He wouldn't hurt her, would he?

If he tried, Xander *would* kill him.

Rannick's yellow gaze landed on her, and she gave a slight nod, against her better judgment. Concern furrowed his dark eyebrows, but he obeyed and slid her door open.

"Get my cousin, please, Rannick."

The guard offered a curt nod.

Alana appreciated his open scowl toward Seamus. Perhaps it was foolish to send him away, but because of the magic soundproofing her suite, Rannick wouldn't be able to hear her scream, anyway.

The door was barely closed when the prince whirled on her, invading her personal space, but she wouldn't allow him to push her against the wall again.

She grabbed the poker from the fire-tending tool rack on the smaller hearth in her sitting room. She brandished it until the space between their bodies widened.

Seamus threw his head back and laughed even as he retreated. "You will stab me?"

Alana squared her stance and held the poker like a sword, as her cousin had shown her years ago. "If you force me to defend myself, I *will*. What is your issue with me, *Your Highness*?" she spat the honorific like a curse.

He smirked and moved closer, but instead of trying to touch her or grab her weapon, he sat on the purple chaise facing her and the fireplace, then crossed his legs. His emerald stare never wavered, and he sat tall, as if on a throne.

She didn't relax but lowered the poker a few

inches. Stared right back, fighting the urge to swallow.

His expression couldn't mean anything good. Anger simmered below the surface, and he could pop up off her lounger and jump on her. He was stronger, despite her make-shift weapon. He'd proven he could best her strength when he'd pinned her to her own wall. The prince wasn't as big as Alex or Xander, but he was muscled like them. Still towered over her.

"You've been naughty, my dear princess." Seamus' smile held no humor as it spread across his wide mouth. His voice was low and even, with a deadly edge.

Unease crawled up her spine and her limbs shook. "Wh-wh-what do you mean?" Alana cursed the shake in her query.

He whistled. "Did we, or did we not, discuss discretion?"

She straightened her shoulders and lowered the poker until the tip hit the stone floor with a *chink*. "Stop speaking in riddles, Seamus," she barked. Her heart skipped and sped up.

The prince smiled again, but his eyes were narrowed to slits. "Well, my *love*, it seems—"

The door burst open and Xander filled the frame, his sword drawn, wings vibrating. He wore armor, as if he'd come from the fighting yard—or a battle. He took one look at the fire-poker in Alana's hand and glided into the room, glaring at the prince. "What's going on here?"

Seamus stood and brushed himself off as if he didn't have a care in the world.

Alana lifted the poker again, despite her cousin's

much larger sword, and the fact he'd moved in front of her to shield her from her betrothed.

"Rannick said you put your hands on the princess," Xander growled, in a tone no one should dare to address a royal with.

Thank the Goddess he doesn't care.

She didn't either. She wanted to cheer. Or order him to use his huge weapon on Seamus.

"I'm glad you've arrived, Sir Xander," the prince said, a smile back in place that made her skin prickle.

Xander's sword never faltered, but her cousin looked from her to Seamus and back, confusion stamped all over his face. "What's going on here?" he repeated.

"It seems we've got ourselves a predicament," the prince announced.

"What are you talking about?" Alana snapped, not hiding the annoyance washing over her. She flexed her fingers on the poker's curved handle. Bumped it against her thigh a few times.

Her only *predicament* was standing in front of her, clad in green from head to foot and now frowning. His hair was long and loose, the dark waves dancing over his shoulders. Handsome as sin, but *he* was the worst sin she could think of.

"*My* hands on our princess should be the least of your worries, Sir Xander." Seamus' expression was placid, but his eyes flashed, and his hands were fisted at his sides. His aura still shouted rage, the red hue throbbing as if he fought to keep himself under control.

Her cousin shot her a look and arched a fair

eyebrow.

Alana wanted to shrug, but her gut dipped.

"Alana has broken her vow to me, despite my generosity in allowing her to keep her *human*." Seamus spat the last word, as if being human was the worst offense in existence.

She bristled. "What are you talking about? I'm very discreet." She didn't bother pointing out how she'd gained skill at sneaking back and forth between realms; how she'd never been caught…well, after that first time, anyway. It didn't matter, and it was none of Seamus' damn business.

He chuckled, long and deep, and shook his head, making his hair float around him.

When he pinned her with an intense gaze, she froze. Clutched the poker tight to her side.

Seamus had never looked at Alana with such…malevolence…in his green eyes. The expression belied his laughter and made her belly somersault. The meager contents of her stomach threatened to make themselves known to the shiny floor.

Xander was uncomfortable too, shifting on his booted feet, and his wings fluttered, the iridescence catching the light in the room. He narrowed his eyes on the prince and lifted his sword again, apparently ready for anything.

"The filthy half-human *thing* in your womb states otherwise."

chapter nineteen

lex was floating…weeeel if a man could do so. He couldn't stop smiling. All he could do was nod and broaden his grin at the odd looks he was getting because of it. Aye, his mood had improved, so it was no wonder all the MacLeods were noticing.

He hadn't even complained to Hamish about his latest round of demanding scrolls. Alex chuckled. He'd almost suggested the steward scrape his jaw from the floor of his ledger room when presented with his time-consuming task that morning. He might've allowed the tease if the man wouldn't have been offended—and likely complain to his da.

Instead of Alex's usual grumbling, he'd cheerfully received the duty; even thanked the old man. Hamish had looked at him as if he'd gone mad.

"Alex?" Duncan had his head cocked to one side, his long hair dangling at the same angle, and a hand resting on one hip as he regarded him from the entrance of his ledger room.

Alex smiled for his twin and leaned back, resting the quill next to the now needed-to-be-refilled inkwell in front of him. He'd just finished his last required signature and rolled the scroll back up. He still needed to affix wax and the MacLeod seal. "Afternoon, brother." He threw him a nod.

"Erm…"

"Have a seat." He gestured to the usual chair Duncan occupied.

That froze his brother about ten feet from his desk.

"What's go' inta ye this time?"

Alex just grinned.

Duncan narrowed his eyes. "What've ye done with my brother?"

He chuckled and put up a beckoning hand. "Come, join me. I've jus' finished here."

His twin made no moves. Just stared, his mouth half-agape.

That made Alex laugh harder. "Ah, usually I'm tha more suspicionin' of tha two a'us."

"Aye," Duncan said slowly. "But I see nothin' *usual* 'bout tha way yer actin'."

"What? I dinnae be permitted ta be happy?"

"*My* brother? Nay." Duncan shook his head. "Did Bán toss ye on yer arse…nay, more like yer head?"

"Nay."

"'Tis yer lass, then? Yer princess?"

Alex could only beam like an idiot.

Duncan rolled his eyes, looking very much like their younger sister.

"Come, come, I've news."

His brother's gaze was still much too wary as he lifted the chair and planted it alongside the desk like he always did, and the expression didn't fade as he folded his big body to sit. He crossed his arms over his chest and hunched his broad shoulders.

"Ye look as if yer bracin' fer bad news." Alex tried not to frown. He wouldn't let his twin dim his good mood. He was to meet Alana that night, and he was going to press her about their marriage.

Where didn't matter, as long as it was soon.

"Should I be?" Duncan asked, still studying him.

The back of Alex's mind whispered she wasn't free from the Fae prince—an Irish bastard no less—who held her captive by a false agreement, but he tried not to focus on that. Part of him called himself a fool. She'd told him her plight and explained if she ran away permanently, his life—and all the lives of his clan— would be in grave danger.

Her gorgeous violet eyes had been filled with such fear when she'd spoken those words. Even if that hadn't been the case, he would've believed Alana, but that genuine terror had rocked him—at the time.

She *loved* him.

Alex loved her, too. Wanted to have her as his wife. *Would* have her.

She was *his*.

He'd spoken the truth that he wasn't afraid to fight, but what would that really cost? He growled and pushed those thoughts away.

They loved each other, and they'd be together.

Alana believed them fated, or so she'd told him. So, it had to be true, right?

The strength of his draw to her couldn't be explained any other way. How she'd felt in his arms had been unmatched by any other lover—another sign that his love, his heart, had been correct. They were *supposed* to be together.

Damn the Irish prince and his threats.

Alex would have Alana as his own. Soon.

She'd *never* belong to another.

"Alex?" Duncan prompted softly.

He'd taken too long to speak. "Nay, no' bad news. Only tha best kind of news."

"Oh?"

"I'm ta be wed."

His twin sputtered and pushed back in the chair until two of the legs rocked off the floor and slammed into the stone with heavy *thunks.* "What?" he gasped.

Alex tried to convince himself not to be offended. "Aye. I've asked Alana ta be my wife and she's agreed." He didn't need to go into anything more...at the moment. Guilt niggled. He *should* tell his brother the *whole* truth.

He didn't doubt the dangers to their clan. He just cared more about making his princess belong to him officially than he was worried about Fae Warriors—as she called them—coming out of the shadows.

That voice again whispered, this time calling him selfish.

Is that true? Am I?

"Are ye mad?" Duncan's question was half-bark, half filled with almost wonder.

As if his twin *did* think his mind had fled.

Alex frowned. After all his brother's demands to meet her, his reaction wasn't what he'd expected. "Mad? Nay. I've ne'er been clearer. More sure of anythin'."

"Ye can't wed a lass none of us have met, Alex. Nor a lass Da dinnae approve. Ye dinnae have jus' any match, brother. Yer tha laird. Ye've responsibilities. All tha', a' course, leavin' off the mention of her bein' Fae."

Alex reared back. "So, ye still dinnae believe me?"

"I…"

"What happened ta all tha demands ta meet her? Ye dinnae doubt then!"

"Dinnae be like tha'. Alex—"

"Dinnae, '*Alex*' me, little brother." He scowled. His mood dipped and Alex wanted to grab his brother and shake him. Of all people, he needed his twin on his side.

Needed his support.

"I ne'er said I'd wed without her meetin' ye, Mother, Da, and Janey. She dinnae always be able ta come here, an' I—"

"Bein' tha laird dinnae give ye freedom ta wed whoe'er ye like, an' ye know tha'. Da 'twill have a say."

Alex glowered. "I *am* tha laird, as ye say. Bein' such, I *will* wed who I want." He put his fists on the surface of the desk to resist the urge to plant one in Duncan's face. He rose up, and his brother's gaze followed, looking *up* at him.

His twin remained seated.

Good.

"Alex—"

"As laird, 'tis my duty ta find matches fer my siblings, as weel."

Duncan frowned.

"I can match *ye* wit' who *I* see fit. Janey, too."

"Dinnae threaten me, Alex MacLeod." His brother re-crossed his arms over his chest and stared him down. "Yer no' listenin' ta me."

"What's ta listen ta? I'm ta be wed. There's nothin'

more ta say on tha matter."

"What's this nonsense?" Their father's boom had Alex's eyes shooting to the doorway of his ledger room. The older man stood there with Janet.

Damn, his brother hadn't closed the door when he'd come in.

He swallowed but wasn't about to squirm. He was a man, and he *was* the laird.

"Da—" Duncan gasped—much like he had earlier with Alex's declaration. He scrambled to his feet as if they'd been caught in mischief. His twin paled a little, but Alex didn't pay it any mind.

"Yer ta be wed?" his sister asked as father and daughter slid into the room and Janet closed the door.

Their father's bushy eyebrows were as high as they could physically go without jumping off his face. His blue stare never wavered from Alex's.

Alex squared his shoulders and nodded. "Aye." He'd planned to tell the rest of his family about Alana. It wasn't like he could keep their upcoming nuptials a secret forever.

Might as well be now.

His father was always touting the Fae were real…Alex was about to confirm it.

"Ta whom?" Iain demanded.

"How could I not have known?" Alana plastered both hands to her lower still-flat stomach. Her body had betrayed her.

Her hands, her arms, her spine, even her legs trembled, although Xander had lifted her and carried her to her bed as soon as Seamus had stormed from her suite with more dark vows.

The prince had been so angry his face had been the same color of his glowing red medallion, but he'd not stated what move he'd planned next. He'd just…left.

Xander had asked if she should go after him, but she hadn't wanted to.

Then, or now.

Alana was reeling with the news she should've been able to sense.

She sat up against her pillows, but the softness behind her might as well have been an abrasive surface. Her back was scepter-straight, and her chest was tight, her heart still pounding against her ribs. Breathing was labored, too. She had to concentrate to get air down.

Chaos reigned, taking over her mind and jarring her like her quivering form.

I'm carrying a child.

Alex's child.

Hope, love and joy bloomed, only to be quashed when her bodyguard spoke.

"You have bigger things to worry about than that." Her cousin shook his head, his frown so deep it jolted her to the edge of the bed. His wings vibrated, and his wide shoulders held a fine tremor, too.

He was scared, and *that* rocked Alana to her core.

The strong Fae Warrior was like a rock most of the time. Xander *didn't* scare.

Any Fae would kill her child on site. Some — like

Seamus, evidently—could sense pregnancy with the barest touch, and it was said her race could smell human blood. Maybe some could, she never had.

As the Crown Princess, she was always around members of the Scottish Court with great magic, and talents usually varied vastly. Being pregnant with Alex's child could get her killed if other Fae could also sense mixed parentage within her.

Not to mention the unwed-Crown-Princess-reality.

Even if she could pass the child off as her betrothed's, she and Seamus would be frowned upon. That wouldn't help the situation anyway; her father would no doubt demand their nuptials take place immediately to cover the impropriety.

Fae could be promiscuous before marriage, but procreation was for *after* the vows. Young Fae were supposed to be careful, and Alana didn't exactly have youth to use as an excuse, she'd long since shed girlhood. Seeing a healer for contraception was acceptable. She'd never thought to be careful with Alex. She didn't have a justification; she'd simply let her feelings and passion for the human laird carry away her sense.

Alana shuddered.

In any case, the prince would never agree to claim Alex's babe, even if they could get away with the half-human issue. He'd been too angry.

At birth, it would be obvious to anyone in her realm that her child wasn't pure Fae.

A death sentence. For them both.

She told herself to breathe in and out. "How could

Seamus be the one to discover—"

"Alana."

Her name was all warning, and her gaze flew to Xander's.

"You're carrying a child."

"Aye, I am aware." Alana tried to keep her voice wry, but his tight expression held real fear, and ice slid down her spine.

"*Are* you?" He cocked his head to one side, narrowing his violet eyes.

Her heart skipped. "Of course. What—"

"A child who is half human."

"Xander—"

"Your life has never been in graver danger."

Alana fought convulsions and didn't dare answer him. "I have to tell Alex. Now." She hurried off her bed to stand on shaky legs and reached for the bedpost at the same time her cousin grabbed her other arm to steady her.

"Nay, Alana."

Their eyes locked.

"Aye, Xander. I promised to meet him up on the ridge tonight anyway. Now my reason is different. I'd merely wanted to see him, but now I *have* to see him."

He frowned. "You have to stay here, and we have to deal with this."

She stilled. "Deal with it? What do you mean?" Her pulse throbbed.

Xander couldn't, wouldn't—

His braid danced when he shook his head. "I'm not cruel enough to suggest you end your—"

"Don't even *say* it," Alana snapped. "I won't do it." Tears threatened and she blinked, then hastily swiped at her cheeks. They remained dry. For now.

Her cousin sighed. "What're you going to do if Seamus goes to your father? He could be there right now. He didn't say he wouldn't."

"He didn't say he *would*, either."

"Your Highness—"

"Seamus has too much to lose—namely Scotland. He wants my father's throne too badly to give up the betrothal because of my…indiscretion." She flattened her palm on her lower stomach. "He'll keep the news to himself for now. He needs to plan and regroup."

Xander studied her. "You suddenly know your intended well."

"It's not sudden. I've known him for years."

He sighed. "You'd better hope you're right. *I* hope you're right." The alarm in his voice was still thick, and he flexed his wings.

"He can't kill me."

"Nay, he cannot wed a corpse."

She straightened and swallowed. "Nay, he cannot." Alana closed her eyes and took a breath. She didn't want to think about Seamus and marriage. She pushed off the bedpost still in her grip. "I need to go to Alex."

Her cousin cast his eyes to the ceiling. "I'll go with you."

"Are you sure you want to do that?"

"Aye, to ensure you come *right* back, so we can decide what to do about your idiot prince."

Alana scowled. "He's not *my* prince, and I want to *ensure* he goes to every level of Fae Hell."

Xander smirked and moved the hearth with a spell to reveal the secret passageway.

chapter twenty

She'd taken him to the cave of the Faery Stones, and when she'd not returned his kiss up on the ridge quite enthusiastically enough, Alana had felt Alex's nerves. She'd called him to their meeting spot hours early; it wasn't quite twilight.

He might be young, but he had good instincts, her love knew something was wrong.

Xander's presence when they were supposed to meet for lovemaking had probably given it away, if nothing else.

Alana had asked her cousin to stay on the beach, so she'd be alone with her laird, but she wasn't foolish enough to think they had true privacy. She could've cast a soundproofing spell, but it was smarter not to. Xander would worry.

Alex had taken the news about their child well. Her magic had told her he was happy, but his expression betrayed his nerves. Apprehension that was probably due to her double betrothal, as much as being a first-time father.

She tried not to wince at the guilt churning her gut. She busied her gaze with glancing over the Faery Stones. She was only a few feet from the crystals, and their magic called to hers, she could hear the humming in her head, and the main Stone brightened.

Alana would rather be on the beach with her cousin, the fresh sea wind on her face, even with the evening chill in the air. It would shuffle her hair and caress her in relieving waves. She loved sitting up on the ridge and watching the crashing waters smack into the rocky beach of Skye. It'd calmed her from the first time she'd waited for Alex up there.

"Ye will marry me now." His hard tone was unrelenting, and Alex made fists at his sides.

Her eyes shot back to his determination. Tears blurred her vision again, as if she'd never known any other existence. She couldn't focus on his demand, or how happy it truly made her. Alana was far from *free*. "Alex…"

He frowned, and her heart thumped.

Her love had no doubt misinterpreted her wet cheeks. She *wanted* to marry him, as she'd already agreed. More than *anything*. Despite the initial panic, she was happy she was carrying his child, too.

Alex crowded her, but his hands never wavered from his sides, as if he was afraid to reach for her, but Alana wanted nothing more.

"Now. No' next week, or in a fortnight, or a month from now, but *this day*. Ye will be my wife. Yer gonna birth my bairn as my *wife*."

She sucked in her bottom lip and ordered her wobbly emotions to every level of Fae Hell. Nothing worked. Her relief warred with her fear and the desperation to scream, *"Aye!"* and jump into his arms.

If Alana disappeared, Seamus *would* go to her father, and an army of Fae Warriors would come here.

Wipe out Clan MacLeod, her love along with the rest of his people.

"I cannot stay. Even as your wife." The words made her knees buckle, but when she was about to fall, her laird's hands shot out and supported her, then pinned her to his hard chest.

"Alana—"

"I've told you everything, Alex. Nothing has changed…I want to wed you more than anything, but I cannot run away. Seamus made vows, my love. Vows he will hold to, I promise you that."

His mouth crashed down on hers and she clung to him, to their fused lips.

Alana couldn't pull away from his kiss, but she shouldn't get lost in it, either. Yet, she didn't have the strength to deny the man she loved and gave herself over to the movement of his mouth over hers, how he possessed and gave at the same time.

He slanted down again, shoving his tongue into hers, and heat shot down her limbs, warmth settled low. Alex continued to kiss her until they were both trembling and restless.

Arousal was thick in the air, but they couldn't undress and be together, her cousin was too close, for one thing.

Alana panted and gripped him, trying to distract her mind from her singing pulse, thrumming body.

"I care no' *mò chridhe*," he breathed, resting his forehead against hers.

She shuddered, and fear shimmied down her spine, chasing away desire, despite the warmth of his chest and his arms around her. "You should."

"Nay," Alex whispered. "Yer mine. We're supposed ta be tagether. Now there's a bairn."

She swallowed. Oh, how she wanted to agree with him. "I love you," was all she could push out.

"I love ye, as well." He dipped down and kissed her again, this time achingly sweet and tender. Soft, and bearing his love for her.

Alex was holding her up; she wanted to burrow into him and never let go.

"So…you want this babe? You're not afraid of what it all means?" she whispered.

"Aye. I want ye both." He pressed his lips to her nose, then her forehead. "Yer both mine."

Alana whimpered and tightened her arms around his neck.

He rubbed her back in long soothing strokes and she melted into his every touch.

"Alana…" He sucked in air, pressing against her breasts even more.

"Alex…"

They stared at each other, and silence filled the cave.

She refused to shed more tears.

Alex was right, they *were* supposed to be together, and as he'd said, there was a child now.

They were having a child.

"Ye said we're fated, dinnae?"

"Aye." Her voice quaked. "I did. I believe we are. *You* are my fate, Alex MacLeod."

"Aye, as yer mine."

That was the third time he'd reminded her she belonged to him.

Perhaps, she'd needed to hear it.

Alana managed a smile, but it was tremulous.

"We will marry now, *mò chridhe*. Ye will be my wife. Taday."

Introductions were awkward, but not many questions were asked or answered as Alex's family gathered with them in the MacLeod chapel—save his sister and mother.

Janet would probably be cross with him later for missing his wedding, but she was keeping their mother company in her rooms.

Alex didn't know what she'd been told to keep her there, but only his brother and father had joined them in the chapel to be witnesses.

Explanations and answers would be for later—as well as revealing that he'd soon be a father. Due to her health, his mother couldn't be there to witness their nuptials, but she'd been happy when he'd told her he would soon marry. The day his father and sister had walked in on him and Duncan in his ledger room felt like months ago.

The same relief and delight had radiated in her eyes as when his stupid brother had told her he had a lass. Lady Caitriona couldn't wait to meet his wife.

Sorrow and joy mixed in his gut and forced his pulse to throb in his temples. Alana would be his wife this day, and the mother to his firstborn in the months to come, but she still couldn't stay with him.

Alex wanted to gather men, storm her realm, and slay the bastard prince that was keeping her from her proper place at his side.

If they were fated, perhaps it would all work itself out?

How? Reverberated in his head.

He refused to be desperate at the moment. He was about to be wed to the woman he loved, the love of his life.

Duncan cleared his throat, and his eyes landed on his twin.

Their father stood next to him, wringing his hands in front of his plaid-clad form. The older man's nerves were evident, making the same skitter down Alex's spine, and he fought a shiver.

He should feel crowded with their tall forms surrounding him next to the altar, but they were his family. It was right that they were present.

Neither looked pleased with the current circumstances, although Iain had been validated and quite smug that the Fae were actually real.

When he'd met Alana and Xander moments before, Alex's father had been quiet, as if hesitant to believe they were before him, and he couldn't gather words to speak. Then he'd blurted that there was Fae blood in their line.

Alana had smiled and nodded, before launching into a story about a Fae princess named Sima.

Iain's shoulders had loosened then, and he'd grinned triumphantly at both his sons. That happy sentiment had seemed to dissolve now as tension shot up, filling the usually peaceful space.

They didn't have time to share with him what they really thought about his wife-to-be or her cousin, but he was grateful neither had protested when he'd explained the marriage was to occur *now*.

Alex hadn't shed light on Alana's situation to anyone, not even his brother, and his family didn't know she couldn't stay in their realm after they'd exchanged vows.

They'd rushed the nearest priest to Dunvegan, and the portly balding man was currently on the dais scowling down at them. He had the Bible open, and his glare softened as he scanned the holy words he would soon recite.

Alex tried not to let Father Alban's displeasure make his nerves even worse. The older man was set in his ways, and he could only imagine what his twin had had to promise the codger to get him to come to Dunvegan in the evening on short notice to perform a wedding.

Movement at the chapel doors snagged his attention, but then his eyes were frozen on the most beautiful creature he'd ever seen.

She was walking toward them—to *him*—on Xander's arm.

Alana was still covered in purple, but she'd changed into a fancy gown with long flowing skirts, and a bodice that seemed to be covered in feathers stained the same rich dark hue—royal purple, of course.

The fabric shimmered and caught the candlelight

surrounding the raised altar and two steps, and it had a train that trailed behind her. Her shoulders were bare, and Alex had to suck in a growl of protest at her breasts, which were pushed high, on display.

Her hair had been bound and placed up, and she wore a glinting jeweled tiara atop her head.

She looked like…well, the princess she was.

So gorgeous his breath evaporated.

Mine.

Her smile was brilliant and made his heart stutter.

Alex bid himself to relax. If she could let go of her worries and fear, so could he.

This was his *wedding*.

It was supposed to be the happiest day of his life—and it *was*. He needed to hold that close and push all the negatives away.

They could—and would—deal with it all later.

He grabbed her hands when she reached for him and helped her step up in front of the priest.

"Alana?" Alex whispered.

"I couldn't very well marry you in trews and a cloak."

His brother chuckled and some of the tension lifted.

Alex let himself smile and leaned in to his betrothed. "Magic?" he said into her ear.

"Aye," she said back, and there was a twinkle in her violet eyes that matched the fabric of her pretty dress. Hopefully the priest wouldn't notice—or remark—on how unusual the gown's style was.

Alana's cousin hovered over her with a frown

firmly in place, but he took his position opposite Duncan and Iain beside the dais without a word.

Alex really wanted to dislike the tall fair-haired warrior, but Xander was fiercely protective of Alana, so he had to respect him. The few conversations they'd shared had showed him the stoic man was good, caring. He had no doubt of his skills as a warrior, either.

Father Alban cleared his throat and didn't bother asking if Xander was giving Alana to Alex. "Ye have no contract?" Disapproval coated his tone.

Alana's eyes locked onto his before they both shook their heads.

"I approve of tha union, Father," Iain said. "Just join them in tha eyes a' God."

Relief and gratitude for his father washed over him, and Alex released a breath.

Alana shot a look to the former laird, and mouthed, '*thank you*'.

Then she looked back at Alex, and he got lost in her eyes, her love, her joy. She was radiant.

She was about to be his.

Officially.

chapter twenty-one

alana rounded the corner, headed into the vast guest wing of her father's palace. Xander wasn't with her, but this time she didn't want her cousin there when she ordered Seamus to all five levels of Fae Hell in detail.

If only I could.

She had to be strong enough to face him alone. She prayed to the Goddess for a steady voice for this argument. She wasn't naïve enough to think seeing the prince would be a mild confrontation.

Alana had no bargaining material; she'd have to beg.

Seamus hadn't graced her with his presence in three days…since he'd dropped the information as sure as a blast-spell that she was carrying Alex's child.

Not seeing him had helped in some ways, she'd been able to think and calm, but it was also bad—she was paranoid he'd already told her father, despite her sure words to Xander that he still needed her. She'd been certain…at the time.

Doubt was her new reality. She'd woken in a cold sweat several times during the previous nights—terror had caused her to hear things, such as stomping boots of full Wings of Fae Warriors marching to her door.

She hadn't heard from any source—she'd asked

Rannick to inquire discreetly—that the Irish prince had had an audience with King Fillan, but then again, maybe it wouldn't be an official thing in his throne room. Alana was more frightened it would be—and had been—a small affair in private.

Her father had not summoned her, but she remained on edge, waiting for it to occur. He'd have her locked in the tower instead of her rooms. Or worse.

She told herself to breathe in and out slowly. She placed her hand over her stomach and was able to smile. Alex's child was with her, so even if her new husband wasn't, she had a piece of him to draw strength from.

They were married now. Of course, only by human traditions, but according to Alex's God, their union could not be torn asunder. That should give her strength, too, but it made her more petrified.

Seamus is going to be so angry if he finds out.

'Keeping' her human certainly hadn't allowed for marriage, let alone the babe that her lover had gifted her. Then again, after her indiscretion had come to light, it would only be natural for Seamus to demand she stop seeing Alex, since she'd failed to do so 'responsibly'. She wouldn't, of course, and she'd have to avoid getting caught—again.

For now, their child was safe inside her, but only because she was masked in special magic. It'd taken a trip to the archives to find the right spells. Eirini would never betray her, but Alana's questions had been inconspicuous until she'd found the right scrolls.

She couldn't go to a healer, they would sense her child's sire was of another race with one touch, and the royal healers held nothing sacred above her father, so a report to the king would be immediate.

Xander's mother had healing magic, so he had it in his blood even though it was far from his main magical gift. He'd helped her with the elaborate spell, but it'd taken a lot out of them both. She'd slept most of the day afterward, and no doubt her cousin had done the same.

Alana could only hope—and pray—the magic was strong enough to cover her for the entirety of her pregnancy. She would not be able to give birth in her realm. As soon as the child was born, danger became death sentence.

She sucked back a breath, and her chest heaved. There were so many things she still didn't know how they could move past. *If* they could. *When* they could be together in his realm. *If* they could.

After the short ceremony officiated by the grumpy priest, Xander had whisked her away—Alana and Alex had not been able to consummate their vows. She'd plastered her new husband with as many kisses as she could steal, then had had to leave him standing up on the ridge where they always met.

Alana had not seen inside his home—the castle Dunvegan, nor had she been in more than the small courtyard that lead to the chapel on MacLeod grounds. She ached to see more of his world, and to *remain* in it.

She'd meet him tonight and be with him again. She could ask the numerous questions swirling in her mind, including about his brother who looked so much like him, but seemed so different, even at just a glance and brief introduction.

Alana hadn't gotten to meet his sister, but she already liked his father very much, and couldn't wait until she'd be free to converse with the older man. It was amusing that Iain MacLeod was actually a few years her junior, but looking into the eyes that matched Alex's told her how her husband would likely appear when he reached the same age.

He—and his twin—looked very much like their father.

The noise of a door closing ahead in the wide corridor had her glancing up.

Alana stilled, because it was her destination, and who she was seeing at the exit didn't make any sense. She startled when he turned toward her, so she muttered a quick invisibility spell, and glued herself to the wall before he could look at her.

What's a Scottish *Fae Warrior doing here?*

She memorized his face, because she didn't know his name, but the epaulet on the shoulder of his green breastplate marked him the leader of a Wing of Warriors. He was tall and ebony-haired, with yellow eyes like Rannick's. His build was typical to the soldiers, broad shouldered and well-muscled. His wings were folded, plastered low, as if he was also aware he couldn't get caught in the guest wing. He would've done better to make himself invisible, but perhaps he didn't have much magic. Some Warriors were more brawn.

Alana tried to read his emotions, but they weren't overt, as if he was covered in some mild stealth spell— which would make sense if he was up to no good. She narrowed her eyes and watched him hurry past her, around the corner from the same direction she'd come.

He wasn't a messenger, her father didn't use Warriors in that capacity, and he certainly wasn't Irish, as his uniform was Scottish. His plait had been down to his waist—indicating he had a place of prestige amongst his brothers.

"So, what are you doing here, sir?" she whispered to the empty hallway. She would see Xander as soon as she was finished with Seamus and identify the soldier. Her gut told her his presence with her would-be-husband couldn't be good.

Perhaps Alana had some newborn leverage over Seamus after all?

She cleared her throat and hurried to the door.

Surprise washed over his expression when she answered his call to enter, but he schooled his expression and frowned. "Why are *you* here?"

Thankfully he was dressed this time, his green doublet elegantly embroidered, and his trews a mixture of green and gold-spun threading that made them shine. His wide-sleeved under tunic was ivory and of the finest material.

Alana smirked and curtseyed. "I cannot visit my betrothed? Good morning to you too, Your Highness." Her heart skipped but she tried to hold onto the guise that she was the one in control with both hands. Should she ask about the soldier?

Seamus paused and gave her a onceover. Then he started to pace and mutter how ridiculous she was.

She swallowed and smoothed her gown as she took

a seat on the gilded sofa in his sitting area. As her room had been decorated in colors she loved, this one was all green and gold, no doubt to the prince's preferences, even though he wasn't a permanent resident—unless they actually married.

Alana crossed her legs and rested her hands on her lap while he continued to move around the furniture with a pattern of jerky steps.

Seamus' voice got louder, his accusations more vile.

Alana squared her shoulders and waited. She'd hold her tongue about the Fae Warrior for now, until she could corner him. She'd rarely seen Seamus lose his temper, and at another time, she might've been amused.

He paused in his rant and pinned her with his emerald gaze. "I do not sense it."

"What?"

"The filth inside you. Did you get rid of it?"

Alana blinked.

Should I lie?

Her mind-shields were strongly engaged, so she'd get away with it if she declared, *'aye'*. Would it help her situation?

Of course, there were magical ways—if one went to an obliging healer—to end an unwanted pregnancy, but she'd never do such a thing, even if she didn't love her babe's sire.

My husband.

Most healers were too gentle spirited to agree to perform such a spell, but of course there were always some. Like in most situations, gold and jewels were sufficient motivators, and Alana didn't have a shortage of either.

"You're not touching me, how could you sense anything?" she tried to deflect instead, arching an eyebrow at her nemesis.

It *was* good to know the magic Xander had helped her put in place was working. Seamus had confirmed her pregnancy wouldn't be discovered now.

He narrowed his eyes but came no closer. "Trust me, it's not something I could forget the *feeling* of."

Alana released a humorless laugh. "Oh, Seamus, this is just me. You and I alone, you don't have to pretend to be offended."

The prince let out a breath that made her heart skip.

What's he playing at?

He couldn't actually be *hurt*—she'd never imagined him capable.

Alana had never pretended interest in him, in all the years he'd chased her. There'd been no illusions in their…arrangement.

He'd backed her into a corner; made vows he'd slaughter the MacLeods to get her to sign the betrothal agreement. She would've never agreed otherwise. That wasn't a mystery to *him*, either.

Was Seamus bothered that he'd failed to gain her as a conquest?

Should I bring up the soldier, now?

She rose and skimmed her hand along the back of a chair and closed the distance between them.

The prince all but recoiled.

Alana stilled. Bit back a smile. "What's this? You

don't want to touch me?" Since their betrothal had been made public, he'd rarely kept his hands to himself, to the point she'd slapped him whenever they'd had no witnesses. At first chance she'd gotten. Every. Time. He always laughed, as if the move delighted him to no end.

Seamus scowled. "You're tainted."

She giggled, couldn't help it. Her smile was genuine. "You told me I could keep my human. You didn't consider we were lovers? What purpose would he serve me otherwise?" A man like Seamus wouldn't understand love, so she didn't mention emotional ties. Plus, it would only mark Alex as her weakness in one more way for him to use against her later.

The prince glowered but said nothing.

"You mentioned discretion; you did not say I could not give myself to him."

Her *betrothed's* eyes shot to hers like daggers, and he made a noise in his throat.

Alana caressed the soft upholstery of the chair suggestively, as if touching a man's bare chest. She grinned when he scowled. "Besides, with no experience, how can I please you in bed? You should thank my *human* lover."

Seamus bristled, pitched forward and made tight fists at his sides. "That is *enough.*"

She bit her bottom lip to keep from beaming at his growl. Cautioned herself to put an end to taunting him, because even if she had some new unspoken fuel, the prince was nothing to be trifled with.

Alana should tread lightly, even if she was enjoying herself. "Oh, all right. I suppose we can discuss something else." She waited until he'd met her gaze again. "Would you like to tell me what a Scottish Fae Warrior was doing leaving your suite?"

His eyes widened ever-so-slightly, but he schooled his expression fast—too fast. "I know not of what you speak."

"Perhaps I'm mistaken."

He watched her as she rounded the chair and plopped down in it, then crossed her legs again and rested her hands on her bent knee.

Seamus blew out a breath and sat across from her, mirroring her posture, and sat up very straight. "To what do I *really* owe this little assignation, Alana?" His tone was guarded, and those green eyes were too tight for polite conversation.

She must be getting to him, because he hadn't mocked her by calling her '*my love*' or '*sweet princess*'.

"Did you come to tell me you'd taken care of your little indiscretion?" he asked before she could answer.

Should Alana confirm?

The magic would help her hide her pregnancy; now she had no worries about that. Perhaps it would lessen his leverage on her about Alex. She could even tell him she'd given him up, and Seamus would have no reason to run to her father.

She went for a regal expression, but then tried to appear aggrieved and hiding it. "Aye," she whispered. "I'm not a fool, 'twas for the best."

Seamus studied her, then nodded. "'Tis for the best," he echoed.

Alana   snorted.   "Don't   console   me,   Your

Highness."

He cocked his head to one side, still appraising her. Moments ticked by before he spoke. "I...this is unexpected."

"What else could I do, really?" She swallowed and blinked so her eyes would water. Averted her gaze, and swiped at her cheeks, as if she couldn't stop crying.

"I assumed you would hold to your human until I pried him away from you." His gaze was still shrewd, unapologetic.

Evil wretch.

"I'm not that selfish, Seamus. I won't put his clan at risk, because of you. It's..." She made her voice wobble, "over." Alana called herself a selfish liar for denying Alex and their child, but it would ensure their survival—and protect all the MacLeods from the bastard's wrath.

She could only pray it would work.

"I am pleased."

She tried not to wince. She told herself again, *this plan is for the best.*

"I'm glad you came to tell me." Her *betrothed* had the nerve to smile now, but he still didn't reach for her.

Alana tried not to give into another smirk.

I guess I'm still tainted.

"Is there anything else?" Seamus asked after a new silence fell.

She drummed her fingertips on her knee. Until she'd seen the *Scottish* winged soldier exiting his room, she'd come to beg. Now that her ruse was in place to protect what she loved, Alana didn't need to bluff him about the Warrior. Nor would she.

Maybe she could have *him* trapped for a change.

Alana leaned forward. "I know you're up to something. More than wheedling a betrothal agreement out of me. There's more to your plan, Prince Seamus of the Irish Fae. You and I both know there's no reason for one of my father's Warriors to be in your rooms."

To his credit, Seamus didn't flinch or look surprised, nor did he look threatened, like she'd wanted. He appeared proud of himself; it was plain from the jut of his chin and how he straightened his shoulders.

Maybe she should've allowed Xander to accompany her and held Seamus in his seat by swordpoint. Demand the prince loosen his lips, lest he be run through. However, she wasn't stupid, and she didn't need her cousin's help, even if a part of her would love to see her *betrothed* bloodied.

The presence of a soldier from *her* Court in *his* rooms could only mean her suspicions about his ambitions weren't just a concern.

He didn't plan to gain two thrones through marriage and letting their fathers' reigns run their natural courses.

Seamus was plotting with her own people.

To kill my father?

He didn't have to confirm—not that he would.

Instinct told her there was more to his scheme.

Alana would have to watch and wait.

chapter twenty-two

The babe in her arms made everything worth it. Although she did worry about Xander, and the situation in the Field of Light, but he'd shouted at her to go. She'd have to trust that he'd handled the other Fae Warriors, and used whatever magic was called for.

Besides, it wasn't like Alana had had a choice. Her son had been demanding, and as it was, she'd barely made it to the Human Realm before he'd made his appearance.

Alex sniffled, as if he was trying not to cry, and she looked up into her husband's face, unable to keep the smile off her own.

She'd have to leave the tiny lad with him, but she didn't want to focus on that. For now, she'd hold and nurse her son while her husband had them both wrapped in his strong arms on the loamy floor of the Cave of the Faery Stones.

They sat on a fresh MacLeod plaid, and Alana was clad in a clean chemise, compliments of Alex's sister. Their location was modest, but she'd never been happier.

She'd only met Janet MacLeod a few times, but the lass was loving and sweet, and she'd done a fantastic job helping to deliver the babe. In many ways, she was a warrior like her brothers.

Alana had called out to Alex mentally, clutching her contracting stomach when she'd stumbled through the portal. His brother, father, and sister had come with him and brought supplies, and had stayed for their son's birth.

She'd had to lift the magic obscuring the cave; she never would've made it up to the ridge. *Blinking* during pregnancy could be dangerous, and she'd been in too much pain to concentrate enough for it anyway.

Before Alana left, she'd put her spells back and place and the MacLeods would all forget the location of the Faery Stones, even though they'd all been inside the cave.

His family had quietly receded to give them privacy, but Alex's very brave sister was close by with swaddling and a basket to take their babe when the time came, so they could go on with the ruse they had to carry out to protect them all.

Their tiny halfling would be placed at the massive gates of Dunvegan, with a note that Alex MacLeod was his sire, and his mother expected him to be '*taken in*' by his blood.

It didn't sit well that her husband's clan would assume her child was the bastard of a whore, but they had no choice…yet. No one but his immediate family knew of Alana or their marriage.

"Jesu, he's beautiful." Alex's stubbled cheek rubbed hers as he held her closer, her back plastered to his chest. He rocked her gently as the baby suckled and caressed their son's downy dark head, a soft smile curving his lush mouth. His voice was thick with emotion and made her eyes sting.

"I love him so much. And I love you." Her voice broke and her husband kissed her temple.

"I know, *mò chridhe*. I love ye both as well. My heart his full." His last sentence was whispered, as if he'd not wanted to be overheard.

"What'll we call him?"

"Angus, after my grandda?" Alex asked.

"Angus MacLeod." Alana tested the name on her tongue. "I like it." She smiled.

"'Tis a good, braw name."

"Raise him right, my love." She swallowed a sob as the words broke and sorrow descended.

"Alana." Her name was all fierce warning.

She shook her head as Alex leaned back so he could look into her face.

He wore a frown. "Alana, I need ye."

"I know." She bit her bottom lip to keep it from wobbling and blinked to clear her vision.

They'd talked, argued, shouted about what she had to do dozens of times. Alex would declare he understood one moment and rage about it the next, promising to slay Seamus himself. They'd both cry, hold each other and make love, but there was no light at the end of the tunnel.

Alana still had to return to the Fae Realm.

Now leaving behind her child.

In the months following her witnessing the Scottish Fae Warrior leaving Seamus' quarters, Xander hadn't discovered much. He agreed that the Irish prince was plotting, and like her, assumed it was to vie for the throne, but their quiet investigations hadn't yielded any fruit.

Her cousin was keeping an eye on the Wingleader, whose name was Tamhas, but his dealings with the prince were still very much unknown, as well as how many others conspired with them. They were smart and had magic on their side. She'd not caught them together again, either.

"I dinnae raise him alone." Alex cupped Angus' head in one large hand and caressed his son's little ear with a calloused thumb.

Alana swallowed and sniffled. "You're *not* alone. You have Duncan, and your father. Janet will do well by Angus; I feel it in my gut." Again, her sentence quivered. She was about to leave her newborn in the care of a lass who'd just turned six and ten. Even if Janet was mature, she was still a child.

"I feel as if I've lost ye again," her husband whispered.

"You've *never* lost me, Alex MacLeod. And you never will." She pinned him with a glare, but he was staring at their son.

The light of the Faery Stones glowed behind them, brightening the area, and making his sable locks seem lighter. The crystals called to her magic, and to the magic she sensed in the small body of her son. He would likely have a strong draw to the Stones, like her.

The apple of Alex's throat bobbed. "I ken nothin' about carin' fer a bairn."

"It's a good thing there are female MacLeods."

He met her gaze, and a smile rippled his lips.

At least her attempt at lightening their very serious situation hadn't missed its mark.

She was glad her remark hadn't upset him. Alana wouldn't mention the loss of his mother; it was too fresh, and from what she understood, a long time in coming. She wished she could've helped with healing magic, but some ailments, Fae and Human alike, couldn't be cured. She wasn't much of a healer anyway, although she did know a few spells. Her magic didn't seem diminished in the Human Realm like her cousin's, but powers that didn't come naturally were.

Weeks ago, the day after Lady Caitriona passed, her husband had expressed sadness his mother would never see their child, and Alana had comforted him as best she could. It'd been so long since Alana had lost her own mother, but she remembered the pain and often thought of her.

Her father would never see Angus, either.

To protect him.

Hopefully, even though her husband, his siblings, and father had lost a beloved family member, welcoming the new babe—son, nephew and grandson would ease them in some way.

"Thank ye fer my son, *mò chridhe*. But I wish ye were goin' home with us." His voice was thick again, broken.

Alana's heart plummeted to her gut and burned. "I wish I could. You have to know that."

"I do," Alex whispered. "But it dinnae soften tha blow."

She crushed her eyes shut. She didn't want to

bicker with him, wasting the remaining time they had together. It was going to slay her to walk away from Angus, even if he was safe with his father, aunt and grandfather. Even Duncan would be there for her laddie.

As her husband had said, none of that knowledge softened the blow.

"I'm sorry," Alex croaked. "I know dinnae be easy fer ye. Anamore than 'tis fer me."

Alana stared down at the perfect creature nuzzling her breast. "It's harder. *I* carried him for all these months. Felt him moving inside me—" Her voice broke on a sob and her husband squeezed her against him.

She'd felt Angus' magic growing with him and thought about teaching him everything he'd need to know. Then she cried over what she'd miss, since her son would be with his father in the Human Realm and any visits, she made would be the same stolen hours she'd had to manage since she'd met her husband.

No one else could teach Angus about his powers, or how to control them, so Alana would have to do her best with limited time.

Alex fired off a string of comfort and love in Gaelic, right above her ear and she fought shudders, but was grateful for his physical warmth at her back, of his arms around her.

How was she going to survive this?

"I want ta kill tha' bastard."

"If only you could. Xander feels the same, but we just can't. We need to figure out what he's planning. Since I confronted him, he's been even more guarded."

"Ye know nothin' more?"

Alana shook her head. "I've been very lucky he still doesn't want to touch me, and the magic Xander helped me put in place remained all this time. Hid Angus and my huge belly."

Alex growled. "He'd better nay lay his hands on ye."

She smiled and kissed him lightly. "You have nothing to be jealous of, my love."

Her husband rumbled—something she heard and felt in her shoulders.

"I'm tainted. Perhaps *you* are the reason Seamus has not mentioned nary a word about when we shall marry. Our fathers haven't finalized their negotiations, but the prince is not nearly as eager for them to do so. He hasn't tried to coax me to his bed or come near me in some time."

"'Tis tha' supposed ta comfort me?" He smirked.

She giggled. "Of course."

He grumbled, but a smile rippled his mouth.

Alana shifted their son to her other breast, and he fussed until he latched onto her nipple. She soothed him with soft words in Fae, which Alex echoed above her ear in Gaelic.

She smiled and settled back into his chest, clenching her jaw to stave away negative emotions. She didn't want to go. *Ever.*

"My place is here with you and Angus," she whispered.

Alex didn't speak, but she heard his quick intake of breath.

"I mean, I don't see my fate being the Queen of the Scottish Court. But Seamus will not be a good king. My father is fierce and can be bloodthirsty, but he's a good king, Alex. Seamus' father is also a good king. I'm actually fond of him. I can't abandon my people to Seamus. I have to find out what he's up to, and tell my father, but I cannot do so until I have proof. If my father banishes or executes him for treason, his threat to the MacLeods would have no power. Only then will I be free."

She heard him swallow next to her ear and let him turn her face so he could kiss her. It was a light brush of his mouth on hers, but it still made her heart skip.

"I understand," Alex pushed the words against her lips.

Alana closed her eyes and let him deepen the kiss.

Watching her go nearly buckled his knees, but Alex forced himself to remain upright and not cling too hard to the small bundle against his chest. He looked down at the sleeping babe in his arms and his breath caught.

Fragile. Gorgeous.

His son needed him.

Perhaps all parents thought their new child perfect, but his son was a mix of Alana's beauty and his own features, down to his dark hair, little nose, and big blue eyes.

How was he going to do this on his own?

Alex needed his wife by his side.

"Alex?" Janet's soft voice came from behind him, and his sister sidled up to him and touched his hand. "Are you ready?"

Nay.

Alana was gone, so he'd never be ready.

"Aye, lass," he whispered and gently transferred little Angus to Janet's arms.

His sister quickly swaddled him in an ivory wool blanket and put him in the basket. Under his tiny form, she placed a scrap of MacLeod plaid and the note written in Alana's hand.

Alex's name was scrawled on the outside of it, and looking at it tightened his gut. He swallowed.

"Dinnae fash," Janet said. "Cousin Cormac will find him soon, an' I've already readied tha nursery."

A room he and his brother had shared as wee ones, but he remembered when his sister had joined them as a tiny infant. They'd been seven years old.

Alex hugged his sister when she straightened. "Thank ye, Janey."

Their gazes brushed and the understanding in her blue eyes just about slayed him. She was too young to be that mature. Her childhood had been stolen for over three years now.

"All will be well, brother. I promise." A small smile carved her mouth when she looked down at the basket between them.

His heart skipped for a different reason. Janet had taken their mother's passing harder than he or his twin, so to see the grief lift from her pretty face even a little bit was a relief. His son was a blessing for many reasons.

"He is a bonnie, braw bairn."

"Aye, like his mother." Alex's voice cracked, but he couldn't hold his emotions back. Like he'd told Alana, he felt like he'd lost her.

His sister reached for his forearm and squeezed. "I'll take him now. See you a' home?"

"Aye."

Janet nodded and smiled; this time wider. She pushed to her toes and planted a kiss on his cheek.

Her floral soap teased his nose, and her hair brushed his face, tickled.

She lifted the basket, and Alex watched until she was gone.

"Lad?"

He glanced over his shoulder to see the tired lines in his father's face, but he smiled for the man who'd supported him without question from the moment he'd found out about Alana. "I dinnae be able ta do this alone, Da."

Iain squeezed his forearm, much like his sister had. "Yer no' alone, lad. Ye have Duncan and Janey. An' me. As long as there's a MacLeod, yer ne'er alone, and neither will yer bairn be."

Alex nodded and looked down at the rocky sand covering the beach. The familiar disorientation scrambled his brain when he studied the area below the ridge and thought about the Faery Stones. He knew *of* them, but to protect them all, Alana made it so he couldn't remember where they were or what they looked like. Trying to remember made his head hurt.

Like something locked in the back of his mind, there but hazy.

"I ken it, Da, and I am grateful. 'Tis just…I feel as if I've lost her."

Sorrow darted across his father's face and drew his graying eyebrows tight.

Guilt hit Alex's gut and spread up his chest. Alana was just somewhere else. His father had lost his wife to the hereafter. At least Alex and his tiny son would see Alana again. Hold her again. "I'm sorry, Da." His voice cracked.

Iain's smile was sad. "'Tis no worry, my lad. Ye dinnae lose your wife, no' like I lost mine. Remember tha'. Hold onta her while ye can. Someday soon, Alana will be where she's supposed ta be. In tha meantime, care fer yer laddie, he needs ye as much as ye need him."

Alex smiled and clapped his father's shoulder. "Ye need him, too, I suspicion."

For the first time, the older man's smile was more natural, open. "I do. 'Twill be good ta hear tha laughter and joy of a bairn a' Dunvegan again. With yer mother…ill, we dinnae get ta laugh nearly enough. But I worry o'er yer laddie's name."

Alex frowned. "Why, Da?"

The twinkle was back in his father's tired blue eyes. "My da could be a mean git. Hopin' yer lad will be more like *ye* than him."

He chuckled. "I remember Grandda fondly."

His father laughed. "Ye knew of him less years than I."

Alex shook his head, but he couldn't stop grinning.

It felt good to laugh with his father.

"I shall always miss your mother," Iain whispered, breaking their companionable silence.

"I know, Da. I loved her, too. An' I'll miss her as weel. I'll tell Angus how bonnie she was, dinnae fash o'er tha'."

The older man's eyes went misty, but he still wore a soft smile. "Come, lad, let us go have some ale in the hall. 'Tis a man's proper place when a babe comes."

Alex chuckled again. "Ye jus' need an excuse ta fall inta yer cups."

"Nay, son, I ne'er need an excuse fer tha'." His father beamed.

He shook his head and gestured for Iain to lead the way to their waiting mounts. With one glance back at the waves, Alex was able to give another smile. He had a feeling his wee laddie would carry the light of his mother inside him. He didn't have to worry about Angus at all.

chapter twenty-three

Alana always cried. No matter how long she spent with her husband and son, leaving always *gutted her*, as Alex would say.

Angus changed before her eyes, always bigger, always older. So beautiful, her lad; like his father in miniature. Her fear that he wouldn't know her was never realized.

Thank the Goddess.

He always opened his arms and yelled for her. Rushed into her embrace from the first time he was able and hugged her just as tightly as she did him.

Angus was getting so big, and except for stolen days, Alana missed everything.

The passing years were trying on them all, but she still didn't see the end. Didn't know when she could finally *be* with them.

She'd been able to use the excuse to Xander of Angus coming into his magic to stay longer occasionally, so they could train. Her cousin agreed she needed to teach him control, but it wasn't enough. It would *never* be enough until she could flee her realm and live at Dunvegan as was her right.

As soon as Seamus was brought to justice.

Her husband always told her his bed would be cold until she could join him in it, and even though he'd never meant to hurt her, things like that made her ache.

Keeping the secret, protecting her family was never more important. Alana kept constant watch on Seamus, ensuring he didn't make a move against her, or her father. He'd been plotting with Tamhas, but they hadn't made a move, yet.

They hadn't been able to prove there were others working with them, but that could've been the reason they hadn't acted — as much as Seamus' fear that she and Xander knew what he was up to.

Alana and her cousin stalked quietly, investigated, and shared what they'd discovered with no one. The prince continued to grow closer to her father, spending more and more time at the Scottish Court.

In recent years, he'd rarely gone home to Ireland, and his father only came for celebrations. Now he was acting as Ireland's ambassador officially, replacing the Irish noble who'd held the post. With his appointment, the prince had permanent residence in her father's palace, so he really wasn't going away.

Alana had hidden her son and husband all these years, and Seamus assumed she'd given Alex up, as she'd told him only days after he'd told her she was carrying her lad.

She'd sulked appropriately when she'd been around him, and the sadness was real, so she didn't have to fake her emotions.

The prince wouldn't forgive any other indiscretion, so she had to hold tight to her secrets so he wouldn't find out she'd married the laird and given birth to Angus.

She and Alex had been careful after their son; they couldn't have another child until she could join them permanently, but she did want more children. When she could keep them, raise them. Wipe and kiss away minor hurts, spend more than a day at a time with them and their father.

Alana wouldn't survive another pregnancy where she had to walk away without the babe she'd carried.

Her husband and his family were raising her lad well, but nothing cured the hole in her heart for all Angus' firsts she'd missed.

She sighed and let the earthy scent of the tunnels envelope her. She didn't expect to run into anyone in the secret passageway but couldn't afford even the lowest servant to see her upset, no matter where she could encounter them.

Alana hadn't had alone time with Alex, and they hadn't made love in what felt like months, instead of the fortnight or so it was, so she had another jaunt planned to meet him at night.

She shivered. Kissing her husband was rarely enough. She wanted him, seared for him. Alana needed his hands on her, needed him inside her.

Xander, I'm back, she called to her cousin mentally.

Alana hoped he'd meet her in her rooms. He always asked her a bevy of questions about her son, and she was eager to share what Angus had accomplished during their lesson today. They'd spent time together over the years, and the lad idolized Xander, but her cousin hadn't seen Angus in a while.

Like her, he had the ability to *blink,* but she was

teaching him to control it, focus on where he was jumping to, and how to get there. They were using static points on the beach for now, and his skill was impressive for a lad of nine. He didn't seem to struggle to access his magic like many Fae in the Human Realm, but perhaps that was due to him being half from his father's world, and half from hers.

Angus' blue eyes and happy smile dominated her thoughts as she rounded the natural corridor. Alana only had about twenty feet until her last turn; the spiral staircase that led to her sleeping room would be visible.

Heavy boot-steps had her pausing, but she couldn't see whoever it was just yet.

"Xander?" Perhaps her cousin had decided to meet her.

"Guess again, sweet princess."

Ice slid down her spine and Alana started to pant. She couldn't move.

What was the Irish prince doing here?

How did he even know about the tunnels?

Worse, she had no plausible explanation for being down here, so what would she tell him when he questioned her?

Seamus sauntered into view, dressed pristinely in green as always. "I suspected you were up to something—" The snide smirk fell off his mouth and melted into something dark. He didn't come closer, but his fury hit her empathic magic with so much force Alana winced.

Her hands rose of their own accord to stave him off, although the prince made no move to strike her.

"Who is Angus, and why does he look shockingly like a human you *ended* your indiscretions with *years* ago?" he demanded.

Panic slithered around her limbs and torso like the snake of a prince in front of her, constricting her breathing. Her mind-shields had been lowered, weak, and Alana had pictured her beautiful son—the exact moment she'd heard footfalls on the earthen floor.

Oh Goddess, no.

Seamus had plucked Angus' face from her thoughts, as well as his name.

He knew.

It's my fault.

Her heart shot to her toes in a cold flush. She reengaged her mental defenses, but it was too late. Alana swallowed and tried to brace herself for whatever he was about to say.

Or *do*.

They were alone.

The sense of danger—real terror for her wellbeing—joined her panic and grief, swirling around her.

"You lied to *me*," Seamus barked. "*Lied* for years. *Years*." He stalked to her, towered over her, and all Alana could do was stare into the rage in his expression. His face was crimson, and spittle gathered at the corners of his mouth.

"Seamus—"

"Nay. You do *not* get to speak. How did you manage it? You *hid* a filthy half-blooded child?" His voice dropped. Deeper. Deadly. "A filthy halfling who did not deserve to be born!"

Fear froze her in place and all Alana could do was stare.

Xander! I need you. I...I'm in trouble. He knows everything. Cornered me in the tunnels. She could only pray her cousin heard her mental shout.

Seamus was angry enough to harm her.

Kill her?

His damn magic-proof medallion glared from his neck, as if taunting her to try to defend herself. It jerked and danced with his livid gestures.

"You *will* answer for this."

"Wh-what will you do?" Her voice was barely a whisper, but she already knew the answer.

Seamus would go to her father.

Without delay.

Would her suspicions of *his* plot save her life? Her husband and son's?

Alana fought the urge to crush her eyes shut or double over and sob. She couldn't afford to take her eyes off her nemesis.

The prince had just gained the upper hand again, in the most dangerous way possible.

The *clanking* sounds of metal on metal, like armor, then rushing boots made Alex scan his surroundings. He was up on the ridge, where he was supposed to meet Alana.

Their lad had an uncanny ability to just *know* when

his mother was coming, so he'd had to wait until Angus had gone to bed, lest he have to deal with his son's upset that this trip was just for Alex and his princess. He'd feared he'd be late, but it seemed his wife was the tardy one.

They hadn't made love in what felt like forever, and he was aching to get his hands on her, hold her close, taste her mouth again, hear her scream his name while she came around him.

Alex should be able to see anything coming at him from his vantage point, but the sounds were as if being made by ghosts. He shuddered for reasons other than the desire riding beneath the surface of his skin.

What he heard but couldn't see didn't make sense.

The beach before him was lit by a full moon. He heard and *saw* the waves crashing against the shore, but the sounds of the rushing feet didn't manifest in his line of sight.

He tensed anyway and drew his sword.

As if from nowhere, a group of men *appeared* around him on the ridge. They hadn't ascended from the beach; he would've *seen* their climb.

What the hell?

Bán, who grazed behind him, tossed his head back and whinnied. He didn't run off, for which Alex was grateful, but his stallion was showing the surprise he was eager to not reveal to his new companions.

The dozen men assembled around him and his mount, who was now hoofing the ground and snorting.

Perfect. No escape.

"Easy, lad," he murmured, but he wouldn't mind

if Bán chose to charge. Maybe knock a few of them over and open up a path for him to retreat through.

His horse nickered at the sound of his voice but kept hoofing the dirt.

Alex gripped and re-gripped his sword, darting his gaze around the men. They were all tall and broad. Looked as if they knew how to use the weapons they brandished. He couldn't see their faces, since they all wore helms, but he imagined hard expressions.

They all wore armor, like Xander's, but gold, instead of dark green.

Fae Warriors?

Like his wife's cousin, no wings were visible, but his gut told him he was looking at a full Wing—what the Fae called each unit—of elite soldiers.

Awareness shot down his spine and he forgot to breathe.

After all this time, had they been discovered?

Where was Alana?

Were these men the reason his wife was late to their assignation?

Is she all right?

His heart slid to his feet, but he couldn't be foolish. Needed to pay attention to what was before him. Alex straightened when two soldiers parted to allow someone within the circle.

The man had dark wavy hair dancing over his shoulders in the evening breeze. He was dressed in green armor, but it was elaborate, with gold leafing all over it that glinted in the moonlight. He had a sword in his hand to match Alex's in size, but it wasn't raised to defend, it was along his side — at least at the moment.

He had a torch in the other hand, but the fire dancing atop it couldn't be natural. It was multi-colored; reds, blues, purples, and even yellows, skirting around each other, and a sweet aroma tickled Alex's nose.

He raised his claymore when the man approached. Instinct whispered he needed to be on his guard around this man.

"Alex MacLeod, I presume?"

The Irish inflection made him narrow his eyes. It was refined, like the man's never-been-marked-upon armor.

"Seamus," Alex spat.

The bastard who was keeping his wife under his thumb smiled, slow and wide, as if to welcome him. He didn't seem to be bothered that Alex didn't greet him with a title or any kind of respect. "Ah, I'm so glad my reputation precedes me."

"Where's Alana?" he demanded.

"Oh, don't you worry your wee head over our princess."

Our princess?

"What've ye done with *my* wife?" Alex growled.

The prince's smile fell off, replaced with a scowl. "I should kill you right now."

"Try it." Alex rushed forward, leading with his sword.

Seamus tossed the torch and lifted his large weapon in what seemed the same motion, readying himself for Alex's strike at an unnatural speed.

Magic?

No matter, he couldn't—wouldn't—give it a second thought.

He had an Irish Fae prince to kill.

Their swords came together with a *clash* that resounded in his ears—and his arms. The bastard was surprisingly strong and pushed Alex back with deceiving ease.

Bán reared up on his back legs and screamed. The men nearest obviously didn't want to be victim to kicking feet and pounding hooves, so they parted and released his stallion from the circle.

Alex cursed and rushed Seamus again. His ride had fled, but perhaps arriving back home without him would raise the alarm. He'd told Duncan of his plans to see Alana this night. Hopefully his brother wouldn't laugh at the horse's appearance and assume the stallion had abandoned him for being ignored.

He willed his twin to know something was very wrong, wishing he could call to him mentally like Alana could.

"You're no match for me, human filth." The prince circled him, but put his palm out, beckoning.

"Dinnae be so sure, ye bastard," Alex growled and gave him what he asked for, darting to him and slashing his sword.

They parried each other, moving forward and back like a dance.

Alex was taller, but they were well-matched, and he couldn't deny the scoundrel had skill. He stalked around him, regrouping before he lifted his sword again and charged his prey.

Seamus evaded, but not fast enough. The tip of Alex's weapon sank into the gap of his armor, at his shoulder.

A murmur went through the watching Warriors, but the prince raised his other arm to stop any defensive action from them. He didn't cry out in pain, or curse, but Alex had cut him. Blood glinted on his breastplate.

He widened his stance, ready for another strike, and Seamus stared him down with narrowed eyes the same color as his armor.

The prince extended his palm high and flat and muttered something, but Alex couldn't make it out.

He took a step back.

His opponent frowned but started speaking louder. It was some kind of chant.

A bright blue ball of light appeared from nowhere and flew at Alex.

He didn't have time to dodge; it hit him square in the chest, knocking him over.

Agony exploded between his pectoral muscles, then jolted his limbs straight and burned its way downward, until he couldn't move. His muscles wouldn't respond to any command. Nor could he feel the ground beneath him, but the little points of light in the sky told him he was looking *up*, into the starry night.

The wretched cheat!

Seamus couldn't beat him fair and square with a sword, he'd used whatever his powers were?

Alex's brain processed he'd been hit with magic of some kind, but his mind was slowing, his eyes growing heavy. "Coward," he spat, but instead of the shout he'd intended, his voice hadn't been much louder than a whisper.

Then, the world went black.

chapter twenty-four

a crowd was gathering in the throne room, as if every resident of Court had been summoned, but they were all gossipmongers, so it didn't take much to gain their attention.

The negative murmur made her cheeks heat, but Alana didn't bother looking around. She wouldn't give them any satisfaction of confirming her embarrassment. Not because of Alex, or getting caught, but because Seamus wanted to hold her accountable so publicly.

Xander hadn't come to her rescue in the tunnels, and when the prince had called for his men — a full Wing of Irish Fae Warriors — to seize her, she'd ordered her cousin to stay away.

She hadn't heard from him since but wouldn't put it past him to be watching from the shadows until he could act to free her.

A part of her prayed that was true.

Seamus had captured her husband as well, and two Irish Fae Warriors had him bound between them. Two more held her next to them, but they hadn't tied her up.

From the first moment she'd seen Alex, she'd panicked that the prince had been true to his word and had killed all the MacLeods, but her husband's headshake told her he was the only victim. Their son and the rest of the clan were safe. For now.

Seamus had barked at her father's steward to fetch him. They awaited his arrival, and Alana tried to talk herself out of being a tremoring mess.

The king could order her death, Alex's death, in moments. She had leverage against Seamus that *might* save their lives, but her betrayal was greater than Seamus'—she'd acted; he had not. She recalled how Princess Sima had been wiped from royal records and fought the urge to close her eyes.

Alana looked at her husband and tried to mirror his straight shoulders and squared jaw, despite his bound hands. If he could be strong when they were very much in trouble, so should she.

"What is the meaning of this?" King Fillan boomed. He marched across the hall and up onto his dais, but he didn't take a seat on his throne. He posted in front of it, his captain on his heels.

Her father had on the thick fur-line mantel he only wore when accepting audiences, and she sensed he'd hastily dressed, despite his impeccable appearance. His jeweled crown glinted in the magic lights hanging all over the vast room.

Alana shook in the Irish Fae Warrior's grip at her father's tone. He was *angry.*

More so than she'd seen him in a long time.

The accompanying Fae Warriors from her Court exchanged looks, obviously confused that their Irish counterparts were restraining her, but they glanced at the king, and her uncle, Captain Daegus, before making any moves. Xander's father stood coolly assessing the situation from her father's side in front of his throne.

Of course, no soldier would dare order *their* princess free without approval.

The two that had Alex by the arms shoved him to his knees before her father.

I'm sorry, my love, she told him mentally.

Alana whimpered and their eyes locked, but her husband held his chin high and gave her an almost imperceptible nod, silently telling her to be strong.

The pain in her chest eased but didn't disappear.

This was all her fault.

Seamus strode forward, hands on hips, chest thrust out as if he'd just been crowned king. "I bring you a gift, Your Majesty."

"A gift?"

"The Crown Princess is a traitor, Majesty." Seamus glared at her before glancing back at her father. "The *worst* kind of traitor. She betrayed us all! She never intended to marry me. She married this *human* in secret, but not only that, she bore his filth, a halfling she's hidden in the Human Realm for *years.*"

Everyone in the throne room — a mixture of courtiers, lords, ladies, and even the Fae Warriors gasped and stared. Some of the noblewomen held their hands over their mouths to hide aghast expressions.

King Fillan's face reddened to his ears, and his massive chest rose as if he needed to breathe, or gather himself before speaking.

Of course, he won't question Seamus.

She would never deny Alex — why try at this point, they were captured — but for her father to believe without doubt, without asking *her* first burned low in her gut.

He was the king more than he'd ever been her father.

"Is this true, Alana?" Every word was carefully measured, but his voice got louder, more demanding. Her name was uttered like a deadly curse.

Alana looked at Alex, even though it was dangerous.

Her husband's jaw was locked, and he was openly glaring at the king.

Her father's face went redder, filled with even more rage when she met the violet eyes that matched hers.

She held her chin high and suppressed the urge to swallow.

Do not show weakness.

"Aye, Father." She intentionally addressed him as her father, instead of her ruler. Something Alana usually did not do with an audience, especially in the throne room.

One of the Irish Warriors shoved her, knocking her off her feet.

Alana landed on all fours and a white-hot bolt shot up her knees and wrists at the same time. Her forearms ached, as did her thighs. She pushed herself up but didn't try to stand. She needed a moment and told herself to breathe away the surprise and anger swirling in her gut.

Alex yelled and rushed to his feet, but the Irish soldiers seized him and pushed him back down to his knees, holding him there with heavy grips on his shoulders.

Had his hands not been bound with magic manacles, her husband might've had a chance to grab a sword, but there were too many powers surrounding them.

He'd get himself killed.

Alana couldn't watch that.

Alex, I'm fine. Don't fight them, it will be worse, she told him, but he didn't look convinced.

Even from across the room she could see the worry in his sapphire eyes.

Her uncle nodded at a few of his men, and two rushed to her side, but not to rescue her.

The Irish Warriors backed away and she was blocked in by two soldiers from her own Court. The same happened to her husband.

I don't know how, but we'll get out of this.

Alex didn't look at her, but he gave a slight nod.

"Where is your bodyguard?" King Fillan demanded.

"I know not."

She'd told Xander to stay away. Her father would never believe he didn't know about her and Alex. He had mages who could use magic to get the truth no matter what, so lying was no use. Her cousin would lose his position — if he managed not to lose his life.

His father would not save him. To her uncle, his son was just another Fae Warrior. Xander got no favors due to their blood ties.

"Sir Xander isn't complicit in this, Your Majesty. The *princess* tricked him, as well as me *and* you. I suspect she used great magic."

It took all Alana was made of not to glance at Seamus.

Why would he cover for her cousin?

What did he have planned?

He couldn't believe his own claim, could he?

Unless he was protecting himself.

Xander was the only other person who could substantiate the prince's plot against her father, except for any coconspirators.

Seamus wouldn't want her father's mages to question her cousin any more than she would. They knew the name of one, after all, and the others would come to light.

She prayed to the Goddess her cousin was safe where he was. Alana had spoken honestly when her father had asked. She'd told Xander not to disclose where he was going.

"'Tis a relief there was not more than one betrayal this day," the king said. He narrowed his eyes and addressed his captain. "Take the foul human to the dungeons. Do with him what you will."

Alana shot to her feet, trying to tear away from the four strong hands pulling at her arms. "Father, don't kill him! Please!"

King Fillan froze, then turned his glare on her. "'*Father*', you call me? No daughter of *mine*, let alone the *Crown Princess* would perform such blasphemous acts. *You* are no daughter to me. Not anymore. From this day forward." He glanced at the Royal Scribe, who was already furiously writing on parchment from his pedestal.

"Ye bastard," Alex spat.

The Scottish Fae Warrior grabbed his upper arms and yanked him to his feet.

Her husband fought their hold to no avail.

"Daegus," her father barked.

Xander's father stepped forward, his thick ebony locks free and surrounding him like a dark aura. Unlike his Warriors, he always wore his hip-length hair free of restraint. He backhanded Alex twice.

Alana screamed but she couldn't look away as her husband's head snapped to one side and blood flew from his mouth.

King Fillan scowled. "Enough. I do not want the scent of his impure blood to linger here. I cannot abide the *smell*."

"Aye, Majesty." Uncle Daegus gave a curt nod, but didn't move away from his men, as if unsure they could contain Alex.

Perhaps he wanted a reason to hurt him again. She'd always wondered if her uncle really liked to torture.

"Your Majesty," she called.

Her father paused.

"Please promise you won't kill him."

The king threw his head back and laughed, his face lit up with black mirth. "Why, my *betrayer*, would I ever do that?"

"Because, *I* have news of betrayal as well."

His expression fluttered from disbelief to curiosity. He narrowed his eyes again and she prayed he'd indulge her *here*, in front of the whole Court.

In front of her *betrothed*.

Desperation clawed at her from the inside out. Alana swallowed and ordered herself to stay calm, look him in the eye and *show* him her royal blood.

Especially since he'd just officially disowned her.

"Oh, very well." King Fillan sounded bored, and he gestured with one hand. "What news have you?"

Alana squared her shoulders and looked straight at the prince before pinning her father with her gaze. "Seamus is plotting to kill you."

chapter twenty-five

A lex was tossed forward like rubbish and landed hard, with his arse smarting and his legs high in the air.

Two cell doors slammed shut at the same time and he heard the Irish prince's "Oomph," as he must've landed in much the same position.

Alex found his feet and righted himself, brushing his rear end and wincing at the throb there. His plaid hadn't been enough padding to save him a sore rump. His mouth hurt, too, from where he'd been hit. He sent his tongue on gentle exploration of the area and discovered a split lip. He winced when it protested the touch and started to pulse.

Footsteps of the oversized Fae Warriors were already receding, without so much as a word.

He blew out a breath and rammed his fingers through his hair. Alex had kept it short for a few years but hadn't had Janet cut it for a month or so. Now it was growing back fast, already touching the base of his neck. Soon it would be at his shoulders, and he'd match Duncan again.

Damn, he'd gotten into a mess this time, hadn't he?

If he and his wife were fated, how had they ended up here?

Had getting caught been inevitable?

The elegance and richness on blatant display in Alana's father's audience room had thrown off Alex's balance. If it stood still, it'd been bejeweled, including the single throne on the dais he'd been forced to be prostrate in front of.

Surely a man who lived like that, a *family* who did, couldn't be a tyrant?

The air of his current environment told Alex how wrong he was, even if the large dark-haired captain's punch hadn't already confirmed it. Like most kings, his wife's father hadn't even done his own dirty work.

She'd always called her father brutal; bloodthirsty. He was grateful their son would never suffer his presence. Angus was safe with his clan. At least he didn't have to worry about his lad, considering his circumstances.

The stone floor of his cell was covered in rushes, but they were old, shriveled, and no longer held a fresh scent. Odors of earth, shite, piss, decay and blood hung low in the air, wrapped in the sense of despair he didn't have to be Fae or have magic in order to feel.

Bile inched up from his throat and he swallowed so he wouldn't retch.

There was a sponge-like pallet in the corner, but it didn't look comfortable; it was thinner than what MacLeod hounds slept on. It was also child-sized, so even if Alex curled in a ball, it would be too short to hold the entirety of his tall form.

The cell itself wasn't iron, or even metal at all. It appeared to be made of crystal, like the Faery Stones, and had a soft internal glow like they did, but it'd been refined, shaped into bars, like any other confinement space he'd ever seen.

It was dark, except for the bars' low light. His eyes were well on their way to adjusting to the dimness, and he explored each corner of his new *home.*

In the very least, it appeared mostly clean, despite the dank air.

What he assumed were curses caught his attention, so he went to the side of the cell that attached his to the one adjoining it. "Dinnae expect this, eh?" Alex held onto the crystal bars and peered at the Irish prince.

"Do not speak to me," Seamus snapped.

He smirked and watched the jilted royal pace his cell. "My lad dinnae pout as much as ye are."

Seamus' fine clothing was ripped, and he gnawed on his thumbnail. He paused, shooting Alex a look. "I would not hold onto those bars, were I you."

A shock of energy went up his fingers, into Alex's wrists and pain zinged along his forearms into his shoulders. He jumped back, shaking his hands. He swore in Gaelic and renewed his efforts when the sting held on.

It was the prince's turn to smirk.

"What did ye do?" Alex barked.

Seamus shook his head. "Nothing a'tall. 'Tis *magic,* daft one. Obviously, Alana did not select you for your intelligence."

Alex growled and narrowed his eyes. The Fae man's Irish inflection was already grating his nerves, and they'd been locked together for mere moments. He might brave the shock and reach through the bars to strangle the prince if the bastard came close enough to reach. "She dinnae choose ye *a'tall*," he muttered.

His new neighbor threw him a scowl but didn't answer. Just resumed his pacing. "I will get out of this," the prince repeated like a mantra as he made circles inside the small space.

Alex sighed and planted his sore arse on the thin pallet, reminding himself not to lean on the bars. "Yer wastin' yer energy," he called, but Seamus ignored him.

Alex… Goddess I wish you could answer me.

He straightened when Alana's voice slid into his head. He wished he could answer her, too, but at least he could *hear* her.

Proof she was somewhere, in one piece, right?

I'm locked in the tower, instead of my rooms. I haven't seen Xander yet, but I hope he comes to me soon. I don't know how yet, but I will get us out of this. My cousin will help, I know he will. I'm so sorry. I love you.

Alex crushed his eyes shut and took a deep breath. He loved her, too. So much it made him ache, but the problem with that was it probably *would*. He had no illusions they'd torture him. He couldn't give them information to help with Seamus' plot or on anything Fae.

His gut told him none of that would matter.

I'm well, but I worry you are not. Regret and concern wrapped around his wife's words, and he wished he could reassure her.

He pictured her sobbing in some unknown place, and he couldn't hold her, or help her. Alex wanted to demand she not worry about him at all, but she'd have reason when her father's men came to lay hands on him.

Hurried heavy boots caught his attention, and Alex found his feet and went to the edge of the cell to see if he could peer into the corridor. He couldn't see much.

"Laird MacLeod." The voice was urgent and familiar.

"Xander?" He took cues from his wife's cousin's volume and kept his tone just above a whisper.

When the big Warrior came closer, their gazes locked.

"Ye are free?"

"Aye." His violet eyes shot to Seamus, who watched them from his cell.

Although the prince had lied for Alana and her cousin, his ease with Alex now would confirm that he *had* in fact lied to the king, if Seamus had actually assumed Xander's innocence.

Alex didn't care right then; was just glad to see the man his wife put so much stock into saving them. "Can ye get ta Dunvegan an' alert my brother a' what's happened?"

Regret crossed Xander's expression. "I cannot risk it. King Fillan has doubled the guard in the Field of Light, where our Stones are located. If I try, I will be caught, and he'll realize Seamus lied to him." He glared at the prince. "Do not think I don't know why you did it, Your Highness." The honorific was spat like an insult. "I have no qualms about telling the king *everything* I know of your plans, worry not. Your days at Scotland Court are numbered."

Even in the absence of adequate light, Alex saw the

prince swallow hard, and apprehension darted over his face as the apple of his throat bobbed.

"That is, if he prefers banishment over execution," Xander said, then looked back at Alex.

"Alana said ye've no' gone ta her. Can ye no' do so?"

"You've spoken to Alana?"

He tapped his temple. "She's spoken ta me."

"Ah. I will go to the tower when I feel I can safely. I must lay low. The king has not summoned me, but he *will*." His mouth set into a hard line.

"Will ye be…weel?"

Xander's eyes widened. "You need to worry for yourself, my laird, not me."

Alex blew out a breath. "They have nothin' good planned fer me."

"Aye." His nod was grim, matching his countenance. "Be strong, Alex MacLeod. I will get you out when I can."

"I shall hold ye ta tha'." Alex cleared his throat when his voice broke. Fearing what would happen to him wouldn't change his circumstances. He was more worried for Alana than himself anyway. He was much stronger than his petite wife, magic or not.

She had to survive for Angus if he could not.

"I cannot dally here; I bribed the guard to let me see you under the guise of angry words for the atrocities you dared commit. Spoiling the princess, and all." His wife's cousin smirked.

He failed to see humor, given his location, but he didn't tell Xander that. "Go ta Alana when ye can, she needs ye."

The Fae Warrior offered a nod, then he was gone.

Alana paced, following a mostly circular path as her prison's walls dictated. She wasn't confined to her rooms, like normal when she'd tapped into her father's ire.

Of course, this situation was more serious than her normal antics, so he'd had her placed in the tower, in one of two small rooms atop it. It had much less space than her palace suite, but it was no less elegant.

She scanned her surroundings and shook her head. "So much for being disowned." It was hard to *feel* punished, because the place was just as opulent as her own, and the engraved four-poster bed just as large. The bedposts gleamed with inset jewels.

A magic crystal chandelier hung from the ceiling. It was crusted with other fine gems that enhanced the light it gave off.

The wooden wardrobe was just as dark and shiny, and the hearth was like the one in her rooms, complete, with winking sapphires, diamonds, rubies, and emeralds.

It was as if each and every last fine stone was chastising her as evidence of what Alana had done foolishly, if she was to believe her father and Seamus.

The wealth was statement of what she'd lost—what she was *gladly* losing when she escaped, and she *would* do so.

However, it was nothing like where her husband was being kept…in the dungeon.

Her heart ached and she fended off tears.

Her father had ordered Seamus seized with her revelation of the assassination plot, but Alana knew no more than that. Not if he believed her, if he'd ask her more questions, so she could turn Tamhas in, or even where the prince had been stashed.

Now that Seamus' plot had been made public, the culpable Fae Warrior would've likely fled, unless he was convinced the prince wouldn't turn on him. Or if he'd underestimated *her* knowing his name. If there were others, they would run, too.

Was the prince with Alex in the dungeons, or did he take up residence in the other room here in the tower?

Frustration made Alana ball her fists at her sides.

They had to get out of the Fae Realm.

Couldn't afford to wait for her father's verdict on her betrothed. Even if he put Seamus to death, it wouldn't undue her *crimes*.

The king had officially severed their blood tie, after all, and had had her de-crowned. Even if she'd wanted it, she'd never be the Queen of the Scottish Fae now. Ironic, since her favorite tiara had been among her things, and she'd donned it when she'd been sealed inside the tower room. It resided atop her head, where it'd belonged since she was a wee lassie.

Alana was like Princess Sima now and would likely be struck from Royal Records.

Xander hadn't come to her yet, but her gut said he would. Perhaps with her evening meal?

If her father had planned on feeding her, that was.

Please, Goddess, let Xander have a plan.

When the Fae Warriors had dumped her in the tower room and slammed the door, she'd run around the place looking for a way out. There was no secret passageway entry that she could find or sense, but she could perform magic within the room.

Alana couldn't *blink* out, she'd tried, and her molecules had bounced off an invisible interior security shield. She'd landed on the stone floor in a heap, but at least her body had reformed. *Blinking* where she couldn't see was dangerous, and some shields could cause death when trying to go through them.

The window was sealed shut, and it was just as grand as the rest of the room. Stained glass with a battle scene depicted. Perhaps since the tower was so high, the king was confident she couldn't scale it to get out.

She called to Alex mentally, and wished with all her might the man she loved could answer. In the very least, he could hear her, but she didn't have a way of knowing if he was unharmed.

He would be tortured.

Alana swallowed to hold a sob at bay and fired off some prayers that Alex would survive until Xander could get them out.

Her cousin *had* to get them out.

If King Fillan had believed Seamus, her bodyguard would remain free, even if he was demoted because of *her* actions. Xander likely would be, but if he remained within any caste of Fae Warrior, no matter how low, he'd still have free movement around the palace.

Her cousin could flee with them, and live in the Human Realm, although she didn't know if he'd agree to live where he didn't have wings. His magic was so strangled there, when hers never had been. He thrived when he flew. Alana never saw the same joy in his expression like she did when he was in the air.

When she'd explored her new quarters, she discovered her father hadn't taken away her garments, the sparkling wardrobe against the wall in the rounded room was full of her gowns, including the fancy feast ones.

Had revealing Seamus' ill intentions saved her from everything but being disowned?

Did her father intend to let her live, but remain in the tower for all her days?

Alana wouldn't put it past him, but he'd never been afraid to exact harsh punishment with *no* exceptions, so she was surprised he hadn't ordered her death. Perhaps he couldn't do so, despite renouncing their blood tie.

Even if he planned to keep her locked away, he'd have to name an heir. There weren't many other blood kin—besides her aunt and Xander—unless the king had hidden a bastard or two. Alana had distant cousins— none of which lived at Court, and all from her mother's side.

Her father had a healthy appetite for females, and even though having a child out of wedlock was frowned upon, it had of course, happened before. Especially from an ambitious mistress to royalty.

The king had never marked a particular official

mistress, but he had many lovers. After her mother had passed, King Fillan had never shown interest in a second marriage either.

Perhaps he would remarry now and have another child. By Fae standards, her father was not an old man. His lovers at Court often bragged about his virility. Something she'd had to endure hearing for years now. Alana had learned to roll her eyes and ignore the talk—who wanted to know of their parent's sexual dalliances?

Her Aunt Aileana, Xander's mother, had also been stripped of her rank as princess, and she wasn't fit to rule due to her Acana addiction. Her cousin had never been acknowledged by her father officially as royal, even though the same blood ran through his veins.

She should probably feel guilty for putting her father in the position she had—public embarrassment and such, but she'd never apologize for Alex. Alana had a right to the love she'd found. Besides, she still believed they were fated.

A noise at the entrance to the room drew her gaze, and Xander slipped into the room and shut the door.

"Thank the Goddess!" Relief washed over her, and she rushed into her cousin's open arms for a quick embrace. Her frantic gaze met his when she tugged free. "Alex?" she demanded.

His mouth was a hard line. "I've just come from the dungeons. He's fine for now, but—"

Alana swallowed and looked down. "I know, they will torture him."

"Aye, he's prepared."

"Seamus?"

Xander smirked. "His *Highness* is next to your husband."

"Good. And you're free?"

"I have not been summoned by the king or the captain. Yet." His voice betrayed no nerves, but he felt some unease; it tingled over her powers, and Alana fell into pacing again.

"What're we going to do?" She tried to keep the helplessness that suffused her words at bay. She couldn't lose her strength now.

"I don't have much time; I talked my way in here. I'm going to wait to be summoned, take my lashes for my ignorance of your dealings, and then tell your father about Tamhas. Pray to the Goddess that King Fillan believes Seamus regarding my lack of knowledge, and does not put the mages upon me, especially Wardric."

She swallowed, fought a shudder, and averted her gaze. The mage he'd mentioned loved to inflict pain and terror. "You will be demoted."

He smirked again. "Well, there's no other princess for me to guard."

"You'll have to admit to being inadequate." Alana winced.

His pride would have a hard time accepting that, no matter the lashes he'd likely receive.

"Demotion is preferred to death. The same is true of lashes." Xander cupped her face. "Don't worry about me, cousin. I'll be fine and I *will* get you and Alex MacLeod out of this."

"I pray your words are true," she whispered.

"For the sake of my young cousin, I do as well. Angus needs *both* his parents."

chapter twenty-six

In all the months she'd been in the tower, the king hadn't shown his face, summoned her, or done anything close to making his presence known. The only orders regarding her had been on the day he'd locked her away.

He'd spoken his piece, and Alana assumed he intended to keep her confined for the rest of her life. She was his stain now.

She no longer thought the word *father* when referring to the Scottish Fae King. He'd disowned her, after all, and she didn't want to consider that his blood flowed through her veins. She was nothing like him, and neither was her son.

Thank the Goddess.

Perhaps sparing her was the only gift she'd ever received from King Fillan, but being imprisoned was the worst thing he'd ever done to her. Aye, Alana had her gowns, and she was fed, but pacing the rounded room didn't relieve the antsy-ness that lived inside her and her worry for Alex was a live thing, wriggling around her, worsening daily.

She glanced over the opulence of the room and guilt rose to bite her. She was stuck in a small space, but at least her meals were regular — if simple — and she was left unharmed.

Alana was permitted to bathe and use limited magic, and she was allowed to be visited by Xander at this point. He'd gained permission after a few months of her captivity.

Her bodyguard was cooperating in the investigation of Seamus' plot and had gained forgiveness from the king for his *'ignorance'* of her marriage and child.

Her husband was kept in a small cell, but it was dark and nasty in the dungeons, and even though her cousin refused to regale her with the whole truth, Alex was being tortured and beaten, probably often.

She winced and scrawled *'I love you'* on the parchment she'd written him a missive on. Her cousin had access, and he'd promised he was ensuring that Alex ate regularly. It was common knowledge at Court that people got what they deserved when in the dungeon of the king's palace, and that certainly didn't include *food*.

Especially for the human who'd dared to defile the princess.

Guilt took another bite from her heart. Alana would never regret meeting her laird—he was the love of her life, and if they hadn't met, sweet Angus wouldn't exist—but his current plight was entirely her fault. *She* had put him in danger.

The peril his life remained in only increased with every passing day.

If Alex died, she didn't know what she'd do.

Alana had always been strong, but even the idea of losing him made her insides shrivel. If she didn't have her lad, she would take her own life in a world without her husband.

She'd fight to get back to her child with or without his father, but she didn't want to contemplate losing Alex permanently.

Alana glanced down at the parchment. She didn't know what else to say, other than repeating her love for him and her vow to get them free, so she folded it and sighed.

Xander had made it possible for him to write her back, and Alex had several times. She read those letters over and over, trying not to be aware of how messy the script was, or how her husband's fatigue seemed to melt off the parchment to make her empathic magic ache.

She swiped at her cheeks; she was so sick of crying. Enough tears to fill an ocean wouldn't free them.

The notch-sound of the door's latch had her gaze flying to the entrance of her prison.

The kitchen maid caught her vision first, and she set a covered tray down on the floor and bowed, backing out of the room slowly. As if Alana would attack her at any moment.

That was always the same, and very tiresome.

Xander emerged behind her, but instead of leaving with the servant, he paused right inside the room. "Go without me, I shall have words with the traitor."

Alana winced, even if the sentiment was for show.

The maid said nothing, just tugged the brown hood of her uniform robe over her head and disappeared.

Her cousin nodded—she assumed to the guard outside—then closed the door. He lifted the tray from the shiny floor and carried it to the small desk she sat at. "I have news," he said without preamble.

When their eyes met, her heart skipped. "Alex?"

Xander shook his head, and his braid slipped over his shoulder. "Nay, your laird is fine. Your prince, however, is not."

"I do not have a prince," Alana spat.

He smirked. "No one does, anymore."

"What?"

"Your father, after one last exhaustive interrogation of Tamhas, declared Seamus a traitor and ordered his execution."

She gasped. "When?"

"He was decapitated this morning, with his father in audience."

Sorrow washed over Alana, and she looked down. "I've always respected King Ciaran. I wish he didn't have to witness that. Seamus was a wretched bastard, but his father shouldn't have had to see his life ended."

Xander nodded, and his expression softened. "All is not lost for the Emerald Isle."

"Oh?"

"You recall how the king remarried last year?"

Alana frowned. "I believe my fa—King Fillan—attended the wedding, since you mention it, but I did not. That being said, yes, I remember."

Her cousin's mouth rippled, as if he was trying not to smile. "Aye, you were not permitted to attend—you were secured to your rooms."

She rolled her eyes. "Aye, I've always been a thorn in the king's side." Alana couldn't recall what she'd been accused of *that* time.

Xander snorted. "I can't argue with that."

"Sod off, Xander," she murmured, pulling words from her husband's armory.

Her cousin chuckled and shook his head. "I do not like the laird's influence on you." His chest rose as if he'd taken a breath. "The new Queen of Ireland gave birth to a son last sennight, so even though it was obvious King Ciaran was distraught over the death of his heir, he now as a new one."

"At his age?" She tried not to imagine having to lay with someone as old as the Irish king. She felt bad for his bride—she had to be much, much younger than he to be of childbearing age.

Again, Xander laughed. "Perhaps it was a love match."

"Get out of my head."

He arched an eyebrow, unrepentant for reading her thoughts. "King Ciaran agreed with your father's actions when the proof was presented as undeniable, so we are not worried about going to war. After all, his death was also included in the plot, according to Tamhas."

"And what of Tamhas?"

"The same—as well as two Irish, two more Scottish—that were involved. They all died this morn."

Alana blew out a breath. Xander had mentioned when others had been arrested in the recent weeks. She and Alex had been confined for almost six months, and her cousin had been deeply involved in the inquiry. "So, six were executed this morn?"

"Aye."

"'Tis really over?" she breathed.

"Nay."

Her gaze shot to his. "Nay?"

"It will not be truly over until you're free."

The months passed slowly. He'd become used to the torture and having to scramble for scraps so he wouldn't starve.

Days before, they'd taken the prince away; of course, Alex wasn't told why, or if Seamus had been executed. He only knew the Irish Fae man had never been returned to his cell.

He hadn't seen his wife's cousin yet to ask. If Xander planned a visit, he only hoped it would be soon. His gut growled and gnawed on itself, the emptiness hollow and sharp.

Sleep was a relief, but then he'd relive what they did to him.

Wake screaming.

Daily.

Xander kept promising he'd rescue them, but at this point, Alex was convinced he was going to die in this cell, in the dungeon in the Fae Realm, never to see his son or wife — or the rest of his family — again.

He only prayed Alana would survive for Angus' sake and escape to Dunvegan.

Their lad was a sensitive, and part of his magic was visions, or premonitions, so he could only pray his son was saved from knowing what was going on in the Fae Realm. He had no need to see his father being tormented and bleeding.

As for his wife, she talked to him every day. Hearing her voice in his head kept Alex going, especially after she'd stopped apologizing.

She told him she loved him over and over, and even though he couldn't answer her with his mind, her cousin could give her messages, and did so whenever he could. First verbally, but then small missives on parchment, and Xander had given him a magic quill that didn't require an ink well to write her back. No matter how many sentences he penned, it never ran out of ink.

He begged the Fae Warrior not to tell her how they hurt him, but even without the words, Alana would know. She'd been raised by the king, after all. How they lived in the Fae Realm was no mystery to her.

Alex fantasized Duncan appeared before his cell, fighting to free him and Alana from the lands of a king that declared that their marriage—their love—could never be.

He worried that while he was locked away, his would-be-father-by-marriage had sent men to his home and harmed Angus and the rest of his family, but Xander confirmed no one had ventured to the Human Realm, King Fillan had only doubled the guard at the Faery Stones and banned them being opened under the penalty of death.

His wife's cousin swore he'd kept eyes and ears out for a raiding party, but the king had never wanted anything to do with humans in the past, and that hadn't appeared to change, despite their circumstances.

"I've brought you a letter from Alana."

The familiar voice had Alex jerking up off the small sponge-pallet. He'd been healed from the day's torture, but his muscles were sore, and his legs protested as he climbed to his feet.

Xander passed the small piece of folded parchment through the crystal bars.

Alex's dirty fingers grasped and held on, as if for his life. "How is she?" His voice was a thick croak he almost didn't recognize.

"She is well. Worried about you, as always."

"Dinnae tell her," he ordered.

The Warrior's expression softened. "I never do, but she knows, Laird Alex."

"I ken it." He crushed his eyes shut. "They heal me."

"I know. My father can be a sadistic bastard, can't he?"

"The captain dinnae lay a finger on me."

"Everything has his seal of approval, my laird, remember that." Xander shoved a small sack through the bars. "Here. I managed to get you some dried meat and bread."

Alex scrambled to the pallet and dropped the letter from his wife. His stomach snarled, and he needed to feed it first. Alana's comfort would have to wrap around him when the ache in his gut was lessened.

He stuffed a sliver of meat into his mouth and chewed, caring not that it was dry and hard. He closed his eyes and breathed deep as another piece made it past his lips.

"Slow down, lest you retch it right back up."

He didn't scowl at Xander — the Warrior was right.

"I'll get you another skin of water as soon as I can."

"Thank ye," Alex managed as he bit into the small loaf of bread.

"I'm sure you noticed Seamus' absence." His wife's cousin gestured to the empty cell with his head and his long flaxen plait jumped, and his wings, taller than Xander's impressive height, twitched. Even in the dim light of the corridor, rainbow colors danced over his iridescent flesh.

It was startling to see a man with wings. The appendages were deceiving because they appeared thin and weak, but they were not. Alex had seen Warriors take to the sky and their wings were an extension of their bodies, like any other strong muscles.

"Aye." He didn't pause eating, just took another bite of meat and bread.

"He was executed this morning." Xander quickly explained what'd happened to the prince and his coconspirators.

Alex didn't comment — had nothing to say on the matter.

Over the months of their shared captivity, Seamus hadn't learned to be more bearable. His tongue had been as sharp as ever, and his stomach as empty as Alex's. Except Xander didn't sneak the prince food.

Humility had escaped him even after he'd been tortured, so they'd been equal, and Alex had almost felt bad for the Fae royal. After all, *he* had Alana's love, and the prince had no one.

Nothing to save him.

Xander grabbed the crystal bars, and they threw blue sparks under his touch, but didn't seem to harm him as they did every time Alex touched them for too long. He didn't so much as flinch. "Something's coming, I feel it."

He looked up from the small chunk of bread remaining and met the eyes that were so like Alana's. He popped the morsel into his mouth. "Meanin'?"

"Just hang on a while longer, my laird. I'll hold to my vow and get you both out of here."

Alex didn't answer.

Xander's footsteps faded; he never stayed long. Couldn't afford to get caught.

Alex hid the small now-empty food sack beneath his pallet and opened the missive from his wife.

The tiny window high above his head on the wall of his cell didn't provide enough light that he didn't have to strain his vision, but he struggled to read the words anyway.

He scanned the short note three or four times, his eyes and his heart clinging to, *'I love you'* written in her neat script.

Without that, Alex would've gone mad months ago.

chapter twenty-seven

lana frowned.

Was that some kind of noise right outside her room?

Before she could react, the door to her prison flew open and smashed into the wall with a loud *bang*. She shot to her feet from her seat on the giant bed.

The petite figure that rushed inside held a full tray, complete with a steaming bowl, and was wearing the normal kitchen maid's uniform of a brown hooded robe, but Alana's evening meal had already been brought.

The remnants of it were on a trencher by the door that'd just been — forced? — open.

The maid appeared to scan the room, and her gaze landed on Alana. She tossed the food and didn't pause as it hit the stone floor, splashing stew and mead everywhere. The small loaf of bread bounced before it bumped the hearth and stopped.

She dashed to her, shoving off the hood, and Alana met a pair of wide leaf-green eyes. The lass was young and had fair hair, a blonde hue only slightly darker than Alana's own. She was also a bit too short to be Fae — probably within an inch or two of Alana, who'd always been considered small.

"What—"

"I'm Claire. Let's go." She grabbed her arm and

tugged.

"Wait!" Alana shouted as the woman attempted to drag her across the tower room.

Who's Claire?

"We don't have time!" she yelled before Alana could voice her question.

She told herself to go with it, because *'Claire'* was obviously a part of her escape. Xander had said he'd get them out *soon,* but he hadn't been specific.

"I packed a bag. Been waiting for my cousin to make his move," she said, then pulled free of the lass' grip and snapped her fingers.

Her purple day-dress *poofed* into lavender trews, a dark purple bodice and soft white leine beneath it. The fabric settled over her body and fastened itself where necessary. Her magic satchel found the appropriate place on her arm. The bag looked small, but the interior was spelled to hold an almost infinite amount of items.

She wasn't trying to be vain, but there were a few gowns she wanted to bring with her to the Human Realm. Since her father hadn't kept her from her normal attire, she didn't want to part with it, either.

"Handy," Claire whispered.

She flashed a grin. "*Now* we can go. Where's Xander?"

"Dealing with your guard." The lass thumbed over her shoulder, toward the rounded corridor.

"Good. Where's Alex?"

"My husband—Duncan—is getting him." Her fair brows drew together, as if she was worried, but Alana focused on what she'd said.

"Husband?" She reared back. From what Alex had always told her of his brother, Duncan MacLeod was a bit of a scoundrel with the lasses and wasn't likely to marry.

Her son adored his uncle, and Duncan was always friendly to her, so she hadn't given it more thought. Her visits to the Human Realm were always focused on Alex and Angus, so she'd not actually spent much time with his family, or other MacLeods.

That was about to change.

She'd finally be *free* to be with her love and her lad and the rest of their clan.

"Aye." Claire nodded. "Long story. We need to go."

Despite the familiar word, the lass' inflection was off. She wasn't Scottish. With the raised voices and excitement of finally getting away, it hadn't dawned on Alana until then. Something about the woman was off… She had to remind herself that staring was rude.

Xander's large frame filled her prison's doorway, snatching her attention from her new sister-by-marriage. He gestured. "Claire, cousin. Come." His voice was more urgent with every word.

He didn't have to tell her twice.

Alana was sick of being locked away.

Her bodyguard kicked the door to the other room at the top of the tower open.

Alana's eyes darted to the oversized Fae man-at-arms slumped against the wall. He was one of the regular guards, but she'd never gotten his name. For months she'd missed Rannick; he'd not been assigned to keep watch on her in the tower.

The guard's neck was at an odd angle, but she didn't think her cousin had killed him. He had a magical aura floating over him, so he'd likely been put to sleep with a spell. It wouldn't last long, so they needed to move.

Xander urged her to enter in front of him, and Claire stayed close, too. There was no one inside, but its level of grandeur mirrored the other room.

Alana snapped her fingers and said a spellword silently. The multicolored pane of glass in the window disappeared. Sunlight flowed into the now open space.

"I gotta learn how to do that. What else can you do?" Claire stared.

She opened her mouth to answer, but her cousin was faster.

"We can discuss magic later. We must go." He wrapped his arms around them and lifted them into the air with two great pumps of his wings.

"I'm going to put my arm around your waist," she told the lass as Xander flew straight for the window.

"Okay," Claire said, and Alana moved closer.

She'd never heard the odd word before, but since her new sister-by-marriage had also nodded, she took it as an affirmative. Although, her unusual accent really jumped out.

Her cousin muttered a spell that would increase his speed and make them invisible.

Claire gasped and clutched at her as Xander abruptly changed direction.

"Worry not," Alana said in the vicinity of her ear.

"He's made us invisible. He won't drop us, either."

Again, the lass nodded, and her body softened against Alana's. "So, can you read minds?"

The query shook, and her magic tingled with Claire's nerves.

"Nay, but I can speak mentally. Among other things." She offered a slight smile. She didn't know Duncan's wife, but she wanted to make her feel better.

"Alana has much magic," her cousin murmured.

"I can *blink*, as well, although my father had the tower spelled so I could not do so to leave."

"Blink?" Claire's pretty green eyes went wide again.

"Oh, *blinking* is a form of travel, I suppose. I think about where I'd like to be, then appear there. I can't jump between realms, but I don't have to, due to the Faery Stones. It's a rare trait, but my lad can as well."

"Angus?"

Alana nodded and beamed. She couldn't wait to see her son again. Hold him, and kiss him, although he was getting too old for that. He'd protested last time she'd done so. Not that she'd been over-bothered and had told him so.

"You're not wrong about that, Claire," Xander said. "That is a part of her magic as well. My cousin has empathic magic. Sometimes she projects what she feels."

"Geesh, stay out of my head."

Alana smirked.

Her cousin didn't answer, but he hovered over a clearing in the forest. He landed gently and released her and Duncan's lass.

She assumed they were waiting for Alex and his brother, but the long blue grasses were undisturbed. In her peripheral vision, she caught Claire and Xander scanning the area while they waited, and she did the same.

They waited.

The passing moments made her heart skip and she didn't like the look on her cousin's face.

Where were her husband and his brother?

Had they failed to get free?

Alex, my love, we wait for you. Please hurry. She pictured the clearing in her mind and tried to project it to him.

Xander's mouth was set in a hard line. He drew his sword. The *swishing* sound it made as it cleared shot up her nerves.

Alana forced a breath, than another.

Claire was just as worried, and her emotions spiked, washing over her magic and making her stomach jump. The lass stood next to her, fists clenched to her sides, and her pretty face contorted with concern.

They both needed to calm.

Alana paced. Her forehead was bathed with sweat, but the same appeared to be happening to her companions.

"Where're Duncan and Alex?" Claire's voice trembled.

His twin growled as yet another key failed to open Alex's cell.

"Duncan, ye've got ta hurry." He grabbed the crystal bars with white knuckles, but released his hold before they could sting him. He couldn't let nerves allow him an injury that might delay them when their time was already limited.

"Yammerin' like a lass dinnae help, brother," Duncan muttered.

Alex managed a smirk. "Aye, I missed ye, too."

His brother glared up from the rattling ring of keys and met his gaze. "Ye think somethin' 'tis amusin'?" he snapped.

"Laughin' is better than despairin'."

"Just a moment ago, ye were orderin' me ta free ye."

He sighed. "That dinnae change. Get me outta here, will ye? They'll know somethin's wrong. Alana has been freed by her cousin—and a lass claimin' to be yer *wife*? From the *future*, my wife says?"

"Aye. My wife." His twin grunted. "I wed, what of it? And how do ye know about *yer* wife?"

Alex snapped his mouth shut to keep it from hanging open. Duncan had *married*? He almost wanted to demand if his brother had been the victim of a changeling. "What do ye mean, '*what of it?*' Ye? *Wed*?"

"Are ye hard a' hearin'? I already said *aye*. I'm goin' ta strangle ye as soon as I free ye."

He laughed; couldn't help it. "I'd rather ye no'. I'd like to see my wife and my lad again."

"I came fer ye, dinnae?"

"Alana says they're ta tha clearing. Brother, please hurry. Tha royal guard will be alerted tha magic on tha tower locks were tampered with. We've run outta time."

Duncan rattled the keys again. "They all look tha same!" His voice was little more than a frustrated growl. "I've lost track a' which I tried. An' how do ye know where they are?"

"Alana can speak inta my mind. Limited by distance, a' course." He took a breath. "Duncan."

His twin met his gaze. "What?"

"'Tis magic. Ye must concentrate ta see past it. The key glows blue. Concentrate, little brother." He'd seen it a dozen times when the guards had come to get him for his daily dose of torture.

It'd gotten so they'd stopped asking questions and would just beat him, then have a healer come put him back together. Healing magic had fascinated him at first, and would be handy to have at home, but with every broken bone and gash knitted, the angrier Alex got.

The guards had never noticed how he watched when they thought he was unconscious each time they reopened his cell to allow the healer in.

The woman had never said a word to him as she worked, but she had very kind eyes.

His brother took a breath. When he looked back down at the giant ring of keys, Duncan stared. Waiting.

Alex too, watched. Waiting for the blue glow.

Finally, the pale sky-like aura radiated in his twin's grip.

"I have it!"

"'Tis a trick ta it. I've watched tha guards. Ye must

turn it ta tha right, then tha left, an' rotate it completely. If ye fail in tha' order, alarms will sound."

Duncan followed the instructions and turned the key so slowly it felt like an eternity.

Finally, *finally*, Alex heard the lock pop.

His brother pulled the door open, flashing a grin.

He was hauled into a tight embrace, and Alex hugged him back, slapping his shoulder. "Thank ye. Captivity was tiresome."

Duncan shook his head, snorting. "Took me six months ta find ye, I'm sorry, brother." His blue eyes reflected regret, but then his gaze went keen, and he wore a frown.

It wasn't a mystery what he was looking at.

They were no longer identical.

Alex had lost too much weight and muscle; his frame was no longer one with his brother's. His plaid was in irreparable scraps, and his leine was so packed with filth it was arguable if it'd ever been anything but black and grimy.

His face was crowded with a thick beard, unlike Duncan's clean-shaven cheeks. He didn't *feel* weak, but he didn't want to see distress in the eyes that matched his own, either. "Dinnae look a' me wit' pity, Duncan MacLeod. I'm as braw as ever. Let us hie ta our wives." He patted his arm and urged him out of the dungeon.

They were almost out of the maze-like place when a shout went up from behind, the voice echoing in the cavernous corridor.

"Halt!" The word was close enough to Scottish Gaelic to be recognizable.

Duncan unsheathed his claymore and ordered Alex behind him.

The rush of feet was too close, so he couldn't argue. He had no weapon, so even if it grated, he'd have to let his brother protect him. He just hoped the problem was dispatched before they gained more attention; he was intimately familiar with the sheer number of Fae men-at-arms.

When the guard came into view, Alex let loose a chuckle.

He was as naked as a new bairn, *and* he didn't have a weapon.

Duncan yelled the MacLeod battle cry and rushed the guard.

His pale blue eyes went wide as his brother knocked him over and brought the hilt of his sword down on his head.

The Fae man slumped to the stone floor, blood trickling down his forehead.

"Ye dinnae kill him." Alex arched an eyebrow. After what the bloodthirsty lot had put him through over the past six months, he wouldn't mind seeing every last one of his torturers dead and buried. Or burned. They'd done things to him he'd never speak of.

"I dinnae kill an unarmed, *naked* man, even a Fae guard."

Alex smirked. "Marriage has made ye soft."

His brother frowned, then whipped the guard's armor up and off his body, draping it over the unconscious Fae man. "Let us go ta our wives, as ye say."

chapter twenty-eight

Claire's yell had Alana's eyes locking onto what the lass had seen first. Two men — *their* men — had broken through the line of thick Acana trees.

Her peripheral vision told her their movements were mirrored; Duncan pulled his wife into his arms at the same time Alex's embrace encircled Alana.

Then there was only her laird.

She whimpered but kissed her husband back with all her might, caring not that his face was rough with a thick beard against hers, his clothes were soiled shadows of what they'd once been, and he needed a bath. She remembered how he always smelled of sandalwood and leather and clung to him.

"Alex, oh, Alex," Alana chanted into his mouth as the hair there tickled her cheeks. She grinned when they parted and tugged on the black fuzz. "This needs to go, my love."

He flashed a fatigued smile and she frowned at how his leine, and plaid hung from a much-too-lean frame.

She couldn't weep for what the king had ordered done to him yet — they were free from their prisons, but *not* from the Fae Realm.

Alana didn't protest when he pinned her to his side and glanced at his brother.

The other couple was still kissing. Holding onto each other with passion and love that would've been obvious even without her empathic magic.

"Weel, weel. My little brother chose a fine wife," Alex said, and at least his amusement was genuine. His lopsided grin didn't seem so tired.

It had her smiling.

The lass looked from Duncan to Alex and back, reddened and gasped. "Twins?"

Alana's smile slid to a grin. Claire's confusion and wonder washed over her magic and made her arms tingle.

"You never thought to mention your brother wasn't *only* your brother, but your twin? You said he was older than you."

Her inflection was so obviously foreign Alana should've known she was not only not Scottish, but from a different century right away, but Claire had confessed such as they'd waited for their husbands. She was from what she'd called America.

Duncan slid his arm around her shoulders but shrugged. "Alex *is* my older brother. We shared a womb, aye. He was born first."

When she rolled her eyes, Alana giggled.

Alex and Duncan side-by-side made a striking pair. Even if her husband's prowess was diminished — temporarily until they could get food and rest in him — the MacLeod twins were the handsomest men she'd ever seen, even though the Fae as a race were beautiful. No Fae man held a candle to Alex and his brother. She and Claire were lucky to have married them.

"We must get to the Faery Stones," Xander urged. "The longer we linger here, the more chance our magic will be discovered."

"I can take one person if I *blink*," she said. Alana glanced up at her husband.

"Go with tha princess, *mò gradh*." Duncan cupped his wife's cheeks.

The lass' panic was obvious as she blanched. "No. I want to stay with you."

"Alex an' I will go wit' Xander, join ye shortly."

"*Blinking* is fast and undetectable. You'll be safe with me." Alana kept her voice soft, reassuring, but her magic told her she hadn't convinced her new sister-by-marriage.

"I'll see ye in moments, Claire-lass," Duncan said.

Alex tugged Alana to him and covered her mouth with his again.

She kissed him back and held on tight as their tongues mingled. She told herself they weren't saying goodbye, so she didn't have to crush his now-leaner waist.

He put his forehead to hers and squeezed her against him. "As my brother said, I shall see ye in moments, *mò chridhe. Tha gaol agam ort.*" His voice was a whisper for her ears only.

The Gaelic words weren't so different than Fae. She smiled. "I love you, too." Alana took a breath and reluctantly stepped away from him. She caught her new sister's green eyes. "Take my hand and hold on tight."

"What's going to happen?"

"You can help me by thinking about the Faery

Stones. Do you remember what they look like on this side?"

"Yes." Claire nodded.

"Good. Close your eyes and picture them. We'll be there in seconds." She entwined their fingers, and the lass' grip tensed. "Claire, breathe deep with me. It'll help." Alana *blinked* without warning her, because the longer they waited, the more anxious Duncan's wife would get.

Their molecules scattered on the wind, only to be carried over the colorful trees and their bodies reformed in the orange and blue grasses of the Field of Light.

Claire went down beside her, landing on her bottom, and breaking their physical contact.

Alana reached for her, cupping her cheeks. "Claire, are you all right?" Green eyes were hazy when they finally met hers.

"Aye," she croaked.

"You must stand. We need to move." She tugged the lass to her feet, but Claire swayed, so Alana steadied her.

The clash of swords was the reality behind them, and one glance told Alana Fae Warriors were fighting a multitude of—humans? Were they MacLeods?

At second glance, she didn't think so, none of the men fighting—or the one's staining the Field's grasses red wore plaid—MacLeod or otherwise.

Their clothing was rough, dark colors. Pirates? Why would her brother-by-marriage have brought human pirates with him to her realm?

Fae Warriors hovered in the air and dove after

fleeing men.

She didn't see any of her people dead, just humans littering the colored grasses.

"Come, lass." Alana took Claire's hand, and they sprinted to the far side of the platform the Faery Stones were perched on. "I must go and turn the red glow off. It'll cease the alarm, and no more soldiers will come. Only then can I open the gate to the Human Realm."

"Okay. Does it take long?"

"Nay, but there's no way to be invisible. The Faery Stones are warded against stealth magic."

"Great. So, they'll be able to see you."

"Aye. I must be quick. Our men and my cousin will be here to defend me if necessary."

Her new sister simply nodded and buried her hands in her trews' pockets.

Nerves—probably her own as well as Claire's—shuddered down Alana's back and she told herself to breathe as she looked at the dais holding their only route to freedom. "I shall wait until they arrive."

"They said it wouldn't be long."

"Thief! Thief!" someone yelled in Fae.

Alana whipped her head in the direction of the shouting and gasped. She slid to the edge of the platform and peeked around it.

"What? Do they know you're here?" Claire asked.

"Nay." Alana didn't look at her, but she sensed—rather than saw—her sister-by-marriage join her. The chant of *thief, thief,* was constant now, and some of the Warriors left duels to fall in behind their shouting brethren.

A pair of humans—a dark-haired woman, and a redheaded man—were running toward the Faery Stones, both had satchels over their shoulders.

Fae men-at-arms gave chase.

"What are they yelling?"

"Thief." She still didn't spare Claire a glance.

"Ah. Duncan suspected Bridei wasn't coming *home* to see long lost relatives."

Alana smirked.

Her sister-by-marriage quickly explained who Bridei was and why Duncan had brought pirates with him. The lass was part Fae. She'd opened the Faery Stones for them.

A Fae Warrior she didn't know swooped down, grabbed the man and sped into the air. The bag slipped from the pirate's grip, losing shiny objects as it plummeted to the colored grass.

Claire gasped beside her when the winged soldier snapped the man's neck.

He slumped in the Warrior's arms; hadn't even had a chance to struggle. Then the soldier dropped the body to the ground.

An anguished scream rose above the din of the fighting.

Bridei dropped her sack of stolen goods and pointed at the Fae Warrior who'd killed the man. Wind kicked up out of nowhere.

Alana sensed magic from the lass, but like Claire had said, she wasn't full-blooded Fae.

Her skirts swirled, then her dark hair, until her skin began to glow, and the Fae Warrior's body started to contort in the air.

He fought back, flapping his wings and throwing a blue blast spell at her, but it bounced off the golden glow around her.

"What the hell?" Duncan's wife muttered.

"Her magic. It's stronger here." She winced as discomfort rolled over her in waves. She fought doubling over as it had a sting to it. Sweat rolled into her eyes and she swiped at it, then tightened her gut to fight off Bridei's magic. Alana gripped the edge of the dais in front of her with both hands.

The lass was projecting her anger and pain—probably because of the redheaded man's death.

"Hey, are you okay?" her new sister shouted.

The wind was gaining whirlwind-like proportions.

"Aye, but you might want to hold onto something."

"Something's wrong." Xander's voice was strained. His hands hovered over his middle, as if in pain.

Alex caught his brother's eye.

"What?" Duncan asked.

"Magic. A huge surge. One of my brothers—a Fae Warrior—is being harmed."

"Alana?" Alex's voice had an edge of panic even to his own ears.

"Nay." Xander's long plait slipped over his shoulder when he shook his head.

"Let's hie to the Stones," his brother ordered.

His twin's expression was worried—for Claire no doubt—and he couldn't feed off that concern. Alex had to believe their wives were fine and waiting for them.

Maybe Alana had even opened the Faery Stones. She could use her magic to defend them, too. She was clever and resourceful and would be well when they joined her and Claire. There was no other option.

He gave Xander a onceover. He'd gone green. "Can ye fly us, Xander?"

"Aye. Get close. We'll go."

Alex threw his arms around his twin.

Duncan made a face. "Ye need a bath."

"My wife dinnae seem ta mind." He smirked as Xander wrapped his arms and magic around them and rose into the air.

"Aye, she must love ye more than I."

Alex chuckled.

His brother's mouth rippled as if he fought a smile. "Ye might be my womb-mate, but I dinnae remember ye e'er smellin' like this," Duncan mumbled.

"Ye dinnae remember anathin' a'tall."

Their banter was discarded when Xander's face contorted with pain. His iridescent wings were pumping twice their normal rate.

Alex gasped. "Yer gonna drop us?"

"My power—my magic—is being sucked away."

"Get as close as ye can ta tha ground, we'll roll." Duncan said, but his expression was wrought with fear.

Alex tried not to panic as well.

The Fae Warrior nodded. Sweat poured from his

forehead and his arms shook around them.

"Tagether?" he asked his brother.

Their gazes locked.

Duncan nodded. "Aye. Count."

"One…two…"

Before *three* exited his mouth, Xander hovered about six feet off the ground. He released them with a groan; he could no longer remain in the air.

Alex tucked and rolled into the oddly colored grass. He couldn't see his twin, but he felt Duncan beside him.

"Xander!" The shout was Alana's.

Her cousin crumpled to the ground, unmoving. His wings were tight around him like a cocoon.

They all reached the fallen winged soldier at the same time.

The wind whipped around them, battering Alex's clothes, and forcing him to squint against the searing air on his face.

"I'm fine, cousin." Xander didn't sound so as he forced words loud enough to be heard over the rushing gusts.

"What's happenin'?" Duncan asked.

Alex gestured to his twin, and they managed to get the Warrior to his feet.

"Riley was killed by a Fae Warrior," Claire said. She touched her husband's forearm. "She…kinda went tornado."

What's a tornado?

Alex didn't voice his curiosity.

Duncan kissed his wife's knuckles, then helped

him support Xander's weight on the opposite side.

"Open the Stones, *mò chridhe.*" He nodded to Alana and slipped his arm around the Fae Warrior's middle.

"I'm weak, my love." Her voice was heavy, strained, like her cousin's had been. "But I will try."

Bodies of pirates were scattered over the area, but all the winged Fae Warriors were crumpled in the colored grass, their wings wrapped around them as they writhed in obvious agony.

The lass his brother had told him was a Fae halfling seer, and a pirate wench, was so radiant, a ball of white light, Alex couldn't look at her.

"Help her, Laird Alex, I'm fine," Xander choked out.

Alex's gaze landed on his wife. She was having trouble ascending onto the dais. He nodded and dashed to her.

He gripped Alana's slender waist and lifted her. He carried her to the glowing crystals that looked just like the ones in the cave where they'd made love so many times, and their son had been born. Even though he usually couldn't remember the Faery Stones—due to his wife's spells—they were clear in his mind.

"Closer, love. I need to touch them."

He swallowed but obeyed. Alex didn't like the tremulous tone of her voice. "Alana?"

She patted his arm. "I'm well, we need to hurry."

He held her up against him, her back to his chest as Alana started touching the glowing Stones in sequence, and the humming got louder, as well as a warm gale that seemed to slam against the seer's winds, and threw them around the dais. He planted his feet and clung to his wife.

The popping sounds started; the portal would be open soon.

Alex glanced over his shoulder when the sound of tearing parchment skidded over his ears. His brother and Claire had Xander propped up between them, but they were too far from the platform. He slid one hand to Alana's stomach to steady her and gestured to their companions.

The bubble-orb opened and hovered as it widened and cleared, but he couldn't see through it just yet. It was right next to the dais.

"Hurry, Alex." Alana was urgent, and she tugged against him, prompting him to turn them toward the magical doorway.

He jumped to the ground with his wife in his arms.

Freedom.

They were almost home.

Alana entwined their fingers when they stood in front of it, waiting for the others. She could stand on her own, but she was still too wobbly on her legs for his liking.

Xander, Claire and Duncan were still so far away.

Alex waved his arm wildly.

Wind picked up speed, pushing and pulling at their bodies as they fought through it to move closer to the waiting portal.

Buffeting air jerked Alex off his feet, but he gripped his wife to him as they were sucked through to the Human Realm.

He could only pray the rest of their family was right behind them.

chapter twenty-nine

his family — hell, the whole clan — was grateful to have him home, and Alex was grateful to *be* home, in more ways than he could say.

He'd never complain about Hamish's scrolls ever again.

Of course, he'd settled into being the laird in the real sense years ago. The loss of his mother and the birth of his son so close together had finally shoved him to growing up, into his rightful role, if nothing else.

Now his wife was at his side in his realm, at Dunvegan, so he was *complete*.

Alex hovered over Alana.

She was in his bed. Naked and ready, *in his bed.*

Joy rode below the surface of his skin as much as arousal.

"Alex," his wife whispered. "Why are you staring, my love?"

The six months in her father's dungeon had been worth it, for *this*.

Alana, his princess, his heart, his wife, was home at Dunvegan.

Finally.

It didn't matter that this wasn't the first, the second, or even the third night she'd been in his bed, every night since they'd been home washed more wonder over him. If Alex was dreaming, he prayed not to wake.

Everything was finally *right* in his world.

"I love ye." His voice broke, and he dipped down to taste her lips.

Alana put her hand on his chest and pushed him back before he could get lost in the movement of their mouths before he could deepen the kiss.

"I love you, too. But...are you well?" She framed his face, and concern glowed in her violet eyes in the light of the fire.

Her thumbs stroked his cheeks as she studied him, and her touch, however slight shot the need for more — for *her* — down his limbs, and heat settled in his already heavy groin, making his cock throb.

He fought through desire and focused on her worry. Alex frowned. "Aye, I'm braw." He'd lost weight and muscle when he'd been her father's captive, but they'd been home for a fortnight, and this wasn't the first time he'd taken her since then.

She'd not questioned him then, why now?

He'd been tucking into more food than he ever had, and had already put on a few pounds, although he'd probably had about a stone more to go until he was normal again.

Alex felt better, and his brother had been working him on the fighting yard. All was well.

"Last time...you were out of breath. It's worrisome."

"Did I no' bring ye pleasure?" Alex demanded.

Alana smiled. "Of course, you did."

He captured her mouth in answer, kissing her hard and deep until *she* was panting to keep up with him.

She broke their kiss and laughed. "You're braw, after all, my love. I shan't question your stamina."

He growled and slanted his mouth over hers again, and the kiss heated his blood. He needed more. Always *more* with Alana.

His wife gasped under him, and her small hands explored his shoulders and back, then she went lower, squeezing his arse.

Alex's skin tingled everywhere she touched him, like every time they'd been together over the course of their marriage. Always as good as the first time he'd taken her.

Many of their couplings had been frantic joinings on the sandy floor of the cave of the Faery Stones, or even against the natural wall, but Alex didn't have to hurry this time — or any time in the future.

Alana's here to stay.

He parted her thighs with his knee and rubbed his cock against her sex, but he didn't join them just yet.

She broke away from his mouth. "Do not tease me."

"Why no'?" Amusement threaded his words at the regal order, and his love mock-glared up at him.

Alana gripped his erection and stroked him. Her talented hands applied and loosened just the right amount of pressure, and she reached below to caress his heavy sac, until his arms, suspending him above her began to tremor.

Alex groaned.

Then her touch was gone, and he shuddered.

"See? 'Tis not nice, my love." Alana smiled sweetly.

He was on her in less than a second, bruising her mouth again and filling her sex with a hard jolt forward.

She didn't pause; just slid her legs around his hips and tilted her own to take him deeper. She kissed him back with the same ferocity and kneaded his rear end for encouragement.

They fell into a hurried rhythm, and Alex tasted every inch of her skin he could reach.

Sweat covered them both and the fire in the hearth made him overheat, but he kept going, thrusting into her over and over, until she was screaming his name like a mantra, and her inner muscles convulsed around his cock.

He pulled back only to shove forward and explode within her, his whole body shaking above her. Alex collapsed and his wife held onto him as if he'd disappear from their bed.

When he could breathe again and his vision cleared, he tried to gently roll away, but Alana held him fast.

"Wait. Please wait."

He cupped her damp cheek and caressed her pinkened skin with his thumb. Her lips were swollen, and her face flushed, but his princess looked gorgeously ravished, and he'd take her again as soon as he recovered.

Alex wasn't even winded. *Thank God.* "I'm goin' nowhere, *mò chridhe.* Dinnae fash."

"I don't want to be parted from you," she whispered. "When we are, my heart hurts." Alana touched her chest, but his eye was drawn to the tempting bud beneath her fingers.

It was still peaked, and he could recall her taste. He couldn't look away, especially when her perfect breasts rose with her breath.

"Ye will ne'er be parted from me again."

She flashed a brilliant smile that had his pulse tripping.

Alex slipped from her body and pulled Alana into his arms. Bed coverings were crumpled at their feet, and he was still too hot to reach for them.

They fell into a companionable silence, and he stroked the soft flesh of her shoulders and back, breathing in time with her. His heart beat with hers, too. They were completely aligned, as they should be.

"I dinnae hardly believe Duncan is wed," he whispered sometime later.

Alana propped herself on his chest, and he shivered as her nipples brushed his. She smiled. "I adore Claire and am enjoying learning of the far future."

Alex, too, had heard some of the wondrous things his new sister-by-marriage had come from in the far future, but a part of him was leery to learn of things he had no business knowing. It was against the natural order. "What of Xander, how is he?"

His wife's expression fell, and she averted her eyes.

A pang of guilt hit, and he almost apologized, but her pretty eyes swung back to his face.

"He mourns more than his wings, but he will not speak with me about it. His magic is not strong in this realm, but he can still read minds, so I've been blocking thoughts for him. It's never quiet for him otherwise."

"Aye, he'd tol' me humans dinnae block their thoughts. Could drive a man mad."

Alana nodded and caressed his chest. "I worry for him. I pray he can find some release. Maybe…love?"

Alex smiled and squeezed her shoulder. "I shall pray fer him, too. What he did for ye, *us*… I dinnae e'er be able ta repay him."

Her eyes closed and her breasts rose again with another breath. "I love him, as I love you and Angus. I do not want him to resent me for giving up his life…his realm. I cannot believe he cut his braid off."

Alex pulled her down onto his chest and she nestled under his chin. He breathed in her scent and closed his eyes, too. "He shall no' resent ye, *mò chridhe*. Yer cousin loves ye, too. If he dinnae, he dinnae be here."

"I made him a traitor." Her whisper was so low he'd almost missed it.

"Ye dinnae. 'Tis o'er, love. Seamus is gone, and *ye* are where ye should be. If we are fated, perhaps 'tis Xander's fate ta live here a' Dunvegan as weel. I could always use another warrior. I shall ask him ta join tha men abou' tha yard."

His wife lifted her head and smiled. "Being useful would be good for him, thank you, my love."

Alex smiled back. "Angus is o'er the moon tha' yer cousin is here."

Alana giggled and his heart lifted a tad more. "I know; I love that. I'm glad they get on so well. It doesn't matter if we're there or here, Alex, he would defend us to the death."

"An' I'm grateful fer tha' and dinnae plan ta take tha' role from him."

Her expression softened and her eyes went misty. "I love you."

"I know." He winked and skimmed two fingers down her cheek. Then he sobered. "Yer da dinnae come after us now?" He'd been worrying over it for the two weeks they'd been home and had secretly readied his brother and their men for a possible attack.

Alex feared her answer, so he hadn't asked.

Alana's flaxen tresses shifted with the shake of her head. "He's disowned me, executed Seamus, and I don't think he has a desire to punish me further. He could've ordered my death; instead, he left me in the tower, and I think in his own way, my father showed me mercy because he couldn't show me affection. I often wonder if Seamus' plot was really the reason I was spared, you were spared. I never knew if he loved my mother, or if he *could* love. Maybe he showed me he can, just a little."

Alex snorted, but he pondered her words. His wife may have been raised in extravagance, but he'd been raised with love. He was grateful Alana had had love from her mother, and from her cousin, who'd both shaped her. She could've turned out more like her father, cold and unfeeling.

She walked two fingers down his chest and his attention snapped back to her when his wife rubbed her pelvis against his. "You're much improved, my laird."

"Meanin'?"

"You've always been a wonderful lover...but somehow 'tis different now. Better. My Alex is like wine, improved with age."

Alex growled and gripped her hips, encouraging her to straddle him. "An' here I thought ye may be concerned fer my health."

Alana winked and obeyed, sliding her leg over him and rubbing her sex on his hardening shaft. "Perhaps I'm too selfish for that. But you *weren't* out of breath." She leaned down and brushed her breasts on him.

He tried not to pant. "I'm braw," he repeated, because his brain had shut down and he wasn't capable of a proper retort.

"Show me."

"Yer ridin' me, lass, so ye show me."

His wife smirked but rose to his challenge and did just that.

Alana woke on a gasp and shot to a sitting position. It took her only moments to orient, but the arousal coursing through her blood captured her focus more than her surroundings or the room—the bed—she was in.

She was naked, and her sex pulsated. The chill in the air was almost welcome on her overheated skin, the gooseflesh on her arms a pleasant contradiction.

Of its own accord, her hand traveled downward. Fingers skimmed her breasts and belly, then she cupped her mons, to support it. To stop the ache there.

Alana parted her already slick folds, but the sense of emptiness only increased, and her sensitive nub gave a throbbing protest.

"Are ye startin' somethin' wit'out me?" The playful rumble made her gaze jump to the end of her husband's oversized bed. Alex's question was wrapped in amusement, but the look in his sapphire eyes was intense. He had not a stitch of clothing on and stared at her over his shoulder.

She studied his bare form as he stood in front of a healthy fire in the large hearth. The light of the dancing flames cast shadows over his broad shoulders, back, thighs, and she tried not to frown. They'd been home for almost a month, but Alex's body wasn't the same.

The king had at least fed her regularly during their six months of captivity, but her love had been in the dungeon where torture was more common than a meal.

Xander had done what he could, but Alana would be eternally grateful for Duncan and Claire as much as her cousin. Her brother-by-marriage and his new wife had gotten them *out*.

Although her husband was gorgeous no matter what, he was still too lean, despite the weight he'd gained in the time they'd been back. Of course, her stubborn laird proclaimed he was fine, but Alana couldn't release her concern entirely.

Alex faced her, and her eyes went up and down his body again. She feasted on his half-mast erection. Worry for his physique dissipated as he stalked to the bed. The play of his muscles was still beautiful and fired her desire, shouting that he was indeed braw, as he always declared.

"Alana…" Her name was a plea, and his manhood

thickened as she watched.

"I was dreaming," she whispered, reaching for him as he climbed onto the bed on all fours and loomed above her.

She dragged two fingers down his chest, caressing the sparse springy hair, and kissed the underside of his stubbled chin, because it was all she could reach.

Alana wanted his mouth, wanted his weight on top of her. She was searing for him from the inside out, and she'd already had him twice since they'd retired to their chambers after evening meal. Having Alex was never enough.

"Dreamin' of what?" He hovered over her, his lips inches from hers as she lay back on the linens, inviting him to come closer.

"You."

"Ye dinnae need ta dream of what 'tis reality."

Alana grinned and cupped his face. "Kiss me, husband. Make my dream come to be."

He growled and took her mouth. Alex wasn't gentle, but she didn't need that. Bruising pressure, full of tangling demanding tongues and nipping teeth was just as well, but maybe even more so, since it was *him*.

Her Alex, her husband, her laird, her love.

The smart of tenderized lips didn't matter, either. Need burned through her, tightening her muscles as she urged him to lower himself on top of her. She kissed him back with that same intensity, nibbling as his mouth slanted over hers.

Over the years, their lovemaking had always been hurried and frantic, not the leisurely sessions of exploration and drawn-out pleasure they'd shared since she'd been in his bed.

The time together had always been stolen, and intimacy less frequent when the purpose of her visits was more focused on their son.

Alana needed this, needed Alex wild, like when they'd first gotten together. Hard and fast and full of ecstasy.

She whimpered and threw her head back when he dragged his tongue along her jawline, and she answered by running her nails down his back.

Her love groaned above her ear, and his encouragement shot anticipation down her spine.

Alana squeezed his rear end and rubbed her pelvis against his. The heated hard length brushing her hip was too much of a tease.

He wasn't in the right place, and she didn't want to wait.

Alex enclosed one of her nipples in his hot mouth and she arched her back, releasing a long moan. Heat blasted lower, until her inner thighs were trembling and her sex pulsing.

Empty.

She needed him inside her.

Now.

Alana cried out and kneaded his biceps, wrapping her legs around him and digging her heels into the perfect globes she'd squeezed moments before.

Her husband got her message.

Alex fumbled, but released her breast and pushed his hand between them. Then he was there, filling her with a firm shove forward, and she clung to him.

He took her hard, driving forward faster with every thrust.

As if he'd read her mind.

The headboard of the four-poster bed smacked into the wall with a rhythmic *thunk-thunk* that was as intoxicating as the movement of his hips.

Over and over, his pelvis rocked, rubbed and hit hers. It didn't take long for her to soar, and Alana tossed her head into the pillows, chanting his name as her sex clenched around his.

Her husband groaned again. Alex pulled out of her only to slam back inside and grunt his release as her body milked his.

He stilled above her, and she couldn't tear her eyes away from the long dark hair curtaining his face, and his cheeks flushed with color. His lips were swollen from hers, and he'd never been more beautiful.

She reached for him, pushing his locks away so she could see his eyes. She traced his lips with her index finger, and then his powerful jaw.

He smiled and kissed her palm. The peace in his sated expression washed over her as he gently separated their bodies and lay beside her.

Alana needed to be in his arms.

Again, as if he'd plucked the thoughts from her head, he pulled her to him, wrapping her in an embrace.

Words failed her, but perhaps they didn't need to speak.

Alex stroked her shoulders, then down her back, sure familiar touches with big, calloused hands that melted her into his side, and she rested her cheek on his chest.

His scent, part Alex, part her, and part *them*, washed over her and she closed her eyes.

"I love ye." Her husband's voice was a low rumble right above her ear.

Alana smiled, and their gazes collided. "And I you."

"'Tis been a month, but sometimes, I still dinnae believe yer here."

The rush of his emotions hit her magic, and she was sad for the time they'd lost—again. "I know. But I am. I'm here to stay." She forced a smile; the other night, he'd admonished her to look forward, not back, and she needed to cling to that.

Alana had a new reason to be happy, and she had yet to tell him.

"*Mò chridhe*," Alex whispered.

She snuggled into his side again and pressed a soft kiss right over his heart. "I'm going to give you another child."

Her husband arched an eyebrow and peered at her. "Aye? Ye can tell already?"

She giggled, and a smile tugged at the corner of his mouth. "I feel it…here." Alana placed her hand over her own heart. "Would that please you?" she whispered.

"A bairn?"

Alana nodded.

"*Ye* please me," Alex growled, leaning over and taking her nipple into his mouth. He laved her, until she wiggled against him and moaned.

"Again?" she breathed.

"Again," he grunted against her skin as he kissed and licked his way over her breasts, paying equal attention before moving across her belly, downward, and nipping her inner thighs.

He teased her some more, making her a wriggling, begging mess in his arms, before he licked her sex.

Heat shot low and hot like before, and Alana buried her hands in his hair. It was thick, but when she tugged, he made a noise in his throat as if to encourage her pulls.

Alex kept working magic at her center, and she focused on how he made her feel, calling his name as she came in his mouth.

His expression was satisfied as he shot up her torso and pushed his erection into her still-boneless body.

Alana gasped, but she'd never refuse him. She'd never get enough of this man.

He caressed her cheek and pressed a soft kiss to her lips. "Aye, a new bairn would please me," he whispered. "Are ye sure yer carryin' one?"

Her core throbbed with a demand for him to move, and passion clouded her head. She had trouble comprehending his words.

"*Mò chridhe?*"

"I…it's…too soon to be sure, truly."

Their gazes brushed and he flashed a lopsided grin. "Then, let us be sure, Your Highness." He groaned with his first thrust into her.

Alana closed her eyes and held on.

epilogue

 lana smiled at her son's laughter and her husband's chuckle as Alex chased Angus with a wooden sword.

"Come face me without magic, ye scoundrel!" he shouted, but their lad ignored him.

Angus shook his head and grinned, and her heart skipped. He looked so much like the man she loved. He took off running toward the castle, with his father yelling empty threats at him.

It'd taken much, much too long to come to this moment. Finally, they were able to live as a family at Dunvegan.

Ten years, wasted.

Seeing the child she'd bore with the love of her life month to month, or even every sennight, had never been enough.

Her son had never suffered from her absence—he'd had his da, loving aunt, grandfa, and now a new aunt, since Duncan had recently married, but the whole Clan of MacLeods didn't fix the ache in her heart.

Her lad had been raised well, but the guilt wouldn't heal for a long time to come. She'd missed so much, but he was a fine lad who showed her as much affection as she showed him.

Neither she, nor her cousin could ever return to the Fae Realm. Alana had happily come to terms with that, but Xander was still struggling, even after the months they'd been at Dunvegan. Her protector had sunk into himself and stayed there, and she was concerned. Hopefully he'd let the love of the MacLeods embrace him like she had.

Alana rubbed her rounded tummy. She carried a lass this time, as her magic told her, and her heart couldn't be fuller.

It shall be different this time.

She'd never leave her husband and son, or her daughter, ever again.

Alex trotted over to her, and his smile fell. "What's wrong, *mò chridhe*?"

"Nothing, my love." She reached for his hand, and when he complied Alana brought his calloused knuckles to her mouth and brushed kisses over them.

He smiled but didn't look convinced.

The laird had finally filled out again, and looking like the handsome, muscular man who'd stolen Alana's heart.

His hair was as long as his brother's and he'd told her he wouldn't give short hair a try again, although that was how Alana would always remember seeing him on the beach all those years ago. Alex didn't think it suited him, but she'd take him as he was, so it didn't matter.

"Stop thinkin', Your Highness." He gently pulled her to her feet and into his arms. "'Tis a fine day, and ye possess magic."

"Magic? What of it?"

He flashed a lopsided grin that had her heart

pattering. "I need it ta pay yer son back."

Alana giggled. "You're trying to take revenge on a lad of ten?"

"Only if ye help me, a' course."

She grinned. "Very well, my laird, let us retrieve your son."

"I dinnae have it any other way." Alex brushed a kiss on her mouth and looped her arm in his.

Together they went toward home.

the end

about the author

USA Today Bestselling, award winning author of romantic suspense, epic and historical fantasy romance, C.A. loves to dabble in different genres. If it's a good story, she'll write it, no matter where it seems to fit!

She's a hopeless romantic and always will be. Risking it all for Happily Ever After is what she lives by!

C.A. is originally from Ohio, but got to Texas as soon as she could. She's happily married and has a bachelor's degree in Criminal Justice.

She's always writing, and helps small business owners by writing their websites, and she loves it!

WEBSITE: http://www.caszarek.com
EBOOK STORE:
https://www.caszarek.com/ebook-store
PAPERBACK STORE:
https://www.caszarek.com/paperback-store

FACEBOOK: http://www.facebook.com/caszarek
INSTAGRAM: https://www.instagram.com/caszarek/
TWITTER: https://twitter.com/caszarek
BOOKBUB: https://www.bookbub.com/profile/c-a-szarek
GOODREADS:https://www.goodreads.com/author/show/5815085.C_A_Szarek
EMAIL: ca@caszarek.com

You can sign up for C.A.'s newsletter on her website, as well as buy all her books!